SMALL TOWN HERO

PATRICK
NEATE

SMALL TOWN HERO

ANDERSEN PRESS

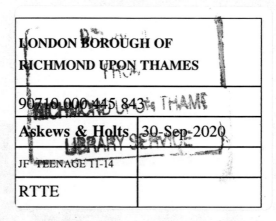
First published in 2020 by
Andersen Press Limited
20 Vauxhall Bridge Road
London SW1V 2SA
www.andersenpress.co.uk

2 4 6 8 10 9 7 5 3 1

British Library Cataloguing in Publication Data available.

ISBN 978 1 78344 967 5

Printed and bound in Great Britain by Clays Ltd, Elcograf S.p.A.

FOR NUTMEG

PROLOGUE

THE FUNERAL

The first time I ever saw Uncle Jesse was at the funeral. He gave a speech all about his brother, my dad.

Mum says this wasn't the first time because he visited when I was little. But I don't remember, so it doesn't really count, right?

I said this to Mum. I was all, like, 'If you don't remember something, how can you be sure it even happened?'

She showed me this photo I swear I'd never seen before. It was taken at the rec: me sitting on Dad's shoulders – not a baby, more like four or something – and Uncle Jesse next to him. They're both smiling, but weird faraway smiles, like they don't really want to be smiling at all. Dad's hair's a bit long, but not as long as Uncle Jesse's.

I wanted to ask Mum loads of other questions, but she was pulling a face that told me that whatever I asked – like, even: *Can I get on the tablet?* – she might get upset. So I stayed quiet. Mum pulls that face a lot these days. She says it's because she's *stressed*. It took me a while to figure out this is just a word she uses so she doesn't have to keep admitting she's sad.

At a funeral, they use all sorts of different words for stuff you already thought you knew: like, a bunch of flowers becomes a *wreath*, a coffin is a *casket* and the kind of speech that Uncle Jesse made is called a *eulogy*. I don't know for sure, but I reckon they use these words so you don't have to think about the funeral all the time. Like, if I'm asked to make a speech thanking Mr Bowler for coaching the team this year, I don't want to have to remember Uncle Jesse's eulogy, because then I wouldn't want to do it.

I didn't see Uncle Jesse come into the church but I noticed him across the aisle from us – this big guy I didn't recognise, just weeping into his hands. I asked Mum, 'Who's that?' But she didn't answer, because she was crying too and trying not to by taking short little breaths.

My big sister Hannah leaned across Mum and hissed, 'That's Uncle Jesse!' like it was obvious. But it wasn't obvious to me. Can you imagine you're thirteen years old and you see your own uncle and you don't even know who he is? Savage, right?

I kept watching him but I couldn't really see his face on account of the way he was crying. Then he got up from his seat and walked right out of the back of the church like he just couldn't take it any more. Nobody looked at him as he went past. It was like they were all embarrassed or something. But I saw him go all the way out of the door.

The priest spoke for a bit. Then he goes, 'Jesse Douglas will now say a few words.' I swear this was only, like, thirty seconds after he'd gone, so I actually looked round to see him come back in. But instead Uncle Jesse just appeared from the side like he'd been waiting there all along and he didn't even look like he'd been crying at all.

2

I was so shocked that I went, 'Did you see that?' I didn't mean to. I couldn't help myself. Mum took no notice – she was lost in her own thoughts. But Hannah bent forward to glare at me. I didn't care. I was looking around for someone to confirm my amazement, but nobody met my eye except this woman across the aisle who must have been sitting right next to Uncle Jesse. She was really pretty – she looked like she was in an advert or something. She gave me this weird little smile without teeth.

Uncle Jesse had to adjust the stand to make the microphone reach his mouth and it made a funny grating noise. He began, 'Billy was my big brother and best friend.' But I don't remember anything else he said because I had too much going on in my head.

First, I felt kind of vex because everybody knows Dad's best friend is Olu Adeyemi from work who buys me the sticker album at the beginning of every season; even though I'm, like, way too old for it now.

Second, I was still trying to work out how Uncle Jesse got from the back of the church to the front like that. I figured it was just about possible if he went out of the back door and sprinted round the side. But that didn't really make it less weird, only possible.

Third, I just stared, because he looks such a lot like Dad, only stretched like people do when they're messing around in an app on their phone. He's taller and thinner and he has a longer nose, longer hair and bigger ears – like a wizard. And he doesn't have sparkly eyes. He's got serious eyes.

Suddenly I felt mad lonely. I glanced at the Adeyemis a

few rows back – Olu and his wife Femi with the baby, Chibs, on her lap, then Juliet who's in Sixth Form, and Pamilekunayo. Pamilekunayo's a bit of a mouthful so he's usually called P. He's been *my* best friend since, like, for ever and I wanted him to look at me but he didn't. I got the idea he didn't dare – some people seem to think grief is catching.

I felt so sad. But I didn't cry.

'I'm sadder than the weeping willow in Misery Park in Sadville.' That's how Hannah said she felt the night before the funeral. It kind of sounds like she was joking, but she wasn't. That's just how she talked. For a couple of months, everything that came out of her mouth was these stupid comparisons: *fatter than a fat man eating fat chips in a fat suit* – that kind of thing. She doesn't talk like that any more.

But me? I felt like I was empty and mostly I still do; not like I'm hungry, but like there's a hole inside me so deep and dark that all my innards, everything I ever wanted, all the love I feel for my dad, even Dad himself, have been sucked inside like matter gets sucked into a black hole in space.

Do you know about black holes? They're crazy interesting. You should read about them, or there're some good videos online. They're parts of space where gravity's so strong that nothing can ever escape – not even light. And I've got a black hole inside me.

After the funeral, everyone went to the church hall and talked in quiet voices and we had sandwiches and tea in proper teacups with saucers (otherwise, I guess, you'd be thinking about the funeral every time you had a brew). There was lots of standing around which I know Mum hates because of her hip, but it's not like she had any choice. All these people came up to her and said *Beth* and gave her a hug. Some of them gave me and Hannah a hug. Some of them didn't.

Uncle Jesse came up to Mum and said *Beth* too, but he didn't give her a hug. He just stood there, looking like he'd rather be anywhere else in the world.

Mum said, 'It was good. What you said about Billy . . .'

Hannah and me both looked up at Mum, because the way she said *It was good* made it sound like she didn't mean it.

But Uncle Jesse didn't seem to notice. He goes, 'Really?'

And Mum said, 'Really.' Like she didn't mean that either. And Uncle Jesse nodded.

Uncle Jesse was with the woman from the church: the pretty one who did that weird smile. She's called Daisy – *his girlfriend*, Hannah said. Daisy's the right name for her because she looks a bit like a daisy – long and thin with an orange face and lots of blonde hair (*platinum blonde*, Hannah said).

Daisy goes, 'Beth', and she put her hand across her chest, fingers spread. Her nails were painted pale pink. Then she gave Mum a hug and it looked awkward, partly because Daisy's so tall and partly, I guess, because they'd never met before. She hugged Hannah and me as well and it was like hugging a bag of coat hangers.

Uncle Jesse cleared his throat. He said, 'If there's anything I can do . . .'

This is how people spoke at the funeral, without finishing their sentences: *Beth . . . What you said about Billy . . . If there's anything I can do . . .*

Mum looked at him. She goes, 'Like what?'

Uncle Jesse shifted uncomfortably, like he hadn't any idea where that sentence had been going. He said, 'I don't know. I'm sure things must be tight right now. Did Billy have life insurance?'

Mum goes, *'Life insurance?'* And she made a noise like a laugh, only it wasn't a laugh and Hannah and me both glanced up at her again. She shook her head and said, 'Right. No. But it's fine.'

Daisy said, 'We should probably . . .' And Mum nodded and Daisy said, 'Friday afternoon. Motorway will be hell.'

Mum said, 'Sure.'

They were leaving.

Uncle Jesse frowned and turned away. But then he turned back and goes to Hannah, 'You're the spitting image of your mum, you know that?' Suddenly he dropped to his haunches in front of me like he thought I was a little kid. For a second, I was worried he was about to give me a hug, but he didn't. He just goes, 'But you're Billy's boy all right.' Then, almost whispering, 'I'll see you soon, Gabe, OK? When you're ready . . .'

Although this was another unfinished sentence, it sounded like a question and he looked at me so hard that I felt kind of awkward. So I said, 'OK.' Because I had to say *something*.

Uncle Jesse nodded, straightened up, and he and Daisy

walked away. Mum put her hand on my shoulder. She goes, 'What did he say?'

'He said he'll see me soon. When I'm ready.'

Mum sniffed and goes, 'Oh, for goodness sake!'

Grandy came over then and he said, 'Beth . . .'

And Mum goes, 'Leave it, Dad,' like she was angry with him, even though he hadn't done anything.

I looked at Mum. She'd been crying all day. In fact, she'd been crying ever since the policeman stood in our hallway and said, 'Is there somewhere we could sit down?' And he hadn't even told her what had happened yet. But she wasn't crying now.

Have you ever been to a funeral? I've been to two – Granny Hannah (who my sister's named after) and now Dad. It's not like I'm boasting; funerals suck. I wish I hadn't been to any and never had to go to another one.

I think Dad's funeral was worse for three reasons.

First, it was Dad. When Granny Hannah died, she'd been sick for ages and people said stuff like *It was her time* and *She had a good innings*. Nobody said that about Dad. It wasn't his time and he didn't have a good innings. He was just there one day and gone the next. I think that's why people said to Mum, *Beth . . .* Because they didn't know what else to say.

Second, at Dad's funeral there were so many people I didn't recognise – all these work colleagues and friends from school and the football. It made me realise that Dad had a whole life before I was born that I didn't really know about, a life full of people I'd never even met. He was twenty-four when I was born and thirty-seven when he died. That means that for most of his life I wasn't there and he didn't know anything about me. That freaks me out.

Third, there was Uncle Jesse and he freaked me out too: because he did that weird thing at the church when it was like he was in two places at almost exactly the same time; because he acted all strange and Mum acted strange around him; because he said he'd see me when I'm 'ready'. I mean, I guess that last one doesn't sound odd to you. Like, he could've meant, *I'll see you when you're ready to come visit* or *I'll see you when you're feeling a bit better*. But you'll just have to take my word for it that he didn't mean it in either of those ways. And I'm pretty sure I'm right because the way he said it, all I could think was: *Ready for what?*

1

STORIES

Sometimes, if I tell a story, it's like I'm right there. I don't mean I'm there in my imagination, I mean I'm *actually there* and I can see everything, hear everything, smell everything and feel everything. It never used to happen. It's only since the funeral and still not always, but if I close my eyes and really concentrate, I start to glimpse a shape or two, or a face, like I'm looking through clouds or deep water; then I hear scraps of noise, maybe voices; then it's like I'm falling and I hear this rushing, whooshing, ripping sound . . .

Say you're lying in bed and you can't sleep and your mum's told you to think cheerful thoughts or whatever, you'll probably picture something really cool. Like, for me, I like football and I support Watford, so I might make up a story about scoring the winning goal in the Champions League Final (Watford in the Champions League? I know. But it's my story, right?).

Before Dad died, I'd picture Moses Hayes (my favourite player) running down the wing and he'd cross the ball and I'd throw myself at it, a diving header into the top corner, and it would be like watching myself on TV – *'Hayes! He fires it across! Gabriel Douglas! Goal!'*

But, last time? I was there; I mean, *I was actually on the pitch*. I was different too – bigger, older; not like a grown-up, but at least like eighteen or something. I heard the thud of Mo's foot on the ball as he sent over the cross. My eyes were stinging with sweat. I felt the centre back's fingernails scratch my back as he tried to hold my shirt (we were playing Real Madrid who are well dirty). I was blinded as my head made contact with the ball and winded as I hit the ground.

I heard the roar of the crowd. I ran towards our fans and I could pick out every face.

You don't believe me? Right at the front, there was this big guy with a shaved head and glasses in a Watford shirt who was shouting all kinds of swear words. I mean, I guess he was happy, but he'd totally lost it and was kind of threatening. That's not the kind of thing you'd picture in your imagination, is it?

The fan leaned forward and tried to grab me, but one of our players pulled me away. I didn't recognise him, which was weird because I know our whole first team squad back to front. But he was ruffling my hair and shouting too – something in a foreign language I didn't understand.

Sounds pretty cool, right? Not always. I'll show you. Let me close my eyes and concentrate.

It's Mum's birthday. Hannah and me should be on our way to school, but Hannah says she can't find her maths book and I'm pretending I can't find my trunks. Mum's at the bottom of the stairs. She doesn't like coming upstairs if she can avoid it because of her hip, which is bad in the mornings. She's getting cross. She says, 'If you can't find your trunks, just swim in your shorts.'

I go, 'We're not allowed.'

Mum says, 'Oh, for goodness sake!' and stomps into the kitchen.

Hannah and me look at one another. We're both kind of hyped because we're in on the secret – this is all part of Dad's plan.

Yesterday, Dad went to Glasgow for work. He's a salesman for Betterwares, who make office furniture. There's a new business park opening and he wants Betterwares to fit it out. He was meant to stay over. He said to Mum, 'Sorry, Elizabeth, I know it's your birthday but there's nothing I can do. Think of the commission.' Dad likes calling Mum *Elizabeth* instead of *Beth* sometimes because he says she's the queen of our house. Then he turned away and winked at Hannah and me.

Three days ago, Dad sat us down in Hannah's bedroom after tea while Mum was loading the dishwasher. He told us he was supposed to be away for Mum's birthday. He told us he was going to drive home overnight instead and be back in time for breakfast. He told us to pretend we'd forgotten about Mum's birthday. He showed us what he'd got – a bottle of champagne and a fancy black dress with sequins that he bought online.

Hannah examined the dress. She thinks she's a fashion expert. Dad said, 'You think it's OK?' He sounded kind of worried.

Hannah said, 'It's perfect.'

The dress is under my bed, wrapped up with a bow. The champagne's in Hannah's chest of drawers.

Dad's going to get home with a big bunch of flowers and say, 'Surprise!' Then me and Hannah will come down the stairs with the present and champagne and say, 'Surprise!' And then we'll go to school and Mum and Dad will drink Buck's Fizz (which is champagne and orange juice). Then because Dad isn't expected at work today, they can go for a walk by the reservoir and have lunch at the Coy Carp, which is Mum's favourite.

Dad said, 'You think it's a good plan?'

'It's a great plan.'

Dad looked pleased with himself and his eyes were dancing: 'This is what life's about – making memories; stories you can tell when you're old.'

I look at my alarm clock and it's eight-thirty. Dad's really late and Mum's getting totally salty, but that will only make the surprise better. The doorbell rings and Hannah and me stumble over each other, rushing to the top of the stairs. We've both had the same thought – *It must be Dad*. He didn't tell us he was going to ring the bell, but it's a good idea because it will all add to the surprise. We're both buzzing as Mum opens the door.

It's not Dad. It's this policeman in uniform who looks too old to be a cop – like, almost as old as Grandy or something. Behind him is a policewoman. He says, 'Mrs Douglas?' Then, 'Can we come in?'

I look at Hannah, but she's not looking at me. She's

holding the banister at the top of the stairs and her knuckles are white because she's gripping it so tightly.

The old policeman goes, 'Is there somewhere we could sit down?'

Mum glances up at Hannah and me. She's started crying and I don't know why. The cop follows her eyes up the stairs. He goes, 'Hello, you two!' in a friendly voice like he knows us, but he doesn't know us. He turns to the policewoman and says, 'Shilpa? Do you mind?'

Shilpa goes, 'Sarge.'

Mum shows him into the front room and Shilpa leads Hannah and me into the kitchen. I'm freaked out. I know something's wrong, but I don't know what it is. I think of the worst thing it could possibly be and, because the cops have come, I think maybe Dad's been arrested. But some bit of me already knows it's worse than that . . .

Hannah goes, 'What's happening?'

Shilpa fills the kettle and puts it on. She says, 'Let's make your mum a hot drink. What does she like, tea or coffee?'

'She'll have a brew,' I say.

'Can you show me?'

I get the tin of tea bags out of the cupboard and the milk from the fridge. Hannah's looking at me like I'm a traitor.

Shilpa goes, 'Shouldn't you be at school by now?'

'We're waiting for Dad,' Hannah says.

'It's Mum's birthday,' I say.

'What's happening?' Hannah asks again. 'What's going on?' She sounds all vex.

Shilpa doesn't answer. She just tilts her head to one side

and does this thin smile. The kettle is boiling. She doesn't know that the button to turn itself off is broken. 'It's broken,' I say. 'The button, I mean.'

Shilpa goes, 'Oh. Right.' She turns off the kettle. There's a lot of steam, which mists up the window and I can see the finger marks where Dad was showing me how to bend my run off the centre back last week.

Then Hannah runs out of the kitchen like she thinks Shilpa might try and stop her. But Shilpa doesn't try and stop her. Instead, she picks up the kettle and starts filling the cup. She goes, 'What's your name?'

'Gabriel,' I say. 'Gabe.'

I watch her pour the water. Her hand is shaking. And this is the moment I know Dad is dead. I don't know how I know; I just do. And my face feels like it's on fire and my stomach is full of ice. And then the fire spreads to my stomach and the ice melts and falls into the black hole that's opening inside me.

You probably figure the first story I told you – about scoring that goal – was just a dream, and the second a memory so terrible that I can't help but recall every single detail even if I don't want to.

But you're wrong. I don't know how to convince you. I don't even know why I'm telling you, except I wanted to tell someone. You might think I'm showing off, or I've gone mad. I'm not showing off and I don't know if I'm mad – how could I? I guess you'll decide for yourself.

2

SMALL TOWN HERO

Have you played Small Town Hero yet? You can get it on every platform, I think.

Everyone at Graycoat's crazy for it. I've never been into gaming. I'm not into Fortnite, Red Dead and that. I mean, I play FIFA with P sometimes, but I get bored pretty quickly – I'd rather just play proper football.

I guess it's partly because I haven't got a phone of my own right now and Hannah and me have this tablet we're supposed to share, only she totally hogs it. But I am into Small Town Hero.

It's not like any other game I've seen. For starters, it's kind of old-fashioned – there's no multi-player, for example, and no different modes. Also, it's hard even to know what kind of game it is. Like, the review on *GamesRadar* says it's a sandbox game, but some of the hardcore gamers at school reckon it's an RPG or a first-person fighter. I'm not an expert, but I reckon it's a bit of all of those. It's almost like it's whatever you want it to be – if you want to fight, you can fight; but if you want to negotiate or just walk away, you can often do that too. And sometimes you won't know if you made a good decision until way later and, even then, it might turn out to be wrong after that. I guess the closest comparison would be something like *Minecraft* in Adventure Mode, or that spin-off, *Minecraft: Story Mode*, but that's not exactly right either.

The main reason I like it is the storyline. I mean, it's not super-original, but it's really smart and funny. I've shown Mum a couple of times and even she likes it, I think.

It's set in Small Town and you're this kid called Prince Prince. At the beginning, you're at a banquet in the citadel when the Fool runs in – Small Town's under attack by the Ineffable, Unstoppable Dragon. The King and his knights mount up and ride off into the night. Then the screen goes black and it says, *Chapter One*. The King hasn't come back, so Prince Prince sets off with the Fool and they find Small Town, like, totally destroyed.

I'm not going to tell you that much about the game right now, because if you play it, you already know and if you haven't, I don't want to spoil it for you. But I think there are three really cool things about it.

First, it's played in 'chapters' and you never get to see the next until you've completed the last. Apparently, it's not even on your device or whatever but gets downloaded depending on the decisions you've taken, so it's as if you're playing a game that's unique to you. I mean, this can't be true, but that's how it feels. There's this famous Korean gamer who does playthroughs on Twitch and he's on Chapter Twenty-three. But there would be no point copying what he's done, because that would be like telling his story.

Also, there's no going back. You can't decide you made a mistake and go and change it. Like, for example, when I was on Chapter Five, Prince Prince met Juju the Witch who set him a riddle. It turned out he needed the answer to open the sliding doors at the Monstrosity in Chapter Nine, but I'd forgotten it by then and that was the end of me (or, rather, Prince Prince). And it's not like you go back to the beginning of the level or whatever. Instead, it's game over, end of story.

Talking of 'End of Story', that's actually an option that's onscreen all the time. If you die, you jump to this animation that shows you the consequences of what you've done up to now. But you can also choose End of Story any time, which does the same thing, like, if you get bored or whatever. I haven't done that yet because that would be admitting defeat. But P's done it loads because he's really impatient. Like, one time, he did it in Chapter One before he'd even crossed the ring road and we flashed to this cool sequence where Prince Prince is standing in Small Town and it's still all rubble, but now gangs are roaming the streets, fighting over snacks. And then you look back at the citadel and it's on fire, burning to the ground, and it's too late to do anything about it – kind of like the opposite of *and they all lived happily ever after* . . .

Right now, I'm on Chapter Fourteen, which is the furthest I've got and further than anyone in my class. Abdul says he's got the furthest because he's been playing every day for more than a month and he hasn't died yet. But, he's full of it because he's, like, really loaded and he's got a Switch which is linked to his mum's credit card, so when he gets stuck he can always just buy another loot box. *And* he's just kept Prince Prince in Small Town: rebuilding the station brick by brick, planning a new mall and having swimming races in the Lido with Psycho Steve.

Anyway, it's a really cool game. If you don't know it, you should Google it.

3

MORE OR LESS

Dad died in a car crash on the motorway. He was driving back for Mum's birthday. It was very late. The cops reckon he fell asleep at the wheel.

When your dad dies, you might think everything changes. Lots of things do, but lots stay the same too, more or less.

Like, I didn't go to school for a bit, but then I went back. I still play in the school team, but this term Mr Bowler's moved me to centre forward, which is what Dad said he should do ages ago. I don't go to every Watford home game any more, but sometimes I go with Olu if P's got kung fu and there's a spare ticket. Uncle Jesse's called a couple of times, but he still hasn't visited. And I still argue with Hannah about who gets to use the tablet, only now Hannah goes, 'Mum! This is *so* why I need a new phone!'

I go, 'Shut up, Hannah!' Because Mum's already stressed, and at least Hannah's still *got* a phone. Mine was nicked (if you ask me) or lost (according to Mum). She says I can earn a new one, but if I ask what I have to do, she kind of tuts like the question's annoying. It sucks, because every Year Nine's got a phone apart from Rainbow Jones and people call her a freak.

Hannah goes, 'You shut up!'

Then Mum says, 'Both of you, shut up!' and storms out, and the room is so quiet it's basically noisy.

Hannah looks at me and makes a sneering face. She goes, 'Well done!' and storms out herself. And I'm so vex because that's unfair and I can't even say anything back.

As for what's changed? Actually, more has changed than stayed the same, but there are two things in particular and, really, I think that everything that's changed is connected to one of these two things in one way or another.

First, there's the black hole inside me, which just won't budge.

Every Tuesday I go and see Mrs Perez, the school counsellor. I told her about the black hole. She said, 'I'm not sure it ever goes away, but you do get used to it.' I must have looked like I didn't believe her, because then she said, 'You know if you cut yourself really badly? At first, it's sore, but eventually it heals and you've got a scar. And that scar tissue is actually stronger than the skin was before, but it's still there, like a permanent reminder. You see what I mean?'

And I did see. But I Googled what she said about scar tissue and it turns out it's an old wives' tale – the skin's not stronger, only rougher – and we haven't talked about the black hole since. Instead, she just asks me all these questions about school, my friends, Mum and Hannah, and things that Dad and me used to do together.

I've already told you about the second thing that's different – the stories I imagine that become real. Eventually, I told Mrs Perez about them too. At least she didn't look at me like I was mad (although she's the school counsellor so she's probably used to it). She said, 'Give me an example.'

At first, I didn't want to, but then I thought, *Why not?* And I told her this story I fell into one night about Mum at work. These days Mum's got a job, you see, and she's always stressed because we never have enough money. So, lying in bed, I closed my eyes and I concentrated really hard until I saw some vague shapes and I felt myself topple forward and I heard that whooshing noise and suddenly there I was – at the twenty-four-hour where Mum works the till.

I'm by the door. There are no cars outside. It must be proper late. Mum's sitting behind the counter, leaning on her hand, almost asleep. But then she sits up like someone prodded her and looks right at me, only somehow she can't see me. I realise I'm invisible. What's that about?

Mum sighs and drags herself to her feet. She comes out from behind the counter and I have to move out of the way so she doesn't walk right into me. She passes so close that I can smell her. She smells like cigarettes, which is weird because she gave up smoking ages ago – Dad and her did it together. The automatic doors slide open and she goes outside to bring in the empty newspaper racks and the black buckets where they keep flowers. There's only one bunch left and they look kind of sad, their petals wilting and turning brown.

Mum wipes her forehead with the back of her hand like she's really exhausted. She returns to the counter but stops by the plastic dispenser where the scratchcards are kept.

She reaches into her jeans and finds a coin. She takes out a scratchcard, then goes back to her chair to scan it, open the till and drop the money in. She pauses for a moment, looking at the scratchcard, turning it in her fingers.

I can hear my breathing. It's so loud I can't believe Mum doesn't hear it too. But she can't hear me any more than she can see me. I go, 'Come on! Scratch it off!' She can't hear that either, but she does bend over the scratchcard and slowly peels the panels with her fingernail.

I watch her face. I don't know what's going to happen but I kind of do too; like when you watch a scary movie and the girl goes outside on her own to investigate a strange noise (only sometimes it's a double bluff because actually nothing happens after all). Mum stares at the card. She shakes her head. She makes a small grunting noise and goes, 'Well, for goodness sake!' Then she starts to laugh and cry all at the same time and she holds up the scratchcard for the security camera on the ceiling, revealing its secret. 'Twenty-five thousand pounds,' she says. *'Twenty-five thousand pounds!'* Then she buries her head in her hands. Finally, she looks up to heaven and she goes, 'Tell me this was you, Billy Douglas! Tell me this was you!' And she's crying and crying. I wouldn't say they're happy tears, but they're not exactly sad either.

When I told Mrs Perez, halfway through she started writing in her notebook. And she was still writing when she said, 'I think that's great, Gabriel.' I didn't say anything and eventually she looked up: 'And you were invisible?'

I frowned. 'Yeah,' I said. 'But that's never happened before.'

'No? So why do you think you were invisible this time?'

'Dunno,' I said. I thought about it. 'Maybe because it wasn't really about me, it was about Mum.'

Mrs Perez goes, 'Right. Exactly.' And she was nodding, like, way too enthusiastically. She put down her pen and did this weird fake smile. Then she said, 'Do you often feel invisible, Gabe? I don't mean *literally* invisible; I mean, do you feel like people don't see you or hear you, and don't understand what you're going through; what you're thinking.'

I stared at her. I'm not thick – I knew what she was getting at. I mumbled, 'All the time.' I should have said, *Like, right now for example*. But I didn't. And she looked at me with that fake smile and she was so pleased with herself, like she just won the school counsellor championships or something.

I'll tell you something about adults: the ones who claim to be listening, who pull those sympathetic faces, lean forward and nod along to what you're saying – they're often the ones who aren't listening at all.

I was mad frustrated. I said, 'It was real! That's the point!'

Then I told Mrs Perez about the next day, when I got back from school and Mum was there because she didn't have a shift and she had this big smile on her face. Hannah was already home, and I asked her, 'What's going on?'

But Hannah didn't know.

Mum said, 'Who wants Chinese?'

Hannah and me looked at each other, because we haven't

had a takeaway for ages because we can't afford it. 'We're celebrating,' Mum explained. 'I won on a scratchcard.'

Now Mrs Perez looked at me like I was mad. She goes, 'You're telling me your mum actually won?'

'Yes.'

'Twenty-five *thousand* pounds?'

'No. It was only twenty-five,' I said. 'But still . . .'

Mrs Perez flickered a real smile, then went back to the fake one, leaned forward, nodded along and said, 'That's a relief.' I blinked at her. I didn't get it. 'I thought you were expecting me to believe in magic,' she said. Then, 'Do you know, Gabriel, in all the times you've come to see me, you've not cried once, did you know that? It's not a problem. Everybody's different. But I just want to make sure you're not hiding how you feel. Sometimes, when an awful thing happens, it's like we grab a shield to show the world how strong we are. Like, I know you want to be strong for your mum, to make sure she's all right. And that's so important. But it's not your job. Your job at the moment is to look after *you*; to make sure *you're* all right. Do you see? That's what your mum needs you to do, OK?'

Mrs Perez was looking at me with such a serious expression that I felt like I had no choice but to say, 'OK.' Like with Uncle Jesse at the funeral.

I don't know if adults know this, but half the time they ask a question, they do it in a way that tells you the answer they want to hear. So you give them that answer because it's easier. But it makes you wonder what the question was for in the first place.

I don't mind going to see Mrs Perez. It's better than being in class and she has these mints on her desk and you can take as many as you want. But I don't know what it's *for*. If she told me when my black hole was going to turn into a scar, that would be useful. I could tell Mum and she could put a note on the fridge like she does for football practice, and it would be something to look forward to. But we don't even talk about that.

And I didn't expect Mrs Perez to believe in magic either. Did I ever use that word? I don't think so. I only expected her to believe *me*. Obviously, I know it's impossible to go somewhere in your head and then find yourself there in real life. But that's what happens. I also know it's impossible to tell a story about your mum winning on a scratchcard that makes her win on a scratchcard. But that happened too, and I don't think it matters whether she won twenty-five quid or twenty-five thousand.

Like, if someone at school said they could fly, you'd laugh, right? But if they really insisted, you'd say, 'Go on, then!' And if they flapped their arms and lifted one metre off the ground, you'd be really shocked. And if you said, 'Fly as high as a plane,' and they said, 'I can't,' you wouldn't say, 'Well, you're not really flying then,' would you? You'd still be thinking, *This kid can fly!*

I suppose what I'm trying to explain is that some people would always rather believe in no magic than a little bit. And, just to be clear, I'm not asking you to believe in magic anyway. I'm just telling you what happened. Why would I lie?

4

NOT LITTLE ANY MORE

One Friday I woke up in the middle of the night and I was terrified. My T-shirt was soaked in sweat and I was kind of out of breath. Maybe I'd had a nightmare, but if I had I couldn't remember it.

I got out of bed and went to Mum's room. I could see the light under her door, so I knew she was awake too. She was standing by the open window. She looked round at me. She goes, 'Gabe? What you doing?'

For some reason, I felt embarrassed, like I was interrupting something. I said, 'Dunno. I got scared.'

She climbed into bed, pulled back the duvet and patted the space next to her, Dad's side: 'Come here.' She gave me a hug. She smelled of cigarettes. I *had* interrupted something, but she didn't want to tell me because she knew I'd give her grief, and I didn't want to say.

Then she did a painful little gasp, so I pulled away. I go, 'Is your hip sore?'

'A bit,' she said. 'You mind if I lie down?'

I shook my head and she lay facing me, propped up on one elbow.

'You take your pills?' I asked. She nodded. 'Are they not working?'

'Not yet.'

'When did you take them?'

'Gabriel!' She used my whole name. She sounded irritable. I know she doesn't like to make a fuss about her hip, but I was worried. She changed the subject. She said, 'It's the middle of the night, love! What are you scared of?'

It was only when she asked the question that I knew the answer. 'I don't wanna be an orphan,' I said, and immediately wished I hadn't because it sounded kind of lame and she looked totally spooked. That was just for a second, then she gathered herself and tried a smile. But it was too late, because I'd already seen the spooked look.

'You won't be an orphan. I know Dad died and it's terrible, but I'm not going anywhere. I promise.'

'How do you know?'

'Because I'm tough as old boots. What about my accident? If I was going to die, I'd have died then. I fell thirty feet onto concrete and I was unconscious a whole week. But then I woke up and I was right as rain.'

'Except your hip.'

'It's not so bad.'

'How can you promise you're not going anywhere?' I asked. 'How can you promise you're not gonna die?'

Mum made this little grunting noise, close to a laugh but not a laugh. She goes, 'We're all gonna die, Gabe.' She must have seen my expression, because she quickly followed this with, 'Sorry. I don't know why I said that.'

'It's OK.'

It's not like I don't know we're all going to die. But it's

still strange to hear your mum say it straight out like that.

Mum said, 'Do you want to sleep in my bed tonight, like when you were little?'

When I was little, I often used to sneak in between Mum and Dad in the middle of the night, waking them both up. Mum usually went back to sleep pretty quickly, wrapping me up in her arms. But Dad didn't. It drove him crazy and often, after tossing and turning for a few minutes, he'd get out of bed, huffing and puffing, and go and sleep in my room instead.

I didn't hear Mum and Dad argue much, but they argued about that. Dad said, 'For Pete's sake, Beth! He needs to learn to sleep in his own bed!'

Mum said, 'He's just a kid.'

'Exactly! He needs to learn! Do you really want him to have to come to his mummy any time he can't sleep?'

I thought about this as I looked at Mum. I'm not little any more. Grandy told me I'm now the man of the house. I said, 'It's OK, thanks.'

I was about to get out of bed and go back to my room. But Mum said, 'It's not for you, Gabe love. It's for me. I could use the company.'

I shrugged: 'OK, then.'

There was a knock at the door and Hannah came in: 'I heard you two talking. I can't sleep. What you doing?'

'We can't sleep either,' Mum explained. 'Jump in. More the merrier.'

So we lay like that – Mum in the middle, Hannah on one

side, me on the other. It wasn't like I remembered from when I was little. If anything, it felt awkward. I don't know why; maybe because Hannah and me are too old and too big to be in bed with Mum; or maybe because we were all so wide awake that it felt kind of stupid to be lying all in a row like fish fingers.

Mum goes, 'Sometimes, if you can't sleep, it's best not to think about it. So let's not think about it. What shall we talk about?'

Hannah and me looked at each other. I knew what I wanted to talk about and she had the same idea. Hannah goes, 'Dad.'

Mum glanced from Hannah to me: 'What about Dad?'

Hannah shrugged. She looked a bit uncomfortable and embarrassed. It was exactly like I was feeling. 'I dunno,' she said. 'You know . . .'

'Anything!' I said.

Mum goes, 'You know what Dad would say if he could see us now?'

'For Pete's sake!' me and Hannah said together, and we all started laughing. Somehow it totally changed the atmosphere to remember something small like that.

'Who's Pete anyway?' I asked.

'No idea,' Mum said, still laughing. Then she lifted up her arms and hugged us both to her. 'So, where shall we start?'

5

WHAT I KNOW (PART ONE)

You probably don't know your mum and dad as well as you think. After all, if you're a kid, they lived half a life before you were born. And, besides, you only ever know them as your parents. I mean, you don't often see them at work, with their friends, at the gym or whatever, right? And, even if you do, *you're there*, so a big part of them is probably still being Mum or Dad.

I bet you don't think about this much – why would you? And when your parents start saying something with *When I was a kid*, you're probably all, like, *Boring!* I used to be like that too. But, since Dad died, the gaps in what I know about him sort of make me panic; like if I don't find out all about him now, maybe I never will.

So I'll tell you what I've found out so far. I'll do it in the order of his life, but actually I've had to put it together like a jigsaw puzzle, because I've discovered things in bits and pieces – from Mum, from Grandy, from Dad's best friend Olu ... and, of course, some of it I knew already. What's more, in telling you about Dad, I'll end up talking about Mum and Uncle Jesse too. That's OK, because Mum and Dad go together like fish and chips, and Uncle Jesse's

Dad's brother and my only other family apart from Hannah and Grandy.

My dad, Billy Mackenzie Douglas, was born in 1983 in a place called Somers Town, which is a part of London near Euston station. His brother Jesse was born three years later. They were really broke: not like we are now – I mean, like, proper poor. Their mum, my grandmother Coral, didn't have a job. She was on Jobseekers and made a bit of cash on the side knitting and fixing clothes; nothing complicated – just scarves, buttons, hems and stuff. They lived in a small flat on the Medburn Estate. Billy went back there once to look for the block, but it was gone. It had been torn down to build new platforms for the station.

Billy didn't know much about Coral because she upped and left when he was seven. That was how he always put it – *She upped and left* – and he used this bouncy tone, which sounded kind of light-hearted but also warned you not to ask anything else. One time I tried: 'Why did she do that?' But he just shook his head and said it again – 'Dunno. Upped and left', all bouncy. He found out that she'd died when he was a teenager and he didn't want to answer questions about that either.

Coral was part Jamaican, which is why Hannah has tight curly hair, although mostly she straightens it with tongs. Billy had no photos and nothing that belonged to her. He said he couldn't even remember what his mum looked like; not really. The only thing he remembered was that she had locks and a small patch of freckles on either side of her nose. I've got freckles like that.

Billy never knew his dad at all. He thought he might have been Scottish because of his middle name 'Mackenzie', which is a Scottish surname, and Jesse has no middle name. But that was just a guess. In fact, Billy didn't even know for sure that he and Jesse had the same dad, but he always thought they must do because they looked alike and, in any case, what difference did it make? Either way, they were brothers.

Quite a lot of this was news to me. Obviously, I knew I didn't have a granny and grandad on Dad's side, but I didn't know everything. When Mum told me about the Scottish thing, for example, I asked, 'But didn't Dad ever want to find out about his family?'

We were in the kitchen and Mum was making sandwiches with her back to me, but when I asked this question she stopped and looked off out the window. It took her a moment to answer. 'Dunno,' she said. 'I think he was too busy looking after Jesse.'

'And then?'

She turned around and smiled: 'And then you guys came along. We had a family of our own.'

Billy and Jesse were taken into care by the council. They lived in a children's home in another part of London called Camden Town. I guess in books this would usually be *an orphanage*, right? But apparently they're not called that any more. After two years, they were fostered, which means they went to live with other people's families. Some of these families had kids of their own, some didn't.

I asked Mum how many foster homes Billy and Jesse stayed in, but she didn't know. She said, 'A lot. I'm not sure. I'm not even sure Dad remembered them all.'

This was how they ended up in Beedon Road and going to St Mark's, which was where they met Mum.

'Everyone was in awe of Billy. I don't know why. Maybe because we knew he'd been in care and he'd come from London and he seemed kind of tough, but he had those sparkly eyes too. Also, he just turned up one year at school and he went straight into the football team. He was like you, Gabe, mad about it – always got a ball at his feet.

'There was this boy called Steve Vickers. He was a right thug, but he was the team captain and some people said his uncle played for Luton. Billy was way better. Steve didn't like that, because he'd always been top man, you know? And then Billy shows up and St Mark's get to the county final for the first time ever and Billy scores the winner.

'I swear, even when Steve lifted the cup he looked kinda angry about it. The whole school was down the rec to watch, but the girls? They only turned out to see Billy, like he was a pop star. I remember Sonya Sullivan and Gemma Something-or-other arguing about whether he looked like Howie D out of Backstreet Boys.'

This was Mum talking that night Hannah and me got into her bed. Her whole face changed as she told the story.

I wanted to ask her who Backstreet Boys were, but she looked so happy that I didn't want to interrupt. So I was kind of annoyed when Hannah goes, 'But Dad only liked you, right?'

It was fine, though, because Mum just burst out laughing. 'Me? No! I was three years younger. He didn't even know who I was. It was Jesse I knew first. Because he was in my year.'

According to Mum, Uncle Jesse was *on another planet*. He was the opposite of Dad – quiet, slight and shy. He was also *too clever* and always getting grief, both from teachers and other kids. It wasn't like he was a troublemaker – he just didn't care what people thought of him. Like, if a teacher caught him daydreaming and said, 'Am I boring you, Jesse Douglas?' Uncle Jesse would shrug and go, 'Sure. But don't worry about it.' That sort of thing made the class laugh. But he also said the same kind of stuff about other kids. Like, if two boys were messing around in comprehension and the teacher got vex, Jesse would go, 'What's the point in getting angry? They don't know what's going on. You know they can hardly read, right?' And the rest of the class would gasp because, even if it was true, saying so in front of everyone was bang out of line.

One Saturday, Mum got a call to work a shift at the last minute and I went with her because Hannah was going round Sapphire's. I didn't really mind, because it gave me the chance to ask more questions, one in particular – 'How come you were friends with Uncle Jesse?' She was serving a customer. She flashed me a look but didn't answer. 'I mean, you said he was *on another planet* and he sounds kind of annoying.'

'He wasn't annoying,' Mum said. 'Just different.' She picked up a box of Starburst and started unpacking them onto the sweet counter. She said, 'I was different too. Two outcasts.'

This was shocking. I said, 'Why were *you* an outcast?'

She shrugged: 'School's like that sometimes, isn't it? You get a label and it sticks.' I knew she hoped that was enough to shut me up, but it wasn't. So she sighed. She goes, 'Look, most of the kids had been to St Mark's primary, so they knew each other. But I'd been to Wilverley Edge and I didn't know anyone. Then, on the first day, Dad picked me up from school and Sonya Sullivan asked if he was my grandad and, when I said he was my dad, she was all, *That's so weird!* That was it. I was weird.'

Mum shrugged again, as if to say, *So what?* Like it didn't matter. But I could tell it did matter and I said, 'People are mean.'

'They didn't know they were being mean. They were just kids.'

'Kids know they're being mean. Trust me.'

Mum gave me a strange look. She goes: 'Very true, Gabe. You're too clever.'

'Like Uncle Jesse,' I said.

She gave me an even stranger look. 'Yeah,' she said. 'Kind of.'

*

I already knew that Grandy and Granny Hannah had been told by doctors that they couldn't have kids, so Mum was a miracle. She was born when Granny Hannah was forty (which is older than Mum is now) and Grandy was forty-seven. That means that at the time Grandy was picking her up from school, he was almost sixty. I guess I might have thought that looked weird too, but I wouldn't have stressed her about it.

Now, Grandy just looks like any other grandad . . .

I reckon that when you get old, age doesn't matter so much. Like, when you're twelve, some of the Year Nines and Tens don't even talk to you because you're *just a kid*. But by the time you reach Under Fourteens, your football matches are eleven-a-side, your voice might have broken, and you could have a girlfriend or whatever – it's totally different. On the other hand, Grandy gets up every morning and goes to the shop and buys a newspaper and a packet of salt and vinegar crisps. He sits in his chair with a cup of coffee and his crisps (which Mum says is *just gross*) and he looks around and goes, 'You seen my goggles, Gabe?' Then, when I've found his glasses, he reads the paper and goes, 'I don't know why I read this rubbish.' And he's done the same thing every day for as long as I can remember, like my whole life.

I told Grandy what Mum said about being an outcast and Grandy said, 'Nonsense. That's not how I remember it. Beth was a lovely, happy, popular girl.'

But I didn't tell him about the other kids teasing her because her dad was so old, because I didn't want him to feel bad. So maybe Mum never told him for the same reason and he never actually knew.

Grandy remembered Uncle Jesse too. He said, 'Nice quiet lad. We thought he was a good influence on your mum. My Hannah – your granny – she adored him. He wasn't like the little hooligans going down the arcade every day. He was round ours; him and your mum, doing their homework at the kitchen table, and afterwards he didn't even want to watch TV, he was always buried in a book. We knew he was destined for big things.'

'Big things like what?'

'I don't know. Whatever it is he does. Earning pots of money.'

'Is Uncle Jesse rich?'

Grandy goes, 'How should I know? Ask your mum. He must be rich. Have you seen the house prices in London?'

6

WHAT I KNOW (PART TWO)

It's funny, but if you've always known one way of doing things or talking about things, you don't know any different.

Like, once, when I went round P's after school, he made some toast, and when it popped out the toaster he laid it on the counter for a couple of seconds before spreading the marge. I go, 'What you doing?' And he told me that it stops the toast going soggy. It works and all.

Like, it was only after Dad died and I saw him at the funeral that I realised I'd never really thought about Uncle Jesse before. I mean, it's not like I didn't know he existed – I knew Dad had a little brother, that he was smart . . . I think I even had some idea that he was minted, though I don't know how. But I never questioned why he didn't come for Christmas or birthdays or even send any cards. He just didn't.

I do remember a conversation Mum and Dad had though. This was ages ago – like, two years at least. We were in the kitchen: Mum, Dad and me. Dad had just got home from work. Mum was cooking. Dad goes, 'I heard from Jesse. He's back from California.'

Mum didn't look round. It was a moment before she said, 'How is he?'

Dad shrugged. He goes, 'It was a voicemail. Just giving

me his new number.' Then, 'We should get him up for a weekend or something.'

Mum goes, 'Sure.'

But Uncle Jesse never came up for the weekend and I didn't think about it again until now.

I know it must sound weird – that I never saw my only uncle and that I hardly even noticed. But, like I said, if you've always known one way of doing things or talking about things, you don't know any different.

Mum picked me up from football practice. I like it when she does, because she'll buy me Maltesers on the way home and ask loads of questions even though she doesn't care about football. But this was the first time in ages and she wasn't asking me any questions today.

She was limping a bit. She limps when she's tired. I offered her a Malteser. She shook her head. She said, 'They're for you.'

We walked on a little. Then I go, 'Grandy told me you and Uncle Jesse were friends.'

Mum stopped. 'Yeah,' she said. 'We were.' At first, I thought she'd stopped in surprise, but she was probably just resting her hip.

I said, 'You don't like Uncle Jesse, do you?' It just slipped out.

'What makes you say that?'

'He's my uncle and I never see him.'

'Do you *want* to see him?' Mum fired this at me fast. She suddenly sounded salty. I felt kind of helpless. Did I want to see him? I had no idea, but I remembered what he said at the funeral – *When you're ready.* Mum goes, 'He knows where we live, Gabriel!'

She started walking again. Her limp was more pronounced. Her right leg kind of slides out to the side and then swings out straight in a wide arc. I can do a good impression which sometimes makes her laugh.

I said, 'Did Dad like Uncle Jesse?'

Mum didn't look at me. 'Of course he did. He loved him. More than anything. We both did.'

I was getting frustrated. I said, 'So what happened?'

Mum hobbled on. She answered the question, but she was talking over her shoulder, like she didn't care whether I heard or not. 'Your dad left school at sixteen. He didn't do A Levels. He didn't go to college. He got an apprenticeship and a part-time job, and he saved up. He rented a flat in town for him and Jesse – so they could leave Beedon Road, so he could look after his brother. That's all he wanted to do: look after Jesse. What Dad did was amazing, Gabe love. He was just a kid himself. Just a kid . . .' She tailed away, but I could tell there was more to come. I didn't know whether to prompt her – *And?* But I was worried that might put her off. Eventually, she goes, 'Jesse got a scholarship to boarding school.' Then, '*He* did A Levels and went to university.' Then, 'And he didn't come back. That's what happened.'

I thought about this: 'Dad must have been pretty vex.'

Mum goes, 'No,' really quickly. Then, slower, 'Not exactly. It's just . . .'

'Just what?'

But she shook her head again.

We'd reached our front gate and Mum did her usual thing of moving the wheelie bin back and cursing the dustmen. I wanted her to keep talking, but she was distracted. Now I felt like I *had* to prompt her, or the moment would be gone. I said, 'Grandy says that Uncle Jesse's got pots of money.' I just blurted it out and immediately knew it was the wrong thing to say.

Mum goes, 'Did he now?' in a sarcastic kind of voice. Then, 'What else did he say?'

'He asked if I'd seen the house prices in London.'

She burst out laughing. She said, 'Sounds about right.' And she took out her door key. And, sure enough, that was that.

To be honest, Mum hadn't told me much I didn't know. I already knew Dad looked after Uncle Jesse on his own in a flat from the age of seventeen, because if Hannah or me ever complained about our homework, not getting what we wanted or whatever, Dad would go, 'For Pete's sake! You don't know how lucky you are!' And then he told us all about it whether we liked it or not. But I did start thinking about Dad in a new way – because Mum was right, what he'd done *was* amazing.

Also, what Mum said gave me some kind of explanation for why Uncle Jesse never visited. I mean, whether Dad was vex or not, I could imagine how hard it must have been – to do all that for his little brother who left and never came back. Like, last year, me and Jeetan were the only Year Eights in the Under Fourteens and we kind of became friends, so at the end of term I lent him my ball to practise, because we were going to Center Parcs for a week and they have loads of footballs. But when I got back, I realised I had no ball and I didn't know where Jeetan lived or have his number or anything. Then I went down the rec and he was playing three on three with his friends with my ball and they didn't want me to play because the teams were fair. I thought Jeetan was a bit selfish, and I was sort of jealous. So maybe Dad and Uncle Jesse were something like that . . . like, Dad tried to make things cool for his little brother and then got totally ghosted. I suppose that kind of makes sense to me; only somehow it doesn't too, because Dad wasn't the kind of person to hold a grudge.

7

I DON'T THINK SO

Now that Mum's got a job, it's like we're hardly ever home. She usually works night shifts at the twenty-four-hour, so me and Hannah stay over at the Adeyemis three or four nights a week. I share P's room, sleeping on an inflatable mattress, and Hannah shares with Juliet who has two beds anyway. It was cool at first.

Aunty Femi's a bit strict. Before, we always just called her Femi. But she goes, 'Now you're staying in our house, you'd better call me *Aunty* and Olu *Uncle*, OK?'

She also sat me and Hannah down: 'I have just one rule: if I ask you to do something, you don't say, *Why can't P do it?* Or, *I'm just finishing this*, or whatever. You just say, *Yes, Aunty*, and do what you're told. OK?'

So we go, 'Yes, Aunty.'

Actually, I don't think Aunty Femi has *just one rule* at all. She's got loads of rules.

But she's still the coolest. Like, another rule is you're not allowed to talk to her when you get back from school (apart from to say hello) until tea's ready (but they call it supper). This is because she works from home and she'll be in the kitchen with her laptop on the table and Chibs on her hip and big heavy pots on the stove and her phone pressed to her ear. She'll be stirring a pot and rocking the baby and saying crazy complicated stuff like *The whole point is to avoid unnecessary litigation* and winking at you, all at the same time.

I told this to Mum and she goes, 'Is that right? She sounds like a proper superhero.'

I said, 'More like Mary Poppins, only from Nigeria.'

And Mum thought this was really funny.

The next time we were all at the Adeyemis, Mum told Aunty Femi what I said, which was mad embarrassing. I wasn't in the kitchen with them, but I heard Aunty burst out laughing and then she came into where we were playing Small Town Hero (or rather P was playing. I was just watching, which was kind of boring because he always chooses to fight Psycho Steve and dies and has to start again). Aunty Femi goes, 'The Nigerian Mary Poppins?' before planting a big kiss on my forehead that left a bright red lipstick mark.

Mary Poppins is lame anyway. We only watched it because it was Mum's turn to choose.

Uncle Olu gets home from work at half-past six and we eat together at the table, never in front of the TV. He sits at the head and asks Juliet, then Hannah, then P, then me, to tell him a new thing we learned at school that day. He listens very carefully and then chooses one to discuss with all of us. I guess it sounds kind of boring, but it's not.

Before we started going to the Adeyemis, I thought it would suck to be away from Mum so much, but it's been OK, and when Mum takes us home she's so pleased to see us that she always wants to hang out, even just watching Netflix or whatever. I also thought Hannah might be unhappy, because she's two years younger than Juliet. But, actually, Hannah thinks Juliet is awesome because she's really smart and she's got her own beauty channel, which has more than three thousand followers, and she does trap dancing and stuff. Hannah's even started talking like her now. She says things like, *I don't think so!* which means *no way!* and *I know you didn't just say that*, which is stupid because it actually means *I know you* did *just say that*.

So if you'd asked me to guess what would be difficult about spending so much time with another family, I never would have thought it would about me and P, because I've known him my whole life and he's my best mate.

It started with an argument about his room. Aunty Femi hung my school shirts in his cupboard, and he took them out and left them on the floor. He said I shouldn't put things in his cupboard because there wasn't enough space. I told him it wasn't me who put them there, but then Aunty came in and goes, 'What's going on?' And when P explained, she got cross and opened his cupboard and started pulling out his clothes saying, '*This?* Doesn't fit you. *This?* Too small.'

P freaked out, because one of the things she took out was his Shaolin hoodie. He goes, 'Mum! They're my garms! You can't just chuck them out!'

'*Garms?*' Aunty said. 'I'm not gonna chuck them out. I'll put them away for Chibs.' When she'd finished, she goes, 'Gabriel's a guest in our house. You have to make him

45

welcome, understand?' He wouldn't look at her. He just shrugged. 'Pamilekunayo!' she said. 'What do you say?'

She used his whole name, which everybody knows is a sign of trouble, so he had to meet her eye and he goes, 'Yes, Mum.'

'That's right, *Yes, Mum.*' And she left the room with an armful of his clothes.

I could tell he was well vex. I said, 'Sorry, man.'

But he turned round and his expression was furious. He goes, 'Just leave me alone.'

Since then, it's only got worse. I mean, it's not always bad. Like, sometimes we can still do stuff together and have a laugh. But then I might play on his PSP without asking or something and he'll switch up just like that. Like, one time he came in and I was looking at his wushu dagger that he'd bought at a kung fu tournament in Hemel Hempstead (even though it was, like, totally illegal to sell it to him). It's his prize possession and he keeps it hidden under his mattress, but this time he left the box out on the bed. I was only looking, but he went mental. He was all, like, 'What you doing? It's not for kids, bruv! It's not a toy!' It was really annoying, because even if he's almost a year older than me and really tall, we're still in the same class.

The Adeyemis live close to Graycoat, so when Hannah and me stay over, we walk to school. Me and P usually walk ahead. Juliet and Hannah walk really slowly and they don't like us to get too close to them because they're having what Juliet calls a *girly chat*. Often, they wait at the bus stop for Shay Rockwell. He's this guy who left last year, but he's always hanging around. Everyone knows Shay because he's a rudeboy and an MC and he smokes weed. Hannah thinks he looks a bit like Joe Weller, but Juliet goes, '*I don't think so!*' And Hannah goes, 'Yeah, but the roughneck version though.'

Me and P used to walk in together, but now he rushes ahead because he's got this bunch of Year Ten friends he meets at the gate. They don't call him P. He's told them to call him 'Pete', which is just stupid because it's not even his name. When I walk in, they all stare and pretend they're not talking about me in a way that makes it obvious they are. It's so lame because I've known most of them since Primary – Jacob Rockwell (Shay's brother), Mirek Nowicki, Barney Something-or-other, David Cole (I even played in the Under Fourteens with Mirek and David last year). I think P might be worried that I'll tell them his real name or something, but why would I do that? Like I care.

Once, as I went past, P goes to Jacob, 'His dad died, bruv. I gotta keep an eye on him in case he loses it.' And I stopped for a second, but I wasn't going to say anything because that's what he wanted. Later, I think he felt guilty, because he let me play Small Town Hero for an hour without even asking for a go. But he never apologised.

P and me went to the rec after school to play three and in. He sucks at football, but he's a lot bigger and faster than me, so it kind of evens itself out. He was in goal and I'd already scored two when he came out to try and tackle me, but I nutmegged him and put the ball into the open goal.

Nobody likes being nutmegged – it's embarrassing. So I shouldn't have run away with my arms in the air, but I was only having a laugh. Then I was thumped in the back and I fell over and, before I knew it, he was on top of me and had totally lost it. He wasn't saying anything, just grunting and snarling. I tried to push him off, but he's really strong and he does kung fu. He pinned my arms with his knees.

Now he was talking: 'What you gonna do about it?'

I didn't think it was going to go any further. He just wanted to make me feel weak and stupid. But then he saw Jacob passing with his big brother and, for some reason, that set him off. He punched me right in the eye. It didn't hurt as much as you might think, but it was a real shock. I mean, we're supposed to be best mates.

P looked almost as shocked as me. He was actually shaking, so I pushed him off quite easily. Shay Rockwell goes, 'Oh my days, bruv!' and he was laughing like it was the funniest thing he'd ever seen, and Jacob laughed too. I just gapped it. I ran all the way home.

I let myself in. Mum was still there. She hadn't left for her shift yet. She goes, 'Gabe, love! What happened?' And I told her as she cleaned me up. She gave me a pack of frozen peas to hold to my eye and she washed a deep graze on my knee that I hadn't even noticed. Then she said, 'Come on.'

'Where we going?'

'The Adeyemis,' she said. When she saw my expression, she suddenly got all impatient. She said, 'I gotta go to work, Gabriel. You're staying at Aunty Femi's. I'm sure he'll apologise.'

I said, 'No way—'

But she interrupted. She goes, 'Kids fight! That's what they do!'

P was already home when we got there. I don't know what he told Aunty Femi, but he'd been sent to his room. I had to wait in the lounge while Mum and Aunty talked in the kitchen. Juliet and Hannah stood in the doorway. Hannah goes, 'What did you *do*?' Even though I hadn't done anything.

Juliet stood up for me: 'It's not Gabe's fault. My brother's such a loser!'

Then Mum and Aunty Femi came in. Mum hugged Hannah and me and left for work, just like that. Aunty told me to come into the kitchen with her. She didn't talk about what had happened, but she gave me a juice and said I should do my homework at the table.

When Uncle Olu got home, Aunty met him at the door. I could hear them whispering. Then Uncle came into the kitchen and he was so angry that when he raised his hand I thought he was going to hit me too. But, instead, he held me by the chin and he said, 'Let me see that?' before turning my face to examine my eye. He sniffed, 'Not too bad.' Then he goes, 'Right.' And his feet on the stairs sounded well vex.

P didn't come down for supper and, for once, Uncle Olu didn't ask any of us for a new thing we learned at school. We ate in complete silence. At one point, Aunty Femi started dishing a plate of food, but Uncle stopped her. He said, 'Let him go hungry. He needs to learn.'

Later, Uncle Olu goes, 'Let's sort this out.' He led me up to the bedroom and opened the door. P was sitting on the bed. He'd totally been crying, although he wasn't going to admit it. Uncle said, 'Pamilekunayo? What you gonna say?'

And P goes, 'I'm sorry.'

Uncle Olu nodded briskly. He said, 'Right. That's the end of it. I'll come back in ten minutes and you better both be in bed.'

When he went out, we just looked at each other. I said, 'I'm sorry too,' even though I didn't have anything to be sorry for – I just thought it would help. Some chance.

At first, P didn't say anything. He just sniffed and got out his wushu dagger from its box under the mattress. He held it in his hand like he was a ninja or something, which was totally sad. He goes, 'You think you're special because your dad died? I hate my dad. And I hate you and all.'

You reckon that's the end of it? I don't think so.

8

THE FOOL

I'm still into Small Town Hero, but it's kind of getting annoying too.

Like, you can't trust the Fool and he's your only ally. I found this out pretty early on, because in Chapter Three he stole all Prince Prince's snacks. I tried taking them back. But that meant that when I fought the Small Giant with Big Feet, the Fool was too weak to help. That was how my avatar died the second time and the End of Story showed Prince Prince's funeral procession through the streets of Small Town and some of the crowd were laughing as it passed.

So, next game, I let the Fool keep the snacks and we killed the giant. But then, when we finally got through the Monstrosity's sliding doors and found ourselves on Long Beach, it was Prince Prince lacking vitality (he was down to, like, eighteen per cent, while the Fool was still at seventy-nine).

I looked at the map and there are only two ways to cross Strait and Narrow. Either you walk all the way round to Harbour Doubts (you need eighty per cent vitality – impossible), or you take the canoe to an island in Strait and Narrow (twenty-five percent) where there's a vending machine and you can buy more snacks and cross to Other

Side. But then you face the problem that the canoe won't fit you, the Fool and your Kit Bag. And surely you've got to keep the Kit Bag, because who knows what's waiting on Other Side?

Anyway, to cut a long story short, I decided my best bet was to let the Fool paddle Prince Prince to the island, then return for the Kit Bag. That was two weeks ago and he hasn't come back yet. I don't mean it was two weeks ago in the game, but *in real life*. For two weeks, I've been stuck in Chapter Fifteen, marooned on the island, waiting for the Fool. Every time I open the game I'm pacing the shoreline, backwards and forwards, peering out to sea. And guess what? Prince Prince can't even use the vending machine because the Small Town tokens don't fit in the slot.

So here I am, watching my vitality drop (it's now at six per cent) and the sea level rise. Soon, there'll be no island left, just Prince Prince and the vending machine, waiting to be swallowed by the water. If you think about it, I'm just watching my avatar and wondering whether he'll starve or drown. That sucks, right?

I could just choose End of Story, but that seems kind of lame considering all the effort I've put in so far. There's also an option to buy a loot box and get another canoe and snacks, but I'd still have no Kit Bag and anyway Mum won't let me use her card.

I tried Googling it, but that was no help. It seems like most people avoid the Monstrosity altogether and take the Road Most Travelled to Harbour Doubts (and that's got problems of its own). The only YouTuber I found who'd done the same as me was a guy in LA called Suarez73 and, after a few days, he tried to swim to Other Side with, like, fifteen per cent vitality. That was suicide. He drowned before he was even near halfway.

9

SECRETS

Hannah told me a secret. Juliet Adeyemi's seeing Shay Rockwell. *He's been chirpsing her for ages, but at first she won't play that, even though he's got mad lyrics. But now they been seeing each other three weeks; in fact, longer than three weeks because it started on a Friday, so that makes it, like, three weeks and four days.*

That's what Hannah said, in almost exactly those words.

She also goes, 'But you can't tell anyone, Gabe; not even P. If her parents find out, they'll do their nut. In fact, I don't even know why I told you.'

I don't know why she told me either. I reckon it just made her feel special, because it's not like I really understood what she was on about. In fact, I only knew it was important because of the way she was talking and looked so excited. I think that's why I said, 'Isn't he a bit old for her?'

I know, right? As soon as I said it, I knew it was lame and I wished I could take it back.

Hannah burst out laughing. She goes, 'What are you, her *dad*?' Then she patted my cheek and said, 'Little Gabe! You're so sweet sometimes!' I felt myself blush. I couldn't help it. She goes, 'You know she's seventeen, right? You know Mum was seventeen when she got married? You do know that?'

I did know. But I hadn't thought about it like that before – that Mum was the same age as Juliet.

Mum and Dad's wedding photo is on the mantelpiece in the front room. After Dad died, Mum put it away for a while. She said it was hard looking at it every day. But Hannah and me complained, so eventually she put it back. And when we said, 'You don't have to,' she goes, 'No. You're right. I was just being stupid.' Even though she wasn't.

In the picture, Dad looks just like Dad, only a bit thinner. But Mum looks totally different. She's so young and pretty, almost like Hannah (though I'd never tell Hannah that). Whenever Mum catches me looking at the photo, she goes, 'What you can't see is Grandy standing just out of shot with my walking stick and you can't see the back of my head where the hair was still growing back. I was a right mess.'

If Dad overheard this, he used to give Mum a big hug and say, 'You were the most beautiful girl in the world. Still are.'

And Mum would pretend to be irritated and struggle to get away. 'You know the only reason I married you? That bang on the head. I wasn't thinking straight.'

But she didn't mean it.

Mum and Dad got married three months after her accident. Dad said he didn't want to risk losing her again.

They'd been walking on the dykes at Penn Reservoir. It was night time and one of the pools had been emptied for maintenance. There were no railings then, so when Mum lost her footing, she fell thirty feet (which is like the height of a house or something) into the concrete basin. It was a miracle she wasn't killed (*Miracle I was born, miracle*

I survived, Mum says) but she landed on her hip and smashed the joint to bits and her head whiplashed into the concrete and she fractured her skull.

The doctors kept her in a coma for seven days because her brain was swollen. When she finally woke up, Grandy and Granny Hannah were there. Dad had to wait outside because he wasn't family. But when he realised that she was sitting up and talking, he burst in, dropped to one knee, produced a ring from his pocket and asked her to marry him.

Me and Hannah? This was always our favourite bit of the story and, when Mum used to tell it, we'd both go, 'What did you say, Mum?'

And Mum would glance at Dad before she delivered the punchline – 'Sorry, do I know you?', pretending she'd lost her memory.

And me and Hannah cracked up every time.

Then Dad would go, 'It's not funny!' Even though he had a twinkle in his eye and his lips twitching a smile.

But, really, he was right. It wasn't funny because Mum *had* lost her memory; although only of the accident. She couldn't remember walking along the dyke. She couldn't remember how she slipped and fell. Dad remembered, but the one time I asked he shook his head and went, 'Let's talk about something else.' I guess I always figured he'd tell me one day, like one day he'd tell me why Coral *upped and left*; but now he's dead.

10

ALL WRONG

I never really saw Dad get vex. I mean, when I was little and I used to climb into bed with him and Mum, he could get pretty salty, but mostly he was easy going and kind of quiet so, actually, if he was angry you probably wouldn't even know. Sometimes, it got on Mum's nerves. Like, if she was all fired up about something, the way he was calm could set her off. Sometimes, he'd pretend to get as vex as her, just to keep the peace. Like, if she was banging on about the bin men and how they could never leave things tidy, he'd go, 'Yeah! What a disgrace!' But Mum could tell his heart wasn't it. Luckily, Dad was such a rubbish actor that it ended up sounding kind of funny. Mum would shake her head and go 'Billy!' and try to stay cross but then start laughing – partly at his bad acting and partly at her own bad temper.

One thing that did make Dad angry, though, was if you ever said something was 'unfair'. He hated that. He'd give you a look like he couldn't believe what he'd just heard and he'd go, 'What do you expect? *Life*'s not fair.'

Whenever he said that to me, I'd just say sorry. But I always thought that what he said wasn't an answer to anything and kind of annoying. Like, *obviously* life's not fair, but what's the point of even having an idea of 'fairness' if you're not allowed to talk about it? And say Mum got caught in the rain and came in dripping wet and complaining about the weather. If I was just, like, 'What do you expect? Rain is wet,' that would be pretty annoying too.

In the holidays, Hannah's going on an outward bound camp in the Brecon Beacons. Mum figured I might be jealous (although I'm not) so she said we'd make a plan of our own.

I asked what I'd do when she had a nightshift and she said Grandy would come round to keep me company. I didn't reply, just nodded, but secretly I thought that was cool. You see, Grandy pretends to be strict but mostly I can do whatever I want because he's totally forgetful.

Like, one time, Mum and Hannah went to an options meeting at the school and Mum left tea for Grandy to heat up on the hob. He was all serious about it, like it was rocket science or something. And when I said, 'Can we eat in front of the TV?', he goes 'No', just like that, even though we always eat in front of the TV and so does he. But when he switched the hob on, he went to watch the news and forgot all about it. He probably fell asleep. I was up in my room when I heard a shout. By the time I got to the kitchen, it was full of smoke and he was scraping our burnt tea into the bin. There was actually a dirty mark on the ceiling. He said, 'Come on, Gabriel!', and we walked to the chip shop, Rock 'n' Roe, where Shay Rockwell's mate Dion works, for cod dinners times two. He even bought me a Coke and when he handed it to me, he said, 'Don't tell your mother.' But there was no hiding what happened to our tea on account of the smoke mark and because he'd ruined Mum's best pot. Now if Mum's going out, she just lets Grandy and me make sandwiches, which I prefer anyway.

When Mum told me that Grandy would keep me company during her nightshifts, she looked all worried like I might think it was boring or whatever. She goes, 'Is that OK, love?'

And I was, like, 'It's all right.'

But I don't think she believed me. That was when she said we'd make a plan of our own. I suppose it was to make up for the outward bound camp, which I wasn't jealous of, and Grandy coming round, which I thought was cool anyway.

Mum told me that, during the day, when she's not at work, we could do whatever I wanted. She said she'd take me down the Intu Centre to look at new boots, although she couldn't make any promises. And, best of all, she booked me on a three-day course at the Moses Hayes Soccer School, which is free because of our circumstances. It has coaches from the Watford Academy and Mo himself giving out the prizes. I was well excited for the holiday.

Then the day before yesterday, it all went wrong . . .

We were round Grandy's when Mum's phone rang. She went into the kitchen to talk. She was gone ages and when she came back she was all hyped. She goes, 'I got it!' Only none of us knew what she was on about. She told us she had a new job. She's going to be a Stock Administration Supervisor for the UK's largest online packaging supplier.

'What the devil's that?' Grandy asked.

'No idea,' Mum said. 'But it pays more than twice the garage!'

Straight away, Hannah goes, 'Can I get a new phone now?'

And I said, 'Hannah!'

But Mum just laughed and gave Hannah a big hug and said, 'We'll see.'

Grandy asked, 'When do you start?'

'Not for a month. But I've got to go on a team building course in Birmingham end of next week, then software training – I'll be away almost ten days!' Then she turned to me. She goes, 'I've spoken to Aunty Femi and she says you're welcome to stay with them while I'm away.'

I felt my blood run cold and the black hole inside me was gaping. I was all, like, 'What?'

After that, it's all a bit of a blur. We had an argument; not just Mum and me, but Hannah and Grandy got involved too. I was so vex. I mean, Mum *knows* what's going on with P, how I hate going there now. But when I tried saying this, she frowned and said, 'What do you want me to do, Gabe? You want me to work in the twenty-four-hour the rest of my life?'

Then Hannah goes to me, 'You're so selfish!'

And I go, 'You're such a cow!'

And Mum goes, 'Gabriel!'

I tried to calm down. I told her that Grandy was already coming to stay, to keep me company. That was the plan. Why couldn't we stick to the plan? I thought she was going to agree. But then she shook her head: 'If Hannah was gonna be there ...' Then, 'I don't think so. It's a lot to ask—'

Then Grandy goes, 'Beth Mulligan! You do know I'm here, do you not?' And he was well cross – you could tell by the way he used her whole name, *including* her maiden name.

Mum turned to him: 'Sorry, Dad. But you know . . .'

I could see in their faces they were both thinking about the time he burnt the tea. Grandy shook his head and muttered, 'Whatever you think's best,' and he walked out of the room.

Then Mum looked at me and her face was hard and her lips were thin and I thought she was going to say, *See what you've done?* But she didn't. Instead, she goes, 'This is happening, Gabriel. I don't wanna hear any more about it.'

I was all, like, 'That's so not fair!'

And you know what she said? 'What do you expect, Gabriel? Life's not fair.' Like Dad, like that was an answer to anything. But she's not Dad and it's not an answer.

11

PENALTIES

I've done this terrible thing, or at least I think I have. And I can't even tell anyone because they wouldn't believe me.

Yesterday was the Under Fourteens Borough Soccer Sixes. This year it was at Graycoat and the whole of Years Seven, Eight and Nine were allowed to come and support. I've been excited about it for ages, because we haven't lost a game all season and I'm captain. But I played really badly and we nearly lost to Twin Rivers (which would've been crazy because they suck and have, like, only sixty kids in a year).

Dad always said, *Don't make excuses. Just try harder next time*. So I don't want to make excuses, but I was feeling really stressed about going to stay with P.

Even Mr Bowler noticed something was wrong. He said I was playing *like a drain* and then he patted me on the shoulder: 'Chin up!' So I tried harder and it just got worse. It was like my boots were on the wrong feet. Mr Bowler reckoned I was trying too hard.

Luckily, we still got to the final. I mean, even though I'm the captain and best player (I'm not boasting, it's true), we're not a one-man team and Jeetan (who's second best) was brilliant. Luckily, in the final against Wallace Road it all changed. I think it was because I'd kind of given up that suddenly everything clicked. Like, Jeetan played a through ball and I got ahead of the defender and I just swung my foot without even thinking about what I was doing. I caught it sweetly and it flew past the keeper right in the top corner. It was such a relief. I scored another in the second half and we won two–nil.

But I should have had a hat-trick.

In the last minute I was chopped in the area. I got up to take the penalty. Everyone was cheering. There must have been, like, three hundred kids on the touchline and I realised it was lunchtime and some of the older kids were watching too. Then, I saw 'Pete' (as he likes to be called) and Jacob Rockwell and I accidentally caught their eye. Jacob made a rude sign at me and P sneered and they did this lame handshake they've been practising. Honestly, it didn't bother me; at least, not until I missed the penalty.

I always do the same thing with penalties. I give the keeper the eyes, drop my left shoulder and then side-foot it to the right-hand side. The keeper goes the wrong way every time. It worked this time too, only the keeper got lucky and the ball caught his trailing leg and bounced away.

I'll tell you something about penalties that really bugs me. If you watch *Match of the Day* or whatever and someone misses a spot kick, the pundits always go, 'What a poor strike!' But if you ask me, that's rubbish, because it has nothing to do with the quality of the strike. Like, there's this kind of penalty called a 'Panenka' (after the guy who invented it) where you run in and pretend you're going to belt it, but actually just chip the ball gently down the middle. Usually, the keeper dives and it loops slowly over his body and you look really cool. Only trouble is, if the keeper doesn't dive he just catches it and you look like a proper muppet. But, either way, the point is that nothing's different about the way you took the penalty, only the outcome; the point is that a good penalty's one that scores. End of.

Anyway, the penalty I missed in the cup final didn't matter at all, because the ref blew for full time straight after and all the team jumped on me and there was a pitch invasion. The only thing that mattered was that when I looked over at P and Jacob they were both killing themselves laughing.

I guess I should have thought, *So what?* But I didn't. Because I realised there and then that P, who's been my best mate our whole lives, must hate me. I mean, I know he told me that already, but I kind of figured he was just vex and would get over it. Now I wasn't so sure.

How many people do you know who hate you; I mean, *really* hate you? Not many. And, what if you've done nothing wrong? Like, the only reason I could think he hated me was that my dad died and I had to share his bedroom sometimes and he got in trouble for punching me in the face . . . Harsh, right?

At first, I was just kind of upset. But by the time I got home, I was proper steaming. It didn't help that Mum had already packed my rucksack to take to the Adeyemis, and when I complained she goes, 'For goodness sake!' And she didn't even ask me about the Soccer Sixes even though I had a medal in my school bag.

Last night, I lay in bed and I couldn't sleep. I closed my

eyes and I thought about the holidays. I was on a total downer. Then I heard voices talking and I thought it must be Mum and Hannah, but it didn't sound like them. With my eyes shut, I saw the vague outline of stairs, like I was looking through mist. I tried to open my eyes, but I couldn't. Then I heard the great rushing, whooshing noise and, before I knew it, I was standing in the hallway at the Adeyemis'.

I hadn't meant it to happen. But there I was.

I'm at the foot of the stairs. The voices I can hear are from the kitchen – Aunty Femi and Uncle Olu. It's Aunty doing most of the talking. She goes, 'She's seventeen. It's totally normal. She just wants a bit of privacy.'

They must be talking about Juliet. I wonder if they know about Shay Rockwell.

Uncle Olu says, 'If she wants privacy, there has to be trust.'

'*I* trust her. More to the point, I trust *us*. We've raised a sensible young woman. She's not gonna do anything stupid.' There's a pause. I can hear water and dishes. I can picture Aunty Femi rinsing plates and stacking them in the rack. Then she says, 'I'm her mother, Olu. You really think I wouldn't know?'

Another pause. Uncle Olu says, 'Pami . . .'

I've never heard them call P *Pami* before. That must suck.

Aunty Femi goes, 'He wants his privacy too.'

'That boy's a problem.'

I hear the tap running. Someone's filling the kettle. Then

Aunty says, 'You know he really doesn't want Gabriel to come and stay? He says he's full of himself. He says he's always taking his stuff without asking.'

My face is burning. I *never* take P's stuff without asking. That's such a lie. And I'm not full of myself. At least, I don't think so . . .

Uncle Olu says, 'What can we do? Beth needs our help.'

'I'm not saying we can *do* anything; I'm just saying. I know Beth's struggling. Perhaps this job . . .' Aunty Femi tails off. Then she says, 'He *is* a bit of a show-off, looking for attention all the time.'

Uncle says, 'What he's been through, it's hardly surprising. His whole world's been turned upside down.'

It's a moment before I realise they're still talking about me and I'm horrified. For P to tell lies about me is one thing, but this is his mum and dad saying I'm *a bit of a show-off*. Is that true? More to the point, is it really happening or is it only in my head? I want to snap out of it, open my eyes and find myself in my own bed. But I'm stuck. I'm so vex. I reckon P turned his mum and dad against me.

I go up to P's room. The stairs creak but I don't care, partly because I'm so angry and partly because I figure no one can hear. I reckon I must be invisible like the time with the scratchcard.

The door is ajar. I find P fast asleep. He's really sweating. I trip over his shoes – he's got feet like boats, size eleven already – but he doesn't wake up. I see my school shirts, hangers still in them, scrunched up in a corner of the room. He did that. He makes this small whimpering noise like he's having a bad dream. I hope he's having a bad dream. In fact, I wish he was dead; not in the lame way people usually say that – I mean, I *really* wish he was dead. And even as I think that, his breathing seems to quicken and he makes this strange strangled whistle from the back of his throat. And suddenly his eyes snap open and it's like he's looking right at me, only I swear he can't see me—

'Gabe love? You still awake?'

Now it was *my* eyes snapping open. I was back in bed. Mum was standing in the doorway. I said, 'Just about.'

She came in and sat on the edge of the bed. She goes, 'I wanted to say sorry. I don't want you to think I'm not listening to you, because I am. But I have to do what's best for all of us. I mean, we wanna stay in this house, right? And the rent and the electric . . . I need this job. *We* need this job.'

I didn't know what to say, so I said, 'OK.'

Mum said, 'OK', kissed me on the forehead and quietly padded out of the room.

I just lay there. I didn't even want to close my eyes in case I went somewhere else by mistake. Also, I was thinking how in the morning it was the last day of term: school would end at lunchtime, then Mum would head to Birmingham, Hannah to the Brecon Beacons and I had to go to the Adeyemis . . .

I didn't get to sleep for hours.

We were having breakfast when Mum's phone rang. It was too early for anyone to be calling unless it was important.

She looked at the screen and answered with surprise in her voice: 'Femi?'

I couldn't breathe. For a second, I couldn't even listen because I imagined Aunty Femi telling Mum how P had seen me in his bedroom last night. Crazy, right? I mean, I swear he didn't really see me and, even if he did, he'd only sound like a nutter if he told Aunty that.

By the time I started listening again, Mum was going, 'No. Of course.' Then, 'No. It can't be helped.' Then, 'I'll figure something out.' Then, 'Thanks.' Then, she just stood there at the sink, staring out of the window.

I said, 'What?' But Mum didn't answer, so I go, 'What's happened?'

'It's P,' she said at last. 'He's come down with something. His mum's called the doctor.' She turned to me: 'She doesn't think you should stay in case it's catching.' Then she put her face in her hands, covering her eyes with the heels of her palms. She said, 'There's no need to look so happy about it.'

I don't know why she said that. I didn't look happy about it at all. Because now I was thinking, *I did this. I went into his room last night and I wished he was dead.* I was thinking it was like what happened with Mum's scratchcard – I told a story about her winning twenty-five thousand pounds and she won twenty-five. This time I'd wished P was dead and now he'd got really sick . . .

Mum still had her face in her hands. Hannah came into the kitchen. She goes, 'What happened?'

Mum said, 'What am I gonna do?' And her voice sounded weird and thin and I realised she was crying. Hannah flashed me a look like it was my fault – maybe it was, but she couldn't know that – and she went and gave Mum a hug. I was stuck in my chair.

The phone rang: not Mum's mobile, the home phone. That was weird, partly because it was still really early and partly because nobody ever rings on the home phone. I went to answer and a man's voice goes, 'Gabriel? It's me.'

'Who's this?'

'Jesse,' the voice said, kind of surprised, like we spoke every day or something. Then, 'I was thinking about you.'

I didn't know what to say to that, but Mum was coming over, wiping her eyes and holding her hand out for the phone, hissing, 'Who is it?'

'Uncle Jesse,' I said, and she didn't look happy about it.

She took the phone and the first thing she said was, 'Hi, it's really not a good time—' He must have interrupted her, because she paused for a moment, listening. Then she said, 'No. You're right. School holidays are starting, I gotta go to Birmingham and Gabriel's supposed to be staying with a friend who's come down with a virus. So, you're right – there's never a good time.' Her voice was hard and cold. You wouldn't have known she'd just been crying. She rolled her eyes. Then she said, *Anything you can do?* She was clearly repeating Uncle Jesse's question, but she said it in a way that made it sound like it was the most unhelpful question ever. She looked at me and frowned and she goes, 'You know what, Jesse? Sure. There *is* something you can do.'

And I wasn't ready for what she said next . . .

12

SOMERS TOWN (PART ONE)

Uncle Jesse picked me up from Euston Station. He was waiting at the barrier. I recognised him at once. He was wearing pointy boots, tight black jeans, a dark shirt and a kind of flappy suit jacket. He stood out from the crowd. He looked like someone who used to be famous; like you'd look at him and go, *Is that the bloke from . . . ?*

Neither of us knew what to say. I think we both wondered if we should hug or something, but we didn't know each other, so we might as well have hugged the ticket guy. In the end, Uncle Jesse frowned and goes, 'You want me to take your rucksack?'

'It's OK. It's not heavy.'

'Come on then.'

We set off towards the exit. At one point, he put a hand on my shoulder. It was like he was testing to see if it felt normal and, without having to say anything, we agreed it didn't, so he took it away again. When we got outside, he goes, 'We're walking. It's not far. You sure you don't want me to take your bag?'

'It's fine,' I said.

The streets were busy and Uncle Jesse had such a long stride that I struggled to keep up. He didn't wait for me. He just marched off, leaving me to bob along in the current, glancing up every now and then to make sure I hadn't lost sight of him. It's not like he was deliberately trying to lose me: more like he was in a world of his own; or, what Mum said – *on another planet*. Then he disappeared for a few seconds and I was just starting to worry when I realised he'd turned off the main road. I caught up with him in a small side street. Now he was waiting. He had this puzzled expression, like it was me who had lost him. I said, 'Sorry.'

The main road was hectic. But the side street was deserted and in the shadow of tall buildings on either side, which made it feel cold. The sudden silence was almost spooky, like we'd stepped out of the real world. 'Where are we?' I asked.

'Somers Town.'

'This is where you were born!' I said. I just blurted it out.

He frowned: 'How'd you know that?'

'Dad told me.'

'Right, of course,' he said. Then, 'We're here.'

We were outside this large glass-fronted building. He led me up a few steps, through automatic doors into an echoing lobby with shiny floors and a man in an old-fashioned uniform sitting behind a desk who goes, 'Afternoon, Mr Douglas.'

Uncle Jesse said, 'Hello, Niki. This is Gabriel, my nephew. Gabriel, this is Niki, the concierge.'

'Pleased to know you, Gabriel.' He had a strong accent – like, Russian or something – but a friendly smile.

We got in the lift. Uncle Jesse pressed a button. I said, 'Is this your office?'

71

He frowned again. He was doing a lot of frowning. It wasn't like he was vex, more like anything I asked him, however simple, took him by surprise. He goes, 'No. Apartments. This is where I live. We're on the twentieth.'

I felt stupid for not realising it was apartments, only it didn't look like anyone lived here – there were no carpets, everything was so clean, and there was no noise but the whirr of the lift. I said, 'So, what's the difference between apartments and flats?'

'Apartments is the American word.'

'But we're in England.'

Now he looked at me and smiled. It was the first time I'd seen him smile except in that photo Mum showed me. It was only for a second and, for that second, he looked really like Dad. He said, 'Good point. I suppose apartments are for people who think they're too important to live in a flat.'

'Are you too important to live in a flat?'

He raised an eyebrow and I thought he might get annoyed. But then he goes, 'I guess I must think so, right?'

I shrugged. How was I supposed to know what he thinks?

I followed Uncle Jesse down a long corridor to 2020. He let us in. I glanced around. It must have been an apartment all right, because it wasn't like any flat I'd seen and it looked like it was in America, or at least how America looks on TV. On the right, there was a passageway with doors, and dim lights along the skirting board; and, on the left, an arch opened into a huge room, about twice the size of a classroom. It had steps down into the middle and then up at the far side to a long dining table and, beyond that, a kitchen that looked like the bridge of a spaceship. The opposite wall was all windows that led out onto a balcony, which ran the length of the apartment and looked out over London. The floor of the balcony was wood decking, and everything else seemed to be stone, although there was a big, fluffy, cream-coloured rug in the sunken bit. The couches were brown leather. The side tables were glass. There was a huge mirror. I hardly dared breathe in case I made something dirty.

I looked at Uncle Jesse and he goes, 'Home.' But he raised an eyebrow again, which made it sound almost but not quite like a joke.

13

UNCLE JESSE

Daisy, Uncle Jesse's girlfriend, was in the kitchen area. She goes, 'Gabriel!' and came clopping to greet me. She was wearing fancy shoes and a clean white pinny. For some reason she reminded me a bit of a chicken.

Uncle Jesse goes, 'You remember Daisy?'

Daisy said, 'Of course he does, don't you?' And before I could answer she gave me a big, bony squeeze. She smelled nice though.

I looked at Uncle Jesse. His eyebrow seemed to be stuck in the up position. He goes, 'I'll show you round.'

It didn't take long. Besides the big room, there were just four rooms off the passageway, which, counting from the end furthest from the front door, were Uncle Jesse's bedroom (with a bathroom attached), his study, another bathroom ('You can use this one,' he said) and the guest room ('This is you').

The only one that was interesting was Uncle Jesse's study, which had a desk with two laptops on it, shelves crammed with books and Post-It notes and photographs stuck all over the wall. I thought I glimpsed a picture of Mum, Hannah and me, but then Uncle Jesse shut the door and said, 'I don't want you coming in here because it's where I work. OK?'

All the other rooms looked like they were from a catalogue. The guest room – my bedroom – had a double bed with brown sheets and grey walls with cupboards that were a different grey built into the walls. Uncle Jesse said, 'It's a bit boring. I didn't know you were coming until this morning.'

After that we had tea. Daisy said, 'I hope you boys are hungry.'

I was starving, because I hadn't had a proper lunch, only a bit of a sandwich Grandy bought at the station that turned out to be gross. Daisy had made cannelloni – big tubes of pasta wrapped around meat and covered in melted cheese and tomato sauce. I don't really like melted cheese, but she couldn't know that, so I just tried to avoid it. It would have been easier if she hadn't kept saying, 'How's the food?'

Uncle Jesse asked, 'Don't you like cheese?'

Daisy goes, 'Of course he likes cheese. All kids like cheese.' She got out a bottle of fizzy water and poured some for her and Uncle Jesse. Then she said to me, 'I bought some Coke. Do you want Coke?'

Sure I wanted Coke, but I also didn't want to do the wrong thing. So I said, 'I'm not really allowed Coke.'

But Daisy was already at the fridge getting it out. She did this weird laugh and goes, 'A little won't hurt. It's a special occasion.'

After tea, Daisy said she was going to a Pilates class. I'd never heard of Pilates, but Uncle Jesse told me it's a bit like yoga. She gave me another hug, then kissed Uncle Jesse: 'Call me, OK?'

'Sure.'

Then she turned to me and said, 'I've been telling Jesse for ages that he had to get you to come and visit.'

Uncle Jesse protested, 'I was just waiting for the right time.'

And Daisy gave me a look that I didn't understand before she goes to him, 'Be nice, OK?'

Be nice? I don't know if I made this convo sound creepy, but it really was and it freaked me out. It was like they were talking in code that sounded normal but meant something sinister. I mean, why would she say 'Be nice' unless she expected him not to be? I couldn't see Uncle Jesse's face, but, as she was leaving, Daisy gave me a last worried glance that made me feel weirder still. But people have been doing that a lot since Dad died, so I tried not to think about it too much . . .

After she left, I asked, 'Doesn't Daisy live here?'

Uncle Jesse turned towards me. But he wasn't really looking at me. In fact, it was more like he was looking a little bit above my head. He said, 'No. She likes her own space. *I* like my own space. I work from home, you see.'

'What do you do?'

He shrugged, 'Nothing very interesting.' Then, 'Daisy wanted to be here. To welcome you. She thinks I don't know about kids.'

'I'm not exactly a kid.'

Now he looked right at me and raised his eyebrow again: 'Fair enough.'

I was beginning to realise that when Uncle Jesse raises

his eyebrow it's generally instead of a smile (except for when he smiled about the apartment/flat thing in the lift). It's like he's trying to keep the smile in, but it just shifts up to his eyebrow instead. If you ask me, it's lame because when you smile it makes other people smile, whereas that raised eyebrow makes him look kind of sinister too.

Uncle Jesse did the washing-up and I dried. We didn't talk much. He said, 'Sorry about supper. Daisy's not much of a cook.'

I said, 'It was fine,' because it was. But he looked like he didn't believe me. So I added, 'I just don't like melted cheese.'

He said, again, 'Fair enough.'

He asked me some questions, but they didn't really lead anywhere. Like, he asked, 'What do you enjoy?' So I told him I like football, only he didn't ask who I support or what position I play or anything. He just goes, 'You're Billy's son all right.' Or, he asked me who my best friend is and I told him it's Pamilekunayo, but everyone calls him P, only now he's started calling himself Pete. When Uncle Jesse raised an eyebrow, I just shrugged and said, 'I dunno. I don't think he's my best mate any more anyway.'

Uncle Jesse said, 'He's the kid who's sick, right?' And he must have seen something in my face because he goes, 'What? It's not your fault, is it?' which made me feel totally weird.

After that, we both gave up. But it turned out not talking was kind of worse. It made the noise of the water and scrape of plates and cutlery sound really loud, as if they were trying to fill the awkward silence.

When we'd finished the washing-up, Uncle Jesse looked at his watch and said, 'What time do you go to bed?'

'It's the holidays.'

'Right.'

'Can I watch TV?'

He frowned. He goes, 'I don't have a TV.'

I was surprised: not because I could really picture Uncle Jesse watching TV, but because his apartment was really fancy and he had loads of other stuff. His fridge had a button for ice and he had a special tap for boiling water – but he didn't have a TV.

There's this girl in my class, Rainbow Jones, who doesn't have a TV because her parents say it rots the brain, so she reads books instead. When I told Mum and Dad this, Mum goes, 'Sounds like they're sensible people.'

But Dad just laughed: 'Sounds like they're showing off.'

And Mum said, 'Billy!' although she was laughing too.

I wondered if Uncle Jesse didn't have a TV because he was sensible, or showing off, or some other reason.

I said, 'Can I go on my tablet?' Mum let me bring it because Hannah was going to the Brecon Beacons.

Uncle Jesse looked relieved. He goes, 'No problem.' Then, 'I got work to do, OK?'

By the time I got the tablet, Uncle Jesse had gone into his study and shut the door, so I had to knock. He said, 'Yes?' And I went in. One of his laptops was on, but he wasn't sitting at it. He was standing by the bookcase, staring at the photo I'd glimpsed earlier. It *was* Mum, Hannah and me. He wasn't working.

I go, 'Can I have the Wi-Fi password?'

'Are you allowed on the internet?'

'It's not for the internet,' I said. 'It's for my game. Anyway, Mum set parental controls. You can check if you want.'

He gave me the password. It was 'G4B3H4NN4H', which is my and Hannah's names if you look carefully. Then he goes, 'Can't you just let me work?' He said this like I lived in his apartment and was always interrupting, which was pretty unfair.

I sat on a leather couch. It was comfy, but kind of cold too. To be honest, I was a bit lonely. I entered the Wi-Fi password and opened Small Town Hero.

Guess what? Prince Prince was still on the island in Strait and Narrow, only now his vitality was down to one per cent, there was still no sign of the Fool, and the sea was so high that the island was a tiny circle of land just big enough for him and the vending machine. It seemed like I'd turned on the game just in time to find out whether I'd starve or drown. I was about to select End of Story, because it was like I didn't want to let the game beat me – weird, I know – when Uncle Jesse said: 'What are you playing?'

I almost jumped out of my skin. I hadn't heard the study door open, but now he was standing behind me. 'Small Town Hero,' I said. 'But it's a stupid game.'

He peered over my shoulder. 'The island's shrinking,' he said. 'You're in trouble.'

I wanted to go, *You don't say?* But for some reason, I didn't dare. The sea was now lapping at my knees and my finger hovered over End of Story.

Uncle Jesse goes, 'Why don't you climb on the vending machine?' Then, 'Just drag yourself up.'

I did what he said and Prince Prince was soon sitting on top of the vending machine. I hadn't realised you could do that. I looked at him, puzzled: 'You play this game?'

He shook his head. 'Uh-uh.'

His face seemed different somehow. It's a bit hard to explain, but I'll try. Usually, Uncle Jesse looked like he could only do two faces – frown and raised eyebrow – but now he looked like he could do all sorts of expressions, even though he wasn't doing them. I told you it's hard to explain.

I looked back at Small Town Hero. The sea was rising around the vending machine with Prince Prince sitting on top. And, of course, my vitality was still at one per cent. I said, 'Now what?'

'Wait.'

I waited. I watched the sea lift the vending machine off what was left of the island until it was bobbing around in the breakers. Then water began to get inside the vending machine and slowly lift snacks out of the slot at the top. Uncle Jesse said, 'Well, go on then!' It was easy for me to pick up four snacks and my vitality was back to one hundred per cent just like that.

Now I really stared at Uncle Jesse. I said, 'How did you know how to do that?'

He was bent over, looking at the screen; only now he

straightened up. For a moment, I thought he was going to smile. But he sighed instead. He said, 'I wrote it.'

I was confused: 'Wrote what?'

'Small Town Hero.'

At first, I didn't believe him. I was all, like, *No way!*

But he didn't look like he was lying, and why would he? Besides, if he was lying, he'd want me to believe him, whereas he didn't seem to care. He just shrugged, looked at his watch and said, 'Time for bed. It's late.'

I looked back at the tablet. 'It's the holidays,' I said. 'Can't I just finish this bit?'

'What you gonna do?' he said. 'You're floating in the middle of the sea.'

'You can tell me!' I protested. '*If you wrote it!*'

But Uncle Jesse shook his head and, out of nowhere, his voice went all strange, like a growl: 'Just do what you're told!' I looked at him in shock – *What are you so vex about?* But that only seemed to provoke him, like he was embarrassed to be angry and that made him angrier still. 'You're supposed to do it on your own!' he snapped. 'See the pattern for yourself! That's the whole point!'

He actually snatched the tablet out of my hand and, because of the way I was holding it, he bent my finger right back and I said, 'Ow!'

He gave me the weirdest look, like this really mean sneer and he goes, 'What's the matter with you?' Then he swore under his breath before marching back to his study with my tablet under his arm, slamming the door behind him.

I don't know if I've made this sound creepy too, but it

really was. I mean, I guess you could just put it down to what Daisy said about how he doesn't know about kids, but I swear it was more than that – because he was so angry and I didn't know why; because he shut himself away in his study and then just appeared at my shoulder (a bit like what happened at the church when he stalked out the back one minute and turned up by the altar the next); because, yeah, he was my uncle, but if you think about it I didn't actually know him from a bar of soap.

I reckon a year ago I might have started crying but I didn't. I don't cry any more; not since Dad died. Besides, I reckon there's a point when you're too freaked out to cry anyway and I knew there was nobody to hear me except Uncle Jesse and, if I started crying, maybe that would vex him and all.

14

WHERE AM I?

At home, I usually read for ten minutes or so and then Mum comes in to say goodnight. I know some people, even grown-ups, don't like the dark and sleep with a light on outside the door or something. In fact, Jeetan told me he went round Tom Forsyth's and he's still got one of those baby nightlights you plug in to the wall – that's *seriously* lame. But when I turn off the light, I like it to be pitch black. The way I figure, if you're afraid of the dark it's because you don't know what's around you. And I'm not afraid of the dark for the exact same reason – I don't know what's around me, and that means I can go anywhere in my imagination and now, sometimes, in the real world too.

But that first night at Uncle Jesse's, when I got into bed in the guest room and turned off the light, for once I was spooked. I wasn't afraid of something I couldn't see though – ghosts, zombies, vampires or whatever. I was afraid of some*one* I couldn't *hear*. Like, I could picture Uncle Jesse in his study, still angry, and my ears were on high alert for his footsteps in the passage, coming towards me. What did I think he might do? I had no idea. That was the problem.

I remembered how Mum talked about Uncle Jesse – that he was *an outcast* and *on another planet*. It seemed to me that could mean he was capable of anything. I remembered how Mum talked *to* Uncle Jesse – like she was angry about something she couldn't mention, like she couldn't quite trust him. But she still sent me to stay with him because that morning she was in a panic and she didn't know what else to do. And I remembered the night before – how I went into P's room and wished he was dead. He got sick and now I was here and, if Uncle Jesse murdered me, maybe it would serve me right. I know this probably sounds stupid, but if you're not careful these are the kinds of things you think about in the dark.

My ears were on high alert, but the silence was deafening. I felt like I had to do something. I closed my eyes. I concentrated as hard as I could. At first it wasn't working. But then, vaguely, in the pitch black, I began to make out this vertical line in front of me that was somehow blacker than the blackness and, very faintly, I heard a *ding* I recognised, and then the ripping, rushing sound.

I'm standing at the lift when the doors open. I get in and press Ground. I'm dressed and I have my rucksack. I plan to go home.

I get out in the lobby. No one's at the desk, but I can see a coffee cup and an open newspaper, so I hurry to the automatic doors, down the steps and I'm on the move. I glance back in through the floor-to-ceiling glass in time to see Niki emerge from the office. He probably heard the doors open and shut. He peers out and he's staring right at me. But his expression doesn't change. I figure I must be invisible again.

I hope I remember the way. I think it's pretty easy – left out of the building, left again at the main road, then across to the station. I see the sign for Uncle Jesse's street on the corner with the main road – Medburn Street. That name rings a bell. I didn't notice it earlier.

The main road's almost deserted. I don't know what the time is, but it's late. I hope I can still get a train. I tell myself that I will be able to because this is my story. I am quickly at the station.

I look up at the station clock, eleven-thirty p.m., then the board – the last train's in fifteen minutes. I stare at the board, trying to change the time of the train, but it doesn't work. I stare at the clock trying to move the hands forward, but that doesn't work either. I'll have to wait.

I sit on a bench. The station isn't busy, but it's not empty either. I look at the different people. There's a man in a suit with a briefcase, talking on his phone; another writing in a notebook; a man and woman hugging and kissing; an old lady with a wheelie shopping bag; three guys drinking beer from cans. I realise everyone can see me now. I don't know how that works. I don't know how any of this works.

Then one of the guys scrunches up his beer can and drop-kicks it across the concourse. The clattering noise echoes. A man in uniform shouts, '*Oy!*' Drop-kick guy shouts, '*Oy!*' back and reels away, laughing. He spots me watching and comes over. He looks me up and down. Maybe I should be scared, but I'm not. He goes, 'You a Watford fan?' I realise he's looking at my rucksack, which has a badge on it. I nod. He goes, 'Who's your favourite player?'

'Mo Hayes.'

He thinks about this for a moment and then holds out his fist: 'Respect.'

I bump his fist with mine and he nods and stumbles away.

I hadn't noticed the man with the notebook sit down on the same bench as me, but now I do. He nods in the direction of drop-kick guy and goes, 'Louts.' Then, 'You OK?'

I say, 'Fine.'

He slides a bit closer. He's smiling and I can see this bubble of white saliva in the corner of his mouth. It's gross. He says, 'It's late to be out on your own.'

'I'm not on my own. Dad's just gone to the Gents.'

He nods, 'Right.' But he's still smiling and I can tell he knows I'm lying.

I look up at the clock. It's hardly moved. I think, *This is my story. I want to look back at this man and find him gone.* I look back at the man and he's not gone anywhere. He's well dodgy. Right now I'd like to open my eyes and find myself back in the bedroom at Uncle Jesse's. But my eyes are already open. I need help.

'Excuse me!' The old lady with the wheelie bag sits down between me and the man with the notebook. The man doesn't move at all, so I have to slide all the way down to the end of the bench to make room. I hear the man make a tutting noise. I figure he's tutting at the old lady and I glance at her, thinking she might say something, but she doesn't. She just takes out her knitting.

Now the man with the notebook stands up. He's looking at me with this mean, puzzled expression. There's something weird about his mouth; like, he's forty or something but his lips are thick, pink and wet like a baby's. He says, 'What's the matter with you?'

That doesn't make sense, but I don't have time to be confused because, at that moment, the old lady jabs me in the arm with a knitting needle, like, totally on purpose. And I go, 'Ow! Get off!'

Now the man's eyes widen and he glances left and right like he's scared someone might be watching, then he hurries away, muttering under his breath. It's a proper relief that he's gone but I don't know why the old lady poked me, so I go, 'What was that for?'

She gives me a look. She says, 'What are you doing, Gabriel?'

Now I do have the time to be confused: 'How do you know my name?'

'Why? Is it a secret?'

I stare at her. She looks familiar. She raises an eyebrow. She looks a bit like Uncle Jesse. She's definitely old, but somehow she doesn't look it. She has this small patch of freckles on either side of her nose, like me.

I say, 'I'm going home.'

She shakes her head, 'Give him another chance.'

'Who?'

She frowns like this is a stupid question. She says, 'Jesse! It's good for him to know you. Keep him grounded.'

Then the strangest thing happens (well, maybe not the strangest, but another strange thing in a long list of them) – it's like I blink and my stomach lurches the same as when you go over a humpback bridge in the car. The station disappears and suddenly I'm not sitting down but standing up outside Uncle Jesse's apartment block. The old lady's next to me and I'm pretty sure this is her doing, so I say, 'Who *are* you?'

But she just does a little laugh and goes, 'For Pete's sake!' And at that moment I know who she is, even though I can't believe it.

'I wanna go home,' I say. 'This is my story.'

I know I sound kind of whiny and she gets kind of irritated. She shakes her head and goes, 'Maybe it's *my* story. What do you think about that?'

Out of the corner of my eye, I can see Niki at the desk in the lobby, reading the paper. Now he looks up and jumps to his feet. I'm not worried because I figure I'm still invisible to him like I was before. It sounds stupid but my first thought is that he's seen the old lady. It's a heartbeat before I recognise my mistake.

You see, earlier, when Niki looked at me through the floor-to-ceiling glass front, he was in the bright lobby and I was on the dark pavement. I was never actually invisible in the first place . . .

Everything happens all at once. I'm turning to the old lady going, 'Is it? Is it your story?'

And she's shaking her head: 'No, it's yours. I'm just watching.'

And the automatic doors are opening and Niki's on the top step: 'Gabriel?'

He looks like he's seen a ghost but he hasn't. I'm not a ghost. It's not me he can't see. I look back at my grandmother, Coral Douglas, who must have died, like, thirty years ago and she raises a hand as she backs away.

Niki takes me up in the lift. He's muttering all these questions in his thick accent – *Where have I been? Do I know what time it is? Does my uncle know I went out?* I don't answer them. He's not expecting me to and I'm too busy thinking about what will happen when we get to the twentieth floor. And I'm not even talking about what Uncle Jesse might do or how angry he'll be . . .

You see, I'm thinking about the time I scored the winner in the Champions League Final. I mean, it's not like I had to fly back from a European city to get back into my bed – it just *happened*. The noise and lights of the stadium slowly faded and I opened my eyes with a gasp. But this time it can't be like that, can it? I try closing and opening my eyes a couple of times, willing myself back into bed. But it doesn't work.

Niki knocks on the door of 2020. Uncle Jesse opens it immediately, like he knew we were coming. He doesn't seem surprised to find me standing there and, when the concierge launches into an explanation of how he found me, Uncle Jesse cuts him off. He just goes, 'Thank you, Niki,' and does this nod. I step inside and he shuts the door. Uncle Jesse doesn't even look at me. Instead, he turns and walks back down the passage to his study, saying, 'Go to bed, Gabe.'

I'm on my own in the passage for a bit. It's totally dark apart from the dim lights along the skirting board. My mind is racing because I don't understand. Obviously, I don't understand what just happened: like, how it's possible I just met my dead grandmother and nobody could see her except me (because now I realise it wasn't just Niki – that man with the notebook didn't see her either). But, more importantly, I don't understand what's about to happen even though I'm pretty certain I know what it is.

I open the bedroom door and, sure enough, I don't find myself lying in bed. Think about it. And if you don't get why that's the weirdest thing ever, think a little harder until you do. Because where have I gone?

15

CHAPTER FIFTEEN

Nothing seemed so weird in the morning; partly because I had other things to think about (like P for starters – *What if he'd got worse or even died?*), partly because Uncle Jesse didn't say anything, and partly because nothing *ever* seems so weird in the morning: monsters lurking in the darkness turn out to be clothes slung over the back of a chair and problems heavy enough to pin you to your bed seem somehow lighter. The difference is that the monsters were never there while the problems never moved – you just stop thinking about them because you're too busy getting dressed, having breakfast and worrying about whether you killed your best friend.

I found Uncle Jesse in the kitchen bit of the big room, beating eggs with a fork. He goes, 'Scrambled?'

'I don't really like scrambled eggs.'

'What do you want for breakfast then? Cereal?'

'OK.'

I sat at the table with a bowl of cereal while he cooked. The cereal was gross. It was this muesli that stuck in my teeth. Uncle Jesse goes, 'Not good?' And I shook my head. He raised an eyebrow, his version of a smile. 'Daisy says it's healthy.'

There seemed to be something lighter about Uncle Jesse too, a better mood. But I didn't trust his mood because I was totally on edge. Obviously, I was waiting for him to raise last night, to give me grief, threaten to call Mum – *What the hell did you think you were playing at?* But he didn't. And I actually began to wonder if I'd made the whole thing up, remembering all the times Mum's said I have an *overactive imagination.* I thought, *Perhaps she's right. Perhaps there's something wrong with my brain.*

Uncle Jesse was eating his eggs. He has really bad table manners, shovelling in forkfuls with one hand and holding the plate with the other. If Mum had been there, she'd have been all, like, *It's not trying to escape, you know!*

He talked with his mouth full too, launching into a conversation from the middle, like we'd already been talking for ages. 'My work,' he said. 'I'm stuck. I can't get the ending.'

'What is it?'

'What is what?'

'Your work.'

He frowned at me like I was being deliberately thick. He goes, 'Small Town Hero. I told you.'

'You told me you wrote it.'

'Yeah.'

I was confused. I said, 'So it's already got an ending. In fact, it's got loads of them – Psycho Steve, the Monstrosity, the Small Giant with Big Feet ... And what about the End of Story option? It's there all the time, right in front of you!'

'But it hasn't got an *ending* ending.'

'Who says?'

'Dino. My boss.' He sighed. He absent-mindedly picked a piece of stray egg off his shirt and popped it in his mouth. 'Look,' he said. 'It was always supposed to be a sandbox. Small Town's been razed to the ground by the Ineffable, Unstoppable Dragon, the King's gone and it's up to Prince Prince to rebuild. Nice and simple. But a basic sandbox is kind of boring, because there aren't any consequences; not really. So I wanted to make something different. That's why I came up with the chapter structure, to make it more like the player's telling their own story.'

'That's what's cool about it,' I said. 'It's kind of like Minecraft: Story Mode. You remember? They did that ages ago . . .'

He'd finished his food. He gave me a look. 'Minecraft: Story Mode?' he said. 'No. Not like that.' He stood up and took his plate and my bowl to the sink. 'It's nothing like that, is it?'

I shook my head. 'No,' I said. 'You're right.' Even though it's totally like that.

Uncle Jesse nodded. 'So, we figured gamers would mostly stay in Small Town. If they explored the rest of the world, it would be to gather tokens and materials. But the feedback we're getting? There's a whole bunch of players just collecting loot boxes in their Kit Bag, like they think it's some kind of quest.'

'That's what I've been doing,' I said. 'It's more fun.'

Uncle Jesse stared at me. I'd said the wrong thing again. 'Dino wants me to write a patch. He wants an *ending* ending – that's what he calls it. He wants a *happily ever after*. That's lame, right?'

'So lame,' I said.

This time I think he knew I was only agreeing for the sake of it. He kept on looking at me like I might crack under pressure, but I didn't. He glanced at his watch. He said, 'What you wanna do today?'

I shrugged.

He said, 'I like to go for a walk in the mornings. Check the lie of the land. Keep me company?'

'OK.'

'Right.' He looked at his watch again. He said, 'Right. I gotta make a phone call. Shouldn't take more than half an hour.'

'Can I get my tablet?' I asked.

He frowned: 'Your tablet?'

'You took it,' I said. 'Yesterday.'

'Did I?'

We went to his study and sure enough the tablet was sitting on his desk. He seemed bewildered to find it there. He said, 'Sorry.' And he still never mentioned last night.

His phone call took a lot longer than half an hour. I had a shower. I opened Small Town Hero. There was Prince Prince, sitting on the vending machine, bobbing around in Strait and Narrow, still no sign of the Fool. I was kind of irritated. I thought, this *is lame*. I made myself some toast and peanut butter. By the time I came back to the game, my vitality had dropped to seventy-five per cent, so I picked up some snacks floating by. And, all the time, I could hear Uncle Jesse, wandering around the apartment with his phone pressed to his ear.

It was clear that the person at the other end was doing most of the talking. Uncle Jesse just said things like, 'Yes, but—' And, 'No, I understand, but—' And, at one point, *'Jerry says?'* Then, at last, 'OK! Two weeks!'

I was sitting on the couch with the tablet. He said, 'Let's go.' I looked up at him. From what I'd overheard, I expected him to be worried. He didn't look worried, but I find his expressions very hard to read. He had no problem reading the question in my face though. He goes, 'Dino likes the sound of his own voice. He's panicking. Given me two weeks to finish the patch. It's not just me, you see – there's coders, graphics guys . . .'

'What you gonna do?'

He shook his head. 'Dunno.' He peered down at my screen. He said, 'Still on the vending machine?'

I nodded. I had a question, but I remembered what he'd said to me last night when he was angry – *You're supposed to do it on your own!* So I just asked quickly, before I could chicken out, 'Does the Fool come back?' He frowned. I said, 'It's just that he stole snacks in Chapter Three. Can I even trust him?'

Uncle Jesse thought for a moment. Then he said quietly, 'I don't think he's untrustworthy, he's a fool.' He glanced down at the screen. He said, 'Look!'

The Fool was approaching in the canoe. He paddled to the vending machine and climbed up as my avatar climbed down next to the Kit Bag. The Fool's vitality was down to one per cent, but he could pick up some snacks floating by. I paddled off with the Kit Bag to Other Side. As I hauled the

Kit Bag onto the shore, I said, 'So, do I go back for him – the Fool, I mean?'

But Uncle Jesse tutted impatiently. I didn't want to make him all mad again, so I quickly switched off the tablet. At least I'd finished Chapter Fifteen.

16

SCHRÖDINGER'S CAT, GABRIEL'S DAD

Uncle Jesse and me go down in the lift together. Suddenly I have the most peculiar feeling, a kind of dizziness. It's almost like I'm about to disappear into another story, but I don't close my eyes and there's no whooshing, ripping sound. Instead, it's more like a memory of a conversation with Uncle Jesse, only – and this is the really crazy bit – I know it hasn't happened yet. It's not very clear. I mean, Uncle Jesse's voice and face are quite clear, but my own words seem to drop in and out, like phone reception on a train.

So, this is the conversation we're going to have. Don't worry if you don't understand everything we say. I don't either. But I can kind of get the gist, so I figure you can too.

Uncle Jesse will ask, 'What do you know about black holes?' And I guess I tell him because he goes, 'It's not true they suck things in. Not really. Or, at least, not especially hard. I mean, the biggest black hole has the mass of about seven billion suns, so yeah, that's pretty sucky. But it's still just gravity. What I'm saying is it's not special. You can orbit a black hole in exactly the same way you orbit the sun, so long as you don't cross the event horizon.'

I don't know what the *event horizon* is. Seems I ask him.

'It's the point of no return. Once you cross the event horizon, you're not coming back.'

I can't hear what I say next, but Uncle Jesse goes, 'That's not the half of it. You want to know something mind-blowing?'

I must do, because he nods. 'OK, then.' He thinks for a moment, frowning, before he says, 'OK. So, you know what science *is*, right? I mean, I'm not talking about physics, biology and chemistry, I'm more talking about what it's *for*. Science tries to find one explanation for everything – one set of rules. Like, at my boarding school, there was this rule that you had to wear your blazer any time you left the grounds. If you were caught without your blazer, it was no good saying it was really hot or you'd forgotten it or whatever, because you'd broken the rule. Science is a bit like that – there's no arguing with the rules.

'But, here's the thing. There are two really important rules that explain the universe – they're called *general relativity* and *quantum mechanics*. You heard of them?'

I've heard of them, but I don't know what they are. I'm rubbish at science.

'Basically, general relativity is good at explaining the big stuff, like how planets move, that scale; while quantum mechanics explains the smallest stuff that you can't even see with a microscope. They're really smart rules and, as far as anybody knows, they're both true. But guess what? *Sometimes they can't both be true.*

'Black holes are a good example. According to general relativity, when something falls into a black hole everything about it is erased – they're like great space dustbins. But quantum mechanics says that's impossible, because you lose time reversibility and—' He looks right at me. He can tell I'm already getting lost. He shakes his head, frustrated: 'Forget time reversibility. It's not important. What's important is that general relativity explains black holes in a way that quantum mechanics says is impossible. Got it?'

I hear myself say, 'Got it.' Even though I don't know what it is I've got. I say, 'So?'

And he goes, 'So? Exactly. So . . .' Then, 'One idea is that black holes don't actually destroy the things that fall into them. Instead, they spit them out into new dimensions. It's one foundation of something called Many Worlds Theory or the multiverse, the suggestion that every possible outcome does indeed happen. Basically, every possible outcome creates a new reality in a new dimension invisible to all the others.'

At this point, Uncle Jesse's face is very clear. I'm staring at him and he has that same look again – the one where his face suddenly looks like he can do all sorts of different expressions only he's not doing them. I hear myself go, 'I don't understand.'

But he shakes his head urgently. 'Don't worry about it. You don't need to understand electricity to switch on a light, right?' Right. I guess. 'So, imagine you're waiting for a bus. You have to wait so long that in the end you decide to walk. Five minutes later? The bus passes you. Typical. Now, imagine you actually took both decisions – you chose to walk *and* wait for the bus. So, you split in two. One of you walked, the other took the bus. Then the one who's walking looks up at the bus passing by and he knows that another version of himself is on the top deck.'

My voice has faded again, but I must say something like, *But he's not!* Because Uncle Jesse goes, 'How do you know?'

I can't see him, I think. So that's probably what I say. Because Uncle Jesse raises an eyebrow and goes, 'But I think you can, Gabe.'

There is a lull then, a few moments silence. I suppose I might be saying something, but I don't think so. I reckon I'm lost for words.

Uncle Jesse goes, 'Can I tell you about Schrödinger's cat?'

Maybe I say, *Sure*. Or maybe I just shrug. Either way, he ploughs on: 'So, there was this guy called Schrödinger who came up with an experiment – not a real experiment, a *thought experiment*.

'Imagine you put a cat in a box and you put something in the box with it that may or may not kill it – let's say a tube of poisonous gas, but it doesn't really matter. The important thing is that you know that there is an exactly fifty-fifty chance that, within an hour, the tube will break and the gas will escape and kill the cat. Then you close the box. After an hour, you come back. How will you know if the cat's alive or dead?'

I hear myself say, 'You look in the box.'

'Right. But what about *before* you look in the box?'

'You don't know. The cat could be alive or dead.'

'Or, it's alive *and* dead.' My voice drops out again. But Uncle Jesse goes, 'It's *supposed* to be stupid.' He raises an eyebrow in place of a smile. 'It's kind of what passes for a science joke.' Then, 'But you remember what I said about quantum mechanics?'

I don't hear my reply, but I do remember – he said quantum mechanics explains really small things. It looks like I remember in the future too, because Uncle Jesse goes, 'Exactly!' Then, 'So, quantum mechanics has some brilliant equations that tell us the position of the tiniest thing we can measure – a sub-atomic particle. But what these brilliant equations show is that the sub-atomic particle is as likely to be in one place as another. So how would you know its real position?'

I hear myself say, 'You'd look.'

'Right! But what if the act of looking itself affected the position? Then you could say that the particle was in two places at the same time until you looked at it.'

'Is that true?'

'That's true.'

'So the cat's both alive and dead until you open the box and look inside?'

'That's the joke. Because everything you know about reality tells you that doesn't make sense.' He pauses. 'But . . .' he says. 'But what if it's everything you know about reality that doesn't make sense instead?'

In my head, I think this must be where I start to see what he's getting at, because, here and now, I'm starting to see what he's getting at. I'm thinking about what this really means – *the consequences*.

My voice has faded away again, but I must be telling him

about the black hole inside me, because, here and now, that's what I want to do. I figure I must say something like – *Since Dad died, I feel like I've got a black hole inside me and it's sucking me in, like all different parts of me – everything I know about him, everything I feel, even Dad himself, like maybe that's where he's gone.*

I reckon I'm right too, because Uncle Jesse's frowning and he goes, 'I know what you mean.'

And my voice comes back, louder than before, and I'm saying, 'So, maybe all that stuff hasn't actually disappeared. Maybe it's just gone somewhere else. Like you said.'

And Uncle Jesse's shaking his head, because he's worked out what I'm going to say next. I don't hear what I say next, but I know what it is – *So, maybe Dad's alive somewhere and I can find him!*

Back in the present moment, the lift has opened and Uncle Jesse's striding across the lobby. I'm distracted for a second and, when I come back to my memory of the conversation that hasn't happened yet, I find I've forgotten the ending.

I reckon Uncle Jesse will keep shaking his head and then say something like, *I shouldn't have . . .* And I'll know what he's thinking – that I'm just a kid who lost his dad and he shouldn't encourage me to believe in something impossible, something that might upset me. But I also know that I won't get upset, because he just told me it's not impossible at all.

17

OUR BEARINGS

When we left Uncle Jesse's apartment, we walked for hours. I couldn't tell you where we went. I don't think we went anywhere in particular, just the streets around Somers Town. At first, Uncle Jesse stalked ahead of me with that long stride going, 'This way,' then, 'Left here,' then, 'Around the square,' and I almost had to run to keep up.

So it was a while before I realised we were only criss-crossing the same bunch of streets. But eventually I said, 'You're going too fast!'

And he stopped so abruptly I nearly ran into him. He turned around. He goes, 'Why didn't you say something?'

He'd stopped by a bench. He turned and looked at it and he seemed surprised to find it there, like he hadn't walked these streets a thousand times, like he'd never seen the bench before. He goes, 'That's a bit of luck.' He sat down, kicked his legs out in front of him, let his head loll back over the top of the bench and closed his eyes. I sat down next to him. Then he said, 'So, are we gonna talk about last night?'

It took me by surprise. *Last night?* I mean, it's not like I really thought it hadn't happened; more like, because he hadn't mentioned it up to now, it may as well not have done. And you think *that* was a surprise . . .

He said, 'You met your grandmother then – Coral, I mean. I saw you both from the window. I see her myself sometimes, but never up close like that; only across a street or through a crowd or something. I don't know why.'

I didn't know what to say. I muttered, 'I thought she was invisible.'

'Not to me.' He shrugged. Then, 'How is she?'

How is she? It was a crazy question. How was my grandmother who died long before I was born? What was I supposed to say – *Yeah, fine, considering*? Instead, I said, 'She's dead, right?' He still had his eyes closed. His eyebrows twitched but he didn't say anything. 'So, that was a ghost?'

A small shake of the head and he sighed deeply. Then he said, 'When did it start?'

You might think that was a mysterious thing to ask, but I knew what he was talking about right away – the stories I tell that become real, that let me go almost anywhere and do almost anything. 'After the funeral,' I said.

'Recently,' he said. 'Right. I didn't realise. I just knew you weren't ready.'

'Ready for what?'

'I dunno,' he said. Another shrug. 'Today?'

'So, you can . . .' I tailed off, but he knew what I was going to say.

'I can do it too. But it's getting harder. Maybe it's an age thing.'

'Getting harder to tell the stories?'

His lips twitched: 'More like harder to tell this one.' He made this sound like a joke, but I didn't get it. Then, 'Who says they're stories, Gabe?' He made this sound like an explanation, but again I didn't get it. Then, 'Ask me whatever you want. I mean, it's not like I understand everything . . . Or anything much. But I'll do my best.'

I thought for a moment. I said, 'You and Dad – didn't you like each other?'

Finally he opened his eyes. In fact, his head jerked forward like he'd suddenly woken up. He frowned. He goes, 'Well, I wasn't expecting that. To think I sat up half the night trying to work out how I'd explain Schrödinger's cat to a thirteen-year-old—'

Schrödinger's cat? I remembered that from the conversation that hadn't happened yet, so I could've told him not to bother. But I felt like he was just playing for time, so I interrupted. I said, 'I asked Mum.'

He looked at me closely. 'What did she say?'

'She said Dad loved you more than anything.'

'Did she?' He nodded. 'There you are.' Then, 'Me too.'

'So, how come you never visit?'

'I don't know,' he said. 'Because I left, went to boarding school, college, moved to London, got a job . . . You know I lived in the States for years?' This didn't sound like a genuine question, so I didn't answer it. I was watching him. He knew I wasn't falling for excuses. He goes, 'What can I say, Gabriel? I'm a fool.' And he smiled – a proper smile – but his eyes were sad. He hauled himself to his feet with a sigh. He goes, 'Come on. Let's walk.'

So we walked, slowly. And we talked, quickly. For hours. Something had changed between us. You might think it was because we now had this thing in common, this shared secret – that we could tell stories (or whatever) and make them real. But I don't think that was the reason; or at least not the main one. It was more like we'd found our bearings – like we each had a map on which we could say, *Right, you're here, and I'm here*. I mean, it's not like we were close or anything, just that we could see our relative positions. I guess that's why people say things like *I can see where you're coming from* and *You know where I stand*.

To be honest, I still thought Uncle Jesse was creepy. But for the moment, that didn't matter. Because, before I knew it, we were having one of those great conversations when you let someone right inside your head to look around, and they're curious and interested, but they don't laugh at you, or criticise. And there's no turning back after a conversation like that. Like, you can't say later, *I didn't mean it*, because the other person's been inside your head and knows exactly what you meant – it's a point of no return.

Actually, it was me who did most of the talking. Uncle Jesse mostly just asked questions and then listened for exactly the right length of time before asking another.

He asked me why I wanted to go home last night. I told him it was because I was going to miss the Moses Hayes Soccer School because I was in London. This was true, but it wasn't the whole truth, and he waited until I said it was also because I thought he was well creepy and I was lonely and I missed Mum, my own house, even Hannah. And he nodded.

I told him all sorts of stuff. I told him about Abdul, who's been playing Small Town Hero for almost two months and hasn't died yet, but it's only because he doesn't dare leave Small Town or do anything interesting. Uncle Jesse raised an eyebrow and goes, 'It takes all sorts.' I told him about Mum; how she said she was stressed when really she was sad; how she starts crying out of nowhere and then stops just like that; how she'd started smoking again and I was worried about her. I told him about Grandy, who forgets things all the time, and Hannah, who's started talking like Juliet Adeyemi and treats me like a kid. And I told him about P, how out of order he'd been, the fight we had, how he ganged up on me with his new mates in Year Ten and took the piss when I was taking that penalty.

Uncle Jesse didn't tell me off for saying *Took the piss* and he didn't just say what Mum said – *Kids fight! That's what they do!* Instead, he goes, 'He sounds like a bully. You really didn't do anything?'

'No! He was my best mate. It's like he's vex for no reason.'

He considered this. 'You told me he's started calling himself Pete, right?' I nodded. He said, 'You don't change your name unless you're unhappy with who you are. He must be scared of something.' I must have looked doubtful, because he goes, 'Really! When the male of the species gets angry, that's generally why.'

I wanted to ask him why he got so angry last night then, what he was scared of. But I didn't; not because I was worried about his reaction, but because I had other things to say. Like I told him about Mum winning on the scratchcard and how I had wished P was dead. I told him that Mum did win, but only twenty-five quid, and P got really sick. I had a nauseous feeling in my stomach as I asked, 'Did I make those things happen?'

He made a noise like he was about to laugh but he didn't. He just said, 'No, Gabriel. You were just watching, right? Do you think you're God?'

I stared at him. I had this overwhelming feeling of something like relief. I mean, it *was* relief, but it was so intense that I almost think it needs a different word – I was numb and dizzy and breathless and I realised that I'd spent the last day or so on the edge of panic and I hadn't even known.

Uncle Jesse put his hand on my shoulder and this time it almost felt normal. We stood like that for a moment without speaking until he goes, 'I'm starting to remember what it's like being a kid.' Then, 'Not a kid; a teenager. I mean, I wasn't like you – I didn't have lots of friends, I wasn't good at football, I was kind of a geek—'

I interrupted: 'You were the two outcasts.'

'Who?'

'You and Mum.'

'Is that what she said?'

'She said that's how you became friends.'

'Really?' He sounded surprised. He frowned. 'Maybe.' He shook his head. 'Anyway. What I was going to say was that everyone gave me grief at St Mark's the whole time I was there. That's why I couldn't wait to get away.' Then, 'There was one guy who made my life hell. Even after he left, I'd see him around town. Even after *I* left . . .'

'What did he do?'

'Threw my shoes on the roof, locked me in the science cupboard, set fire to my school bag in a dustbin . . .' Uncle Jesse listed these things matter-of-factly, like they were no big deal. But he wasn't fooling me. He sniffed. 'But mostly he just wanted people to laugh at me, make me feel weak and stupid.'

'What was his name?' I asked.

'I called him Psycho Steve.'

'Really? Like in the game?'

'Like in the game.'

I had another question, but it took me a moment to get it out. I said, 'You ever wish he was dead?'

Uncle Jesse looked at me. He goes, 'Sure.'

It was when he was living with Dad in the flat in town. Uncle Jesse had gone to boarding school for Sixth Form, so he was almost an adult. It was the Easter holidays (like it is now) and he went to Smith's to buy stationery. He was just looking in his wallet to check he had enough cash when Psycho Steve appeared, snatched it out of his hand, took all the money (like, a tenner or something), dropped the wallet on the ground and swaggered off, laughing. Uncle Jesse decided enough was enough: 'I thought, *I'm gonna show him. He has no idea what I'm capable of.*'

His voice sounded really menacing, like he was remembering how angry he'd been so well that he was getting angry all over again. But I wasn't surprised. I understood. It was exactly how I'd felt about P. I said, 'What did you do?'

'I looked for another version.'

'A different story?'

He gave me a look. He said, 'That's what I thought.'

Uncle Jesse told me he went back to the flat, shut the curtains, closed his eyes and really concentrated. He heard this great rushing sound, like wind through trees, and then vague silhouettes started to take shape before his eyes. The way he described it sounded exactly like what happens to me.

I was listening so hard that I hadn't noticed we'd done another circuit and were back by the bench. Uncle Jesse sat down again, same position as before, feet out in front of him, head back, eyes closed. I go, 'You gonna tell me what happened?'

'I thought I'd try and show you,' he said. 'Shut your eyes.'

18

PSYCHO STEVE

It's night. I know where I am. I'm outside the Odeon in town. I just don't know when. For starters it's open, whereas I've only ever seen it boarded up with posters covering the doors and windows. But, also, everyone's wearing old-fashioned clothes – baggy trousers and stuff – and the first guy I see is talking on this ancient mobile. Uncle Jesse's standing next to me. I ask him, 'Can they see us?'

Uncle Jesse shakes his head: 'We're just watching.' And he nods up the street.

I recognise young Uncle Jesse at once (I'll just call him Jesse from now on, to be clear). At first, I think he looks exactly the same, but as he gets closer, I realise he's not quite as tall and his hair is even longer and he's even skinnier. He's wearing this big dark overcoat and he looks kind of nervous. There's a girl with him. She has her hair pulled back in a pony and she's got a short top that shows her belly button, cargo trousers and trainers. She's smoking a cigarette and wearing so much make-up that it's a moment before I even think I know her. I go, 'Is that Hannah?'

Uncle Jesse frowns: 'No. That's your mum.'

Imagine that, seeing your mum as a teenager! I feel like my heart's stopped beating. 'The two outcasts,' I murmur.

'Your mum wasn't an outcast; not by now. In fact, I'm not sure she ever was. It was all in her head.'

'But you were still best friends?'

Uncle Jesse looks at me. He doesn't frown or raise an eyebrow or smile. His face is frozen: 'I thought so.'

Suddenly we're sitting in the movie, in the row behind Jesse and Mum. It's *Men in Black II*. I saw it ages ago round P's when we were bored and playing pot luck on Netflix. It's not as good as the first one, but we join it right at the end where Will Smith discovers that the world is actually all inside a locker in a giant alien train station – that bit's pretty cool.

It takes my eyes a minute to adjust to the dark. Uncle Jesse is on my left. The guy on my right is about twenty years old. He has his feet on the chair in front. He's not watching the movie at all but talking loudly to a friend on his other side. He can't see me, so I look at him closely. He has blond hair, a big face and small eyes.

I turn to Uncle Jesse. 'Is that Psycho Steve?' He nods. I go, 'And the other one?'

'His mate, Drew.'

Now the girl in the row in front turns round. Mum. She goes, 'Can both of you shut up?'

Her voice sounds exactly like it does now and, just for a second, I think she's talking to me and Uncle Jesse. But she isn't, of course.

Psycho Steve makes this mocking noise – like, *Oooooh!* But he briefly shuts up. Then he kicks the seat in front of him really hard. This is Jesse's seat, but he doesn't look round, so Steve leans forward and flicks his ear, before hissing at Mum, 'What you doing with this loser?' Only he doesn't use the word *loser* if you know what I mean . . .

I say, 'Hey!' My face is all hot. I'm angry, which is kind of stupid, because this has already happened and they can't see or hear me anyway.

Now we're in the foyer. The movie's finished and everyone's filing out. Through the glass doors, I can see Mum already outside on the pavement, looking at her watch, smoking a cigarette (another cigarette!), alone. Here come Psycho Steve and Drew, emerging blinking from the dark cinema. Drew branches off to the Gents. I turn to Uncle Jesse. I go, 'Where . . . ?' But he's white as a sheet.

There's a shout. I turn back just in time to see Jesse appear as if from nowhere, pushing a girl out of his way. Psycho Steve doesn't see him coming and is blindsided by this vicious sucker-punch that sends him sprawling.

It's hectic. Parents try to pull their kids away; teenagers try to get closer. I'm with the teenagers, wanting a better look – *fight, fight, fight!* Jesse's on top of Psycho Steve, making the most of surprise, a fury of action. People are shouting: 'Get him off!' But nobody does anything. Steve tries to cover his face with his hands, but Jesse lands another solid punch. My blood is racing. I'm excited, thrilled – the psycho's getting what he deserves.

But then a voice cuts over the hubbub. 'Jesse! Jesse!' It's Mum and her face is horrified, disgusted. Jesse turns and his eyes are wild and there's something in his face – an unlocked rage – that kind of freezes my excitement right there.

Mum stalks away and Jesse goes after her. 'Beth!' The crowd quickly breaks up. A couple of people try to help Psycho Steve, but he shrugs them off. He's humiliated. His nose is bleeding. He touches the back of his head and his hand comes away bloody too. He's not badly hurt, but he's well angry.

I don't know where Uncle Jesse's gone, but I'm not really looking. I head outside. I see Mum turn down the alley that leads to the car park back of Asda. Jesse's a few paces behind. I go after them.

When I catch up, I can hear him saying, 'What am I supposed to do, just take it?'

Mum stops in her tracks and turns round. She's crying but trying not to. She goes, 'I didn't want to see that stupid movie anyway.' She shakes her head. Then she looks at her watch and stalks away again.

Jesse says, 'Where are you going?'

She answers over her shoulder: 'I told you. I'm meeting someone.'

Jesse stays where he is. He tuts defiance. He's still rushing adrenaline. He looks down at his hand with a wince. His bruised knuckles must be hurting. He flexes his fingers a couple of times. I have a decision to make. I follow Mum.

By the time I reach the end of the alley, she's halfway across the car park, heading for the footbridge across the canal. On the other side, I can see the Coy Carp, which is Mum's favourite pub, only it's not called the Coy Carp. I can see the sign – the Fisherman's Rest.

I am about to follow, but Uncle Jesse steps out of the shadows. He goes, 'Not now.'

And everything fades away.

I opened my eyes first. Uncle Jesse didn't open his eyes and I wondered if he was still there – in the car park, I mean. He flexed his fingers a couple of times, like he had in the alley. I said, 'How did you do that?'

'Do what?'

'*That!* So that we were seeing the same thing!'

He opened his eyes slowly. He said, 'How do you know we were seeing the same thing?' Then, 'What do you think?'

'I don't know. You were really brave, taking him on like that. I mean, he's massive. You must have been bricking it. But that's what you gotta do with bullies, right? Stand up to them.'

Uncle Jesse raised an eyebrow, then he shook his head. He said, 'I wasn't brave. All I did was sit in that armchair, pull the curtains and shut my eyes. I was still like you. I thought I was in control. I thought I was telling a story.'

'And you weren't?'

'Not exactly.' Uncle Jesse looked at me and sat forward. 'That's the point, Gabe. I never opened my eyes in the armchair. That me was gone. I never came back to myself. I'd passed a point of no return. I don't know how else to explain it.'

I stared. I considered the implications. I remembered the previous night, the Gabriel Douglas who got into bed, terrified of his uncle. That me, that uncle – both gone too. It was as if we had crossed an event horizon. And I knew what that was because I remembered a conversation that hadn't happened yet. In fact, this was the precise moment Uncle Jesse goes, 'What do you know about black holes?'

19

JUST DESERT

I decided to go back for the Fool – in Small Town Hero, I mean. Or rather, I decided that my avatar, Prince Prince, should go back for the Fool. He only got there just in time, as the snacks had all run out and the vending machine was starting to sink into Strait and Narrow. So by the time Prince Prince paddled them to Other Side, they were both low on vitality. But there was nothing to do but pick up the Kit Bag and strike out across Just Desert.

I completed Chapters Sixteen, Seventeen and Eighteen pretty easily. I won't describe them in detail in case you're playing yourself. We had to dump the map, because it didn't go as far as Other Side, but we soon came across a fast food joint where we could stock up on snacks and get Our Bearings. We were crossing the car park when we were attacked by a gang called Vicious Rumours and for a moment I thought we were in trouble. But then the gang turned on each other and, in the free-for-all, we were able to capture the Unbreakable Shield and the Dagger of Ultimate Leverage. I was feeling all pleased with myself because they had really important-sounding names, but then I realised I had no idea what they were for.

We ran into Juju the Witch again, lost in the desert. She

posed her usual riddles and I swear we got them all wrong, but she gave Prince Prince something nonetheless – a small box which she said contained the Lodestone. 'When you hold it,' she said. 'It gets you where you need to be.' I was all for taking it out then and there but she said it wouldn't work properly until we reached Place Necessary (which is twisted if you think about it). I wanted to know more, but the witch disappeared when we were distracted by this great whooshing noise high overhead. The Fool said it was the beating of the Ineffable, Unstoppable Dragon's wings.

Finally we reached the other side of Just Desert and the Pavilion at the Edge of the World. It was a rough place, kind of like a town in an old Western, full of Ne'er-Do-Wells, Arcade Hooligans and the remnants of the Vicious Rumours. All of them were up for a fight, but I decided to dodge the lot because we were looking for the Backseat Driver who could take us to Place Necessary. We tracked him down to the bar, but first we had to get past his bodyguard, the Guy That Won't Die. He might not die, but he's a lousy bodyguard, and Prince Prince took him out no problem.

The Backseat Driver was this huge, bald guy in a white suit with a gangster movie accent. We led him out onto the precipice overlooking Infinite Space where he kept his *Mid-Life Crisis*, which turned out to be a small black airship, spitting fire from its engines. He was reluctant to take us, saying we were too heavy. He said, 'You expect this baby to carry that amount of weight? Forget about it!' In the end, we had to give him all our snacks and tokens before he'd agree.

We boarded the airship. It was pretty cramped – two seats in front and two behind, like a sports car. The Backseat Driver climbed in the back with the Fool. Prince Prince took the wheel with the Kit Bag next to him.

We set off into Infinite Space. It was wicked – travelling at the speed of light through solar systems and galaxies, dodging asteroids and space junk, careering ever faster. This was a different kind of game altogether, kind of like a racing game. But it had a typical Small Town Hero twist, because we had to follow Our Bearings instructions ('In one light year, turn forty-two degrees starboard') and ignore a constant commentary from the Backseat Driver – 'Woah! You know you got people back here?' It was really hard to concentrate. And, when Our Bearings said to swing hard-a-port to avoid a black hole, I turned the rudder too late and suddenly gravity was pulling us in.

The Backseat Driver was shouting: 'I told you! We're carrying too much weight!'

Prince Prince tried the reverse thrusters, but they barely slowed us down. He picked up the Kit Bag, ready to heave it out of the airlock. But the Fool and the Backseat Driver were now fighting at the hatch. Before I knew it, the Fool had landed a couple of solid blows and pushed the Backseat Driver into oblivion. As we crossed the event horizon, I saw him stretched like a strand of spaghetti before he was totally obliterated.

I was shocked, but I had no time to think about it because now we were being pulled into the black hole too. I thought it was the end. To be honest, I'd given up and I was already wondering about my End of Story and whether I could be bothered to start again from Chapter One. But suddenly we were out the other side and hurtling down to what Our Bearings called *a small dull rock*. I had Prince Prince deploy parachutes as we accelerated into the atmosphere before crash landing.

It was pitch black when Prince Prince and the Fool climbed out of the wreckage. But as the sun began to rise, I realised we were right back where we'd begun, on the edge of the precipice, only facing the other way, looking back into Just Desert. Prince Prince stood there, gawping across the endless sand dunes like a total loser, but when the Guy That Won't Die appeared for revenge, he sprang into action. In the half-light, it was a tougher duel and my avatar ended up having to use the Dagger of Ultimate Leverage. He finished the Guy Who Won't Die but then, of course, he pretty much came straight back and the sun was still hovering on the horizon like it couldn't make up its mind.

I was concentrating so I didn't hear Uncle Jesse come up behind me until he said, 'Wow. Look at you. You got the Lodestone?'

'I can't see anything!' I said.

'No,' he said. 'It's a false dawn.'

And as he said that, I saw the sun start to drop again. Prince Prince ran through the Guy That Won't Die. I checked Our Bearings. The readout said, 'You have arrived at Place Necessary.' It made no sense.

This was the end of Chapter Nineteen.

20

SOMERS TOWN (PART TWO)

It's the night before Dad goes to Glasgow. I'm in the hallway, barefoot, approaching the kitchen. I can hear Mum and Dad talking quietly. They are sitting at the table. Mum looks up and sees me at the door. She says, 'Go to bed, Gabe!'

I say, 'I want my sticker album.' It's like I have no choice – I can't say anything else. I grab my sticker album from the side, pad back to the bottom of the stairs and . . .

For the next few days after our conversation – the one where I told Uncle Jesse everything and he showed me how he punched Psycho Steve before explaining black holes, Schrödinger's cat and Many Worlds Theory – Uncle Jesse was mostly working: on a mission to complete his patch for Small Town Hero.

And me? I had a mission of my own: to save Dad. Every chance I got, I closed my eyes, concentrated as hard as I could and waited for that rushing, whooshing sound. But it only seemed to work at night and, even then, I could only step into the same place and time – the night before Dad went to Glasgow, going to the kitchen, taking my sticker album, reaching the bottom of the stairs . . . And then opening my eyes with a gasp to find myself back in the spare bedroom at Uncle Jesse's.

In the mornings, we went for Uncle Jesse's daily walk around Somers Town, and in the afternoons we sat on the balcony of his apartment: him on his laptop, me on the game itself. That's when I finished Chapters Sixteen to Nineteen. The weather was really warm and spring-like, so we sat outside until the sun went down.

The balcony's pretty cool. It looks out miles across the city and it's got a metal rail about the height of my chin above clear Perspex panels. I mean, it's not dangerous or anything, but it took me a few minutes to dare to go right to the edge; not because I thought I'd fall but because it's impossible to stand there and not imagine how it would be if you did.

Daisy came over in the evenings. She's actually all right. I mean, she talks *a lot* and sometimes Uncle Jesse seems to get kind of irritated but, secretly, I think he likes it and he gets irritated because that's all he knows how to do. If that sounds weird, it's because Uncle Jesse is totally weird. Although I've also begun to wonder if the whole world's kind of weird that way – often we don't do what we truly feel, so much as what we know how to, and what other people are expecting.

Like, you know that thing grown-ups tell kids about pulling faces? *If the wind changes, your face will be stuck that way.* I don't reckon any kid anywhere has ever fallen for that. But I'm starting to think it might be true for how you behave. Sometimes, if Hannah takes the last strawberry yoghurt or whatever, I'll start going on about how unfair it is, even if I don't actually want it myself. Or if I do something to vex Mum, she'll give me this look and I'll know she's about to tell me how stressed she is, and originally that meant she's sad only now I'm not so sure. What if, at some point after Dad died, the wind changed in her heart and now it's stuck that way?

On one of our morning walks, I asked Uncle Jesse how come he moved to Somers Town, the place where he was born. I asked if he was trying to find out about his mum: how she died.

He raised an eyebrow. He goes, *'You saw her.* Why do you keep saying she died? Who told you that?'

'Dad,' I said.

'And you always believe what your dad tells you.'

'Of course I do,' I said. *'Did.'*

He looked at me. He blinked. He said, 'Fair enough.'

'Are you saying she's alive then?' I asked.

Uncle Jesse shook his head; not like he was denying it exactly, more like it was the wrong question. And then he told me about the first time he saw her himself (since he came back from America, I mean). It was late at night. He'd fallen asleep in the back of an Uber and the driver had to wake him up when they reached his apartment. As he got out of the car, he spotted Coral with her wheelie shopping bag crossing at the far end of the street, just for a moment – then she was gone.

I thought about this. It actually made no sense – it was night, she was quite a long way away, and he hadn't seen her since he was a toddler, when she wasn't an old lady. I asked him how on earth he knew it was her. He goes, 'I don't know. I suppose she's my mum.' That made no sense either, but it was somehow kind of obvious. I was learning there are a lot of things like that – more than you think.

I asked him why he walked the same streets every day and he goes, 'Force of habit. I like to check the lie of the land, because what if I've stepped into another world without realising?'

I stopped. I remembered the funeral, how he rushed out the back and reappeared by the priest moments later. I turned to look at him only to find he'd also stopped and was already looking at me. I said, 'Does that happen a lot – you step into a whole new story by mistake?'

He shook his head, but again it wasn't like he was saying *no*. And, instead of answering the question, he goes, 'The stories you tell that become real, Gabe. You gotta stop using those words – you're not telling them and they're not stories.'

I didn't know what to say. I mean, I guess I already knew this, but hearing him say it? That made it true, only for some reason I wanted to argue. So I reminded him about Mum winning on the scratchcard and P falling sick; and about his own story when he sucker-punched Psycho Steve – at some level we wanted those things to happen.

He gave me another raised eyebrow: 'But we weren't in control.'

I couldn't argue with that.

He told me more about the theory of the multiverse. If it's right, then everything that can happen must and does happen. According to Uncle Jesse, when I take the penalty in the last minute of the Soccer Sixes, reality divides and branches, so there's the me whose spot-kick catches the keeper's trailing leg and another who takes the exact same strike but finds the back of the net and celebrates a hat-trick. *You see? I told you – the only way of judging a penalty is whether it goes in.*

According to Uncle Jesse, there aren't just a few different realities, but a countless number – a world where Mum won £25,000 on a scratchcard, a world where she won £25, one where she won nothing, one where she never bought a scratchcard in the first place, and millions more. 'But the key thing, Gabriel, is that all those outcomes spring from the same timeline. Like, the Mum who won and the Mum who never even bought a scratchcard were the same person until the very moment that timeline split. And those splits happen every single moment of every single day.'

I stared. I felt like my brain was about to explode.

Uncle Jesse went on: 'Time itself – that's the real story: something made up to help people see meaning where there isn't any. Because actually everything that *has* happened, *can* happen and *will* happen is happening all at once.'

'What about death?' I said. 'Are you telling me that's a story too?'

Now it was Uncle Jesse's turn to stare, and he did that face where he looks like he can do all sorts of expressions only he's not doing them. He said, 'Define your terms. What do you mean by death? What do you mean by a story? Who do you think's telling it?'

He sounded like a school teacher. In fact, he sounded exactly like Mrs Naidoo does when she makes a mistake solving an equation and then tries to pretend she did it on purpose to catch you out.

Uncle Jesse raised his voice a bit. He goes, 'Don't get hung up on that, Gabriel. Because there are a lot crazier things to consider. Like, there must be worlds where we were, are, will never be born; worlds where the asteroid misses and dinosaurs keep walking the earth; where mankind doesn't invent the combustion engine and there's no global warming; where we destroy ourselves in a nuclear war!'

Boom! That's the sound of my brain exploding.

I said, 'But I haven't seen any of those.'

He just shrugged. He said he couldn't explain it but the way he had it figured, perhaps we only see realities close to our own. He goes, 'It depends on your point of view, right? You can never see everything. You can't see the whole planet, but it's not like you don't believe that America and Brazil and Cameroon are all out there somewhere.' Then, 'Imagine our reality has a fence round it. Most people can't even see the fence, but you and me, Gabe? We can. It's our great and unusual talent. Sometimes we peer over, invisible to what's on the other side – like when we saw your mum and me at the cinema with Psycho Steve. But sometimes we find a gap and climb right through.' He paused. 'And sometimes? Sometimes we can't find our way back.'

Pffisht! That's the sound of my brain putting itself back together (not great, but it's the best I can do). Because, deep down, I already knew this too. You see, I remembered the other night: going to Euston Station, meeting Coral, finding my bed empty – *I hadn't found my way back.* 'It's like we cross an event horizon,' I murmured.

'Yeah,' Uncle Jessed nodded. 'Like that.'

I suddenly felt very peculiar; not quite scared, but queasy, like I thought I might fall. In fact, I felt exactly like I did standing on the balcony looking out over London.

It must have shown on my face, because Uncle Jesse smiled, proper smiled, and then he did the most unexpected thing – he gave me a hug. And then I did an unexpected thing too . . . Maybe because my brain had just exploded and then put itself back together, or because I felt queasy, or because he hugged me, or because his hug was a bit like Dad's, or because it wasn't really like Dad's at all, I started to cry. I mean, I *never* cry. But that's what happened. And it was so unexpected that we might as well have been in another world.

I was totally embarrassed. I pushed him away and tried to pretend I was laughing. I go, 'If you're right, that means there's a world in which I score the winner in the Champions League.' And I told him about Mo Hayes's cross, my diving header and the way the fans celebrated.

Uncle Jesse raised an eyebrow. He didn't laugh (he never does). Instead, he gave it serious thought. He said, 'Perhaps you're better at this than me and can see realities that are further away.' Then, 'Or perhaps that reality's closer than you think.'

It took me a minute to grasp what he was saying. Because among all the crazy ideas he'd told me, that was probably the craziest of all.

21

APPLE AND PEANUT BUTTER

Uncle Jesse handed me the phone. It was Mum calling to check how I was doing. I told her I was fine. She asked what I was up to and I said, 'Not much.' She asked how I was getting on with Uncle Jesse and I said, 'Cool.'

I could tell that the less I said, the less she believed me. Trouble was, I didn't want to lie, but I couldn't tell the truth. Imagine how that would have sounded: *Yeah. I tried to run away the first night and I got in trouble at the station, but I was saved by Coral – you know, my grandmother who may or may not have been dead thirty years? – even though she was invisible. And it turns out Uncle Jesse can make his stories real like me (not that you know that), only he says that's not what's happening at all, because actually we're stepping into alternative dimensions. Like, he took me back into the past and showed me the time you two went to the Odeon and he beat up Psycho Steve. I saw you smoking, Mum – a lot! You really shouldn't smoke. Oh, and by the way, Dad must be alive somewhere in another world, so I'm trying to work out how to save him . . .*

I don't think so.

Instead, our conversation was really awkward. It was like Mum was finding a hundred different ways to ask the same three questions – *How are you? What are you up to? How's Uncle Jesse?* – and I couldn't think of a single different way to answer. Eventually, Mum said, 'Gabe, love, what's wrong?'

Part of me wanted to say, *Wrong? Define your terms.* But I didn't. I just said, 'Nothing.' Then I had a brainwave. 'Guess what?'

That cheered up Mum straightaway. She goes, 'What?'

'Uncle Jesse wrote Small Town Hero.'

'What's Small Town Hero?'

'My game! Small Town Hero. You know – Prince Prince and the Fool?'

'Oh!' she said. She sounded surprised, but not exactly excited.

'Did you know that?'

'No,' she said. 'No, I didn't.'

'Isn't that mad?' I said. 'I mean, like, totally mad. Small Town Hero's such a big deal right now. Everybody's into it.'

'That's mad,' Mum said, only she didn't mean it – she made it sound about as mad as a pre-season friendly. She said, 'So, is that all you're doing, playing video games?'

'No,' I said. 'Not really.'

And our conversation was awkward again, just like that. There was a brief uncomfortable silence and then Mum goes, 'Is Jesse still around? Could I get a word?'

'Sure.'

'See you soon, Gabe love. I miss you.'

'I miss you too.'

I passed the phone back to Uncle Jesse. I realised I

hadn't even asked Mum how her software training was going or anything.

Later, when Daisy arrived, she goes, 'Why don't we go out for supper?'

Uncle Jesse frowned. He said, 'I was gonna make stir fry. I bought tofu.'

Daisy did a strange little giggle. It sounded fake. She said, 'You hate tofu.'

'But you don't,' Uncle Jesse said, which made her coo like a bird and she gave him a kiss on the cheek.

Then she goes, 'What about you, Gabe? Do you like tofu?'

I shrugged: 'I don't know what it is.'

'It's bean curd,' she said. That didn't help. She did that giggle again. She said to Uncle Jesse, *'You see?* Come on, Jesse. Let's go out.' Then, to me, 'You'd like that, wouldn't you, Gabe?'

'I don't mind.'

'You're so polite! It's too cute!'

I hadn't said anything polite or cute. I just said, *I don't mind.* I looked at Uncle Jesse. He raised an eyebrow. I was beginning to see why he found Daisy annoying. She said, 'It's not every day you're in London, right? Your choice. Anything you like – Vietnamese? Thai? Or there's that Nepalese barbecue?'

I thought about it. I said, 'What about Nando's?'

And Uncle Jesse burst out laughing, this deep throaty laugh that sounded like it surprised him as much as me. I'd never heard him laugh before – I didn't know it was possible. Daisy darted him a look like she was vex, but then she laughed too, almost as deep and throaty as Uncle Jesse and every bit as surprising. She goes, 'Nando's it is.'

We went to Nando's. It was cool. When we were looking at the menu, Daisy said, 'So, Gabe, I've never been here. What's good?'

I said, 'The chicken.'

And she and Uncle Jesse cracked up again like this was the best joke ever and I laughed along, even though I didn't get it because chicken's what Nando's is famous for. Still, looking at them laughing together was like watching their hearts unstick, like getting an answer to a question I hadn't even thought of asking. I already told you that Mum and Dad went together like fish and chips, right? Everybody knows that fish and chips is a top combo. But, have you ever had apple and peanut butter? You cut the apple in quarters and dip it in the peanut butter. Sounds disgusting, but actually it's really good. I reckon Daisy and Uncle Jesse are like apple and peanut butter.

While we were eating, Uncle Jesse goes, 'I've got an announcement: I spoke to your mum, Gabriel. I told her what you said about missing Soccer School, so I'll take you home tomorrow.' I must have looked shocked, because he added, 'Isn't that what you want?'

'Where am I gonna stay?'

He frowned like he was puzzled. 'At home,' he said. 'I'm not explaining very well. I'll stay with you till your mum gets back. It's all arranged.'

I was worried. I couldn't believe Mum wanted Uncle Jesse

staying in our house without her. But he claimed she was actually relieved, because Hannah was due to come back from the Brecon Beacons and supposed to go stay with the Adeyemis, but there was some problem.

Some problem? That didn't help and my feelings of panic came back just like that. I said, 'Is P OK? Is he not better?'

Uncle Jesse gave me a look. He said, 'For Pete's sake, Gabe, he's fine! Beth just said they've got a lot on their plate, that's all.'

But it wasn't just me that was worrying; Daisy looked really worried too. She didn't say anything, but she was looking at Uncle Jesse with wide eyes and she reached across the table to take his hand. He gave her a look. He goes, 'A change of scenery will do me good – work-wise, I mean. I gotta finish this thing. It's only for a few days.' I could tell he was trying to make her feel better and she did a sharp little nod, like she didn't really agree but knew there was nothing she could say.

I suddenly remembered the first time I saw Daisy – at the funeral, across the aisle, the way she smiled at me. It hadn't occurred to me before that she might already know everything about Uncle Jesse that I knew, but maybe she did. In fact, maybe she knew even more.

22

SIX GABRIELS

It's the night before Dad goes to Glasgow. I've managed to climb the stairs and I'm in bed. We have a routine – Mum will come to say goodnight first, then Dad.

I have my sticker album and I'm checking the Watford page, even though I know it's full except for Kiko Femenia. Every time I get a pack of stickers, I check for Kiko, this journeyman Spanish full back who's in and out of the first team. If you think about it, that's a weird thing about sticker albums – like, I've already had eight Kun Agueros for Manchester City and all I want is Kiko. Kun must be worth £100 million, while Kiko was signed on a free transfer. But it's Kiko's sticker I need to complete my team. It's pretty random.

Mum and Dad come in together. I wasn't expecting that. This is the fifth time I've tried this in a row and it hasn't happened before. Or, at least I don't think so. I'm not sure I can remember. I'm so tired I'm getting confused.

Mum kisses my forehead and goes, 'Night, Gabe.' Dad does the same. He turns off the bedside light.

As they're leaving, I go, 'Dad?'

And he says, 'What?' Then, 'For Pete's sake, don't mess about, Gabriel. It's time to go to sleep.'

But he comes back and crouches by the bed and Mum goes out.

I know what I have to say. I know what I have to do. I've already tried truth and lies, persuasion and pleading, so I've got a new plan. I turn on the bedside light and sit up.

Dad goes, 'Gabe! What you doing?'

'Dad. I gotta tell you something. You're not going to believe me, so I need you to promise not to interrupt and to listen, OK?'

He looks at me, surprised. I can tell he's worried, but he says, 'OK.'

'You can't go to Glasgow tomorrow. You're going to be killed in a car crash.' He furrows his brow. He tries to say something, but he promised not to interrupt. 'Dad, please! Listen!'

'OK,' he says. 'I'm listening.'

'I can't explain how I know. I just know. But there's something I can tell you that might convince you. You never see Uncle Jesse. You haven't seen him for years. But I think you know he's special. After you die, I'll go stay with him in Somers Town, where you were born. He'll come to your funeral, you see, and Mum will send me to stay with him because she has to go away for a new job. Uncle Jesse's got this really big apartment near the station. He'll explain what's happening to me. It's not magic, it's science.'

Dad is staring at me with this puzzled expression; not like I've told him he's going to die, more like I've asked for help with my homework. He says quietly, 'So you've come back from the future,' like I knew he would.

I say, 'From *a* future. It's more like everything that *can* happen, *has* happened and *will* happen is actually happening all at once.'

Dad gives a funny little laugh, like I knew he would. He goes, 'Gabriel!' like I knew he would.

'*Dad!* On Mum's birthday, the day after tomorrow, the cops are gonna knock at the door. Me and Hannah are at the top of the stairs. Mum knows what they're gonna say before they even say it. She starts crying. There's this policewoman called Shilpa who takes me and Hannah into the kitchen. She makes Mum a brew. She doesn't know the kettle doesn't work and steam goes everywhere. It's the worst day of my life.

'The funeral is a blur. That's the second worst day of my life. Uncle Jesse is there. He gives the eulogy. He says, *Billy was my big brother and best friend*. And I think how weird that is because I've never even met him. I mean, later Mum shows me a photograph, but it's not like I even remember. Uncle Jesse comes with his girlfriend, Daisy. But you probably don't know about her. This is what's gonna happen, Dad! *It's all gonna happen!*'

I'm talking really fast and getting faster. Dad looks ... *peculiar*. I don't know if it's because of what I'm saying or the fact I'm saying it. Basically, he's either got to believe me or think I've totally lost it, right?

I say, 'If you don't believe me, just call Uncle Jesse. Ask him if it's possible. He knows.'

Dad goes, 'Gabe!'

He tries to hug me. I want him to hug me so badly. I miss

him so much. But I need to see this through or it'll just be a hug, so I push him away. I say, 'Promise me you won't go! Promise me!'

Dad is staring at me, wide-eyed: 'I've got to—' Then, 'I need to—' Finally he says what he always says, 'Let's talk to your mother . . .'

And I say, 'Fine.' And I realise I'm crying, tears streaming down my face. That hasn't happened before. But I'm so knackered and frustrated.

'Come downstairs with me,' he says.

I shake my head. I go, 'Talk to Mum.' Because I've gone downstairs with him before and it doesn't work. And besides, I'm so tired.

Dad doesn't say anything else. He doesn't tell me to get under the covers or turn off the light. He just backs out of the room, like you might back away from a growling dog.

I lie down for a bit. I want to go to sleep. I've not done that before. I wonder what would happen if I did. Where would I wake up? But I don't want uncertainty. And I can't wait for Mum and Dad to come upstairs together and for Mum to hold me and start crying and for them to start talking about bad dreams and hallucinations and doctors and how I mustn't worry and Dad *still* leaves for Glasgow in the morning. I drag myself out of bed.

Mum and Dad are in the front room as I knew they would be. Dad's going, 'I can just call in sick.'

Mum says, 'He's got an overactive imagination, Billy, you know that!' Then Dad must give her a look because she goes, 'Seriously? What about the commission? You said yourself—'

Dad cuts in, 'You didn't hear him, Beth. We have to talk to him.'

'So, let's talk to him.'

I hear Mum's chair squeak as she stands up. But I know Dad will say, 'Wait! Just a minute! Let's think it through – what we're going to say.'

I don't interrupt. I tried that before and it didn't work. I head into the kitchen and get Dad's drill and hammer from his tool box. I go to the front door and open it as quietly as I can. I don't bother to shut it behind me. It's freezing and my bare feet are quickly so cold they're stinging, but it doesn't matter – this won't take long.

There's nobody in the street. Dad's car is right outside. I drill a hole into each tyre in turn. The whirring noise sounds very loud, the rush of air even louder, but there's no one to hear. I put the drill down on the pavement and go to the front of the car. I smash the hammer down on the windscreen. It does surprisingly little damage – a small crack. I do it again, harder and harder, until the whole thing shatters. Now I hear someone shouting: 'Hey! You!' But I don't stop. I go to the headlights. They're easier. One swing each. And then more shouting, and someone running, and Mum's voice: 'Gabe!' I look up and she's standing in the doorway, eyes wide, mouth wider. And then Dad sweeps me up in his arms and I'm screaming and struggling like I'm mental as he carries me back into the house . . .

*

I opened my eyes with a gasp, as if I'd been holding my breath. I was back in the spare room at Uncle Jesse's house. I checked the time on my tablet. It was three a.m. and we were getting on the train home in the morning. This wasn't working and I was so tired I wasn't thinking straight.

I'd been trying all night. I remembered the four Gabes I'd become who predicted their dad's death and were ignored. Their dads would've still driven to Glasgow and been killed in four car crashes. I'd have been proved right and Mum would have looked at me every day, feeling really guilty and probably freaked out too. What kind of life would I have had?

I thought about the fifth Gabe who smashed up the car. What would've happened next? Would the police have come? Would they have taken me away to a mental hospital? Would it have been worth it? I shook my head. I mean, I actually shook my head like it was a ketchup bottle and I was trying to shake out some answers. I told myself that of course it would've been worth it, because Dad wouldn't have gone to Glasgow to die in a car crash on his way home. In fact, the only question that really mattered was this – how come I didn't get to stay in that world like I got to stay in this one the night I walked to the station, or like Uncle Jesse did when he attacked Psycho Steve? And I didn't know the answer.

23

ANOTHER WORLD

It was strange being in our house, just me and Uncle Jesse. At his apartment, walking around Somers Town, talking about whatever we wanted – that was one thing, but this was different.

It was a bit like when we went to Center Parcs last year. I had a really great time and that, but I was still looking forward to getting home. Then, when we got back and I took my rucksack up to my room, everything seemed both familiar and unexpected all at once and I didn't know what to do with myself. In fact, it was more like I couldn't even remember what I'd ever done with myself before. And Jeetan had my football.

I was beginning to think people move between different worlds all the time.

Still, it felt strange to realise that Uncle Jesse didn't know about the broken button on the kettle or the trick with the dimmer switch in the front room. Also – and this sounds super freaky – he just seemed really, really tall; I mean, not like a giant or anything, but just a bit too tall for the house. It was like he crossed the front room in one huge stride, and when he walked upstairs, I swear he had to duck his head under the lampshade. I think Uncle Jesse felt it too (not that he was too tall, the strangeness, I mean), because he seemed on edge, almost nervous.

We don't have a spare room, so Mum had told Uncle Jesse to sleep in her and Dad's bed. But he just stood in the doorway, like he was frozen to the spot.

I said, 'What?'

He frowned. He goes, 'I don't know. It just seems a bit weird. Maybe I'll sleep on the couch.'

I knew what he meant, although I didn't quite know why. I said, 'When I was little, I used to crawl into bed with Mum and Dad and then Dad slept in my room. So why don't you sleep in my room and I'll sleep here?'

Uncle Jesse goes, 'Thanks.'

We went to my bedroom. It looked really small with Uncle Jesse standing in it. I looked at the bed. I said, 'Your feet will poke off the end.'

He goes, 'I'll be fine.'

Gradually everything settled down, just like it did when we got back from Center Parcs. I mean, when Uncle Jesse knew about the kettle, he knew – I didn't have to tell him again. And I swear he even seemed to shrink a bit, or at least that's how it felt.

He set up his laptop on the kitchen table. I said, 'How are you getting on with the ending – the patch, I mean?'

He shrugged: 'Still stuck.'

'You should let me help you,' I said. 'You know I'm pretty good at stories.'

He gave me a look. Then he goes, 'I told you not to use that word!'

I tutted and gave him a look right back. Obviously I wasn't talking about Many Worlds Theory; I was talking about the game. I was just trying to be helpful.

He knew what I was thinking but he didn't say sorry. He just goes, 'You look totally exhausted, Gabe.'

I tutted again – all, like, *whatever* – and left him to it. I *was* totally exhausted on account of last night, but I wasn't going to tell him that.

I went upstairs. There were two things I wanted to do although I wasn't really looking forward to either of them.

First, I needed to call P. I mean, I knew I hadn't made him sick and Uncle Jesse said he was fine, but I still felt like I had to check for myself.

I used the phone by Mum's bed. I know P's mobile off by heart, but it was Uncle Olu who answered. I said, 'Uncle Olu, it's Gabe.'

He said, 'Gabe?' like he didn't remember who I was for a minute. Then, he goes, 'Gabe, were you part of this?'

And it was like my heart stopped beating and then started again at four times the speed. I said, 'Part of what?' But he didn't answer.

I could hear Aunty Femi in the background going, 'Who is it?' And Uncle Olu saying, 'Gabriel.' And then she came on the phone. She goes, 'Gabriel?'

'Hi, Aunty. I wanted to speak to P. Find out if he's all right.'

'All right?'

'Mum said he was sick.'

'Oh!' she said. Then, 'No, he's OK.' Then, 'He can't come to the phone right now. Sorry. We've got a bit of a situation here.'

'Right,' I said.

Then she said, 'I'm sure we'll see you soon.' Or something like that. I couldn't really hear because she was already cutting the call.

And I said, 'OK.'

I sat on the edge of Mum's bed for a minute. I didn't know what a *bit of a situation* could mean. But I had the second thing I needed to do and, if it came off, maybe whatever was going on with P wouldn't even matter.

I lay back on the bed, closed my eyes and concentrated as hard as I could. I was exhausted but I had to save Dad – I had to stop him going to Glasgow. There was nothing more important than that and nothing more urgent.

I don't know how long I lay there, but I couldn't make it work; I couldn't even find my way to the bit where I was in the hallway and went to the kitchen to get my sticker album. Maybe the gap in the fence around this reality had closed up or maybe I couldn't find it; maybe I was trying too hard or maybe I was just too tired (I think I dozed off a couple of times). But the next thing I knew I heard the front door and Uncle Jesse calling up the stairs, 'Gabe?'

Grandy had brought tea – cod dinners times three, eight cans of Guinness and a Coke for me. He goes, 'Lay the table, Gabriel, there's a good lad.' He was doing that thing he does of being super-serious, like he wants to show who's in

142

charge. I always thought it was just aimed at me, but maybe this time it was aimed at Uncle Jesse too.

Grandy made a big fuss of opening a Guinness for him and Uncle Jesse, then he raised his glass and said, 'Sláinte.'

Uncle Jesse goes, 'Cheers,' and I lifted my Coke and said 'Cheers' too.

Then Grandy took a mouthful and smacked his lips: 'That's a nice drop.'

And Uncle Jesse goes, 'So it is.'

I don't know if he meant to, but it sounded to me like he was doing a bit of an Irish accent and I cracked up. They both just stared at me.

Nobody talked while we ate. It was fine at first because we were all hungry. But slowly the silence weighed us down. I mean, I like to talk – Dad used to say I could talk the hind legs off a donkey – while Grandy and Uncle Jesse are both kind of quiet. But I've figured out that just because people don't like to talk much themselves, it doesn't necessarily mean they want silence. Maybe that's part of the reason Uncle Jesse and Daisy go well together even though you wouldn't expect it, like apple and peanut butter.

I had an idea. I go, 'You should see Uncle Jesse's place in London, Grandy. It's so posh. Top floor of this totally smart building in Somers Town – that's Euston.'

Uncle Jesse looked kind of annoyed, but he didn't know my idea and I could see that Grandy had looked up from his chips and narrowed his eyes. I'd given him something else to get his teeth into. He said: 'One of those new monstrosities, no doubt. How much did that set you back?'

Uncle Jesse goes, 'It's not mine. I'm renting. I couldn't afford to buy round there.'

'Renting, then. How much do you pay? Don't be shy. What is it – two, three thousand pounds a month?'

Uncle Jesse raised an eyebrow: 'And the rest.'

'I knew it!' Grandy exclaimed triumphantly, as if this confirmed absolutely everything he'd ever thought about anything. He said, 'You know how much my Hannah and I paid to buy our little house forty years ago? Eighteen thousand pounds. Eighteen thousand!'

'I don't believe it!' Uncle Jesse said. Actually, I think he completely believed it, but he'd cottoned on to my idea.

Grandy goes: 'It makes you think – the world's an upside-down, inside-out, back-to-front kind of place, is it not?'

'It is,' Uncle Jesse said. 'It definitely is.'

I looked between them. I knew Uncle Jesse had, like, zero interest in house prices. But I'm not sure Grandy cared that much either. It was just something to talk about. I'm beginning to think that most conversations aren't about what they seem to be. In fact, most aren't really about anything at all. Instead, they're just a way of saying, *We're on the same side here. Agreed?* Like, when P and Jacob laughed at me missing a penalty, they didn't really think it was funny and they weren't really laughing at me, they were just saying, *We're on the same team.* And if they *were* laughing at me, it was only to say, *And you're not!*

After tea, Grandy drained his Guinness – 'I know my limits' – and hauled himself slowly to his feet.

We walked him to the door. Uncle Jesse goes, 'Do you want some company?'

But Grandy waved this away: 'I can still find my own way home, you know.' On the doorstep, he turned to Uncle Jesse: 'It's good you're back, son. About time.'

24

YOUR STORIES MUST BE TRUE

Uncle Jesse and me quickly loaded the dishwasher. Actually, I did most of it. Uncle Jesse may have all kinds of fancy stuff in his apartment, but he doesn't have a TV and he doesn't have a dishwasher. He didn't know about the drawer at the top for cutlery, or that you have to turn the glasses upside down. Afterwards, he opened another can of Guinness and sat down at his laptop. He didn't pour the Guinness carefully like Grandy, so it had a thick white top.

I thought he probably wanted to be left alone, so I was about to head back upstairs. But he said, 'Where are you going?' Then, when I looked puzzled, 'I thought you were gonna help.'

'With what?'

'Small Town Hero. My patch. Like you said, you're good at stories.'

I sat down at the table opposite him and he pushed the laptop away and sipped his Guinness. He pulled a face. I said, 'Isn't it nice?'

'Not really.'

'Can I have a sip?'

Uncle Jesse shrugged and passed me the glass. I took a sip. I said, 'That's gross!' and passed it back to him. 'Why'd you drink it?'

He raised an eyebrow. He goes, 'Sometimes I think that's growing up – learning to do horrible things for no good reason.'

I couldn't tell if he was joking. As usual.

He took another mouthful, then he said, 'The trouble is, Gabe, Small Town Hero was always supposed to be a sandbox. Sure, I wanted it to have a story, but that was supposed to be generated by the players, using their own imaginations. That's the whole point of a sandbox, right? You build your own world, find your own pattern. I mean, if I try to come up with an ending now, it's like I'm just sticking something on as an afterthought.'

'Like a patch,' I said.

He gave me a look. He goes, 'Very funny.' But, actually, it was pretty funny if you ask me.

He goes, 'A story has to be true, Gabe. Otherwise what's the point? I don't mean true as in it happened, I mean as in *believable* – that's what gives it meaning. Otherwise, it's just a cheap trick, ephemera.'

Ephemera? I didn't know that word. He saw this straightaway and he goes, 'Short-lived, forgettable. Like, it won't last. It won't hold together.'

I stared. I thought about all the times I'd climbed through the fence around this reality and gone back to the night before Dad went to Glasgow. I hadn't made a single one hold together. I hadn't crossed the event horizon. So maybe they weren't true, as in believable.

He said, 'Remind me where you're at?'

I reminded him – Prince Prince and the Fool had landed

the airship at Place Necessary only to find they were looking back at Just Desert.

'But you got the Unbreakable Shield, the Dagger of Ultimate Leverage and the Lodestone?' I nodded. 'What about the Guy That Won't Die? Did you kill him?'

'Twice. So far.'

'What about the Lodestone – did you use it?'

'Not yet.' He nodded thoughtfully. I was getting impatient. I said, 'I reckon the ending's pretty obvious – Prince Prince defeats the Ineffable, Unstoppable Dragon and rescues the King.'

Uncle Jesse raised an eyebrow, but this one wasn't in place of a smile. In fact, he looked kind of sad. 'And they all live happily ever after,' he said flatly. 'That's what Jerry wants.'

'Who's Jerry?'

'Jerry's head of strategy. At the developers. My boss, Dino – Jerry's kind of his henchman. He's the Guy That Won't Die.'

'So that makes Dino the Backseat Driver?'

For a moment, Uncle Jesse didn't say anything. He just kept his eyebrow up there. Then he goes: 'That's just between ourselves.' He drained his Guinness and opened another. He saw my expression. He goes, 'It gets less gross.' I wondered if he might be getting drunk.

I said, 'So?'

He stood up. He put a hand to his head. He declared, 'So!' Then he did a really big burp. He said, 'So how does Prince

Prince defeat the Ineffable, Unstoppable Dragon? On account of the fact he's unstoppable, I mean.'

I frowned. I thought about it. I said, 'Maybe he doesn't defeat him. Maybe he tricks him.'

Uncle Jesse began to stride around the kitchen, but it wasn't really big enough, so he just marched this tight little square – sink, cupboard, door, table. He said, 'But he's also ineffable!'

Ineffable – I didn't know that word either. In fact, all this time I'd thought it was made up. I said, 'What does ineffable mean?'

'It means . . .' Stride. Sink. '. . . you can't . . .' Stride. Cupboard. '. . . describe it . . .' Stride. Door. '. . . in words.' Stride. Table. 'So, how am I supposed to describe the dragon? What's it gonna look like?'

'Right.' I felt like saying, *Why did you call it the Ineffable, Unstoppable Dragon then?* But I didn't think that would be very helpful. So I said, 'Maybe the Ineffable, Unstoppable Dragon doesn't really exist?'

'It exists all right. Who else do you think destroyed Small Town?'

'So maybe it's the dragon playing a trick. Maybe you *can* describe it. Maybe it *can* be stopped.'

'And it's really the Effable, Stoppable Dragon?' Uncle Jesse made this weird noise, like a sneer pretending to be a laugh. He said, 'That's lame.'

I was getting frustrated. In fact, I was getting kind of bored. I said, 'Well, I told you what I think: it's a quest, right?

So Prince Prince has to kill the dragon and rescue the King. That's what it's about. End of.'

Uncle Jesse suddenly stopped striding like he'd walked right into a lamppost. If he ever looked any way about anything, I'd say he looked shocked, almost offended. He goes, 'It's not a quest and it's definitely not about the King. The King's gone. He's not the point.'

'So what's it about then?'

Uncle Jesse turned away and shook his head. He started tossing the empty Guinness cans into the bin. He goes, 'That's the question, Gabe.' Then, 'I need to go to bed.'

25

BETWEEN THE LINES

I had my first session at the Moses Hayes Soccer School this morning. It was amazing, but it wasn't the most amazing thing that happened today.

I'll come to that, but I have to tell you about the football first. After what Aunty Femi said about me being a show-off I don't want to sound like I'm boasting, but Uncle Jesse's not interested and I've got to tell someone.

Moses wasn't there himself, of course. But I hadn't expected him to be (apparently, he's coming Friday) and there were coaches from the Watford Academy. I was pretty nervous. Most of the kids who showed up were really good. I mean, you wouldn't go to Soccer School if you were rubbish, right?

When we first went out with a bag of balls, we were allowed to mess about for ten minutes. There was this kid called Harry who could do crazy stepovers like Cristiano Ronaldo. I was really impressed. I can't do a stepover, or not a good one. I can't get my balance right. But, that's not really my game.

Then we did a whole load of drills for about an hour – left foot, right foot; ball control; boxes. To be honest, most of the kids were being all flash (like, in boxes, Harry kept dribbling, which is so not the point). But me? I just concentrated on my technique and keeping it simple – Dad always said, *Control the controllables.* It was a bit annoying though, because I felt like the coaches were noticing the others a lot more than me.

Afterwards, we split into squads of thirteen for a match – fifteen minutes each way, two subs. I was one of two strikers in my squad, along with a guy called Darren who was really fast but had a lousy touch. I was picked to start and I thought I did OK. But it was nil-nil at half time and the coach told Darren to strip off. I thought I was going to be subbed and I was gutted. But the coach subbed a midfielder instead and took me to one side. He said, 'We'll play two up top, but I want you to drop deeper. Let Darren get on the shoulder, you go between the lines.'

If you don't know about football, that means Darren was to play right up close to their defenders, with me a little bit behind – kind of like what Lionel Messi does for Barcelona. I've never played there before; I'm really an out and out striker. But I said, 'OK.'

When the second half started, I felt a bit lost. It was like no one would pass me the ball. When our midfielders got it, they just lumped it forward towards Darren. When their defenders got it, they could knock it straight past me. But the coach kept shouting to our team, 'Gabe's feet! Gabe's feet!' And eventually I got a pass to my feet.

If you're a striker and you get the ball up towards the goal, you usually have a defender snapping at your heels straightaway. But because I was a little bit deeper, I had space to turn. One of their centre backs stepped out, but I was able to hold him off long enough to glimpse Darren making a run off the last man. I played a short through ball and Darren was away, one on one with the keeper, and he slotted it no problem.

After that, it was like I was bossing the game. If the defender got up close to me, I could lay the ball back into midfield and spin or choose to whip it wide. And if the defender held his position I could turn and run. With a couple of minutes to go, I found myself running at the two centre backs and they didn't know whether to stay with Darren or make a tackle. It was just a second of confusion, but it let me dummy a pass to Darren and open up the goal. The defender tried to get to me, but it was too late, and I curled a beauty into the bottom corner.

We won the game two-nil and at the end the coach ruffled my hair and said to me, 'That's your position, Gabe. Between the lines. You got vision!'

If you don't know about football, you probably got bored with this bit. But I was really made up and I had to tell someone. I mean, one of the coaches from the Watford Academy said I had *vision*? That's huge.

OK. Now I can tell you about the most amazing thing that happened.

When we arrived at the Soccer School about half-past nine, Uncle Jesse said, 'I'll pick you up at twelve.'

But, like I told you, I was nervous, so I go, 'Aren't you gonna watch?'

Uncle Jesse looked surprised at that (at least as much

as he ever looks any way about anything). He said, 'You want me to?' But he could tell that I did without me even having to answer, so he shrugged and said, 'Fair enough.'

I was glad he stayed, because most of the other kids had their dads there – mums *and* dads, some of them. But Uncle Jesse didn't half look funny standing on the touchline with his pointy boots, tight jeans and long hair; like when you see a game on TV and the camera picks out a rock star in the crowd and he's trying to look like he's just another fan. Most of the dads had Puffa jackets and tracksuits and, during the game, they shuttled up and down the touchline shouting stuff like *Man on!* and *Square it!* But Uncle Jesse just stood in one spot with his hands behind his back, kind of looking at the game without watching it at all.

As we all trooped off, some of the dads came up and shook all the kids' hands, going, *Good game, son, good game!*

Harry's dad came over to me and shook my hand. He said, 'You're a proper player. Man of the match.' He was this huge fat man – I mean, like, obese or something – and he had thin blond hair that was raked back over his enormous pink head.

I said, 'Thanks.'

Then he goes, 'You're Billy Douglas's kid. I used to play with your dad.' I was too surprised to answer; partly at the mention of Dad and partly at the idea that this guy ever played football. He said, 'He was a proper player and all.'

Uncle Jesse had come over. He was standing at my shoulder. Harry's dad stuck out a hand. He goes, 'Jesse, right?' They shook hands. Harry's dad said, 'I heard about

Billy. I'm really sorry. Top man.' Uncle Jesse raised an eyebrow but it wasn't in place of a smile. Harry's dad said, 'How's Beth?'

Uncle Jesse shook his head. I guess he didn't actually know the answer. So I said, 'She's on a course. She got a new job.'

Harry's dad said, 'Yeah? That's great.' Then, to Uncle Jesse, 'Please pass on my condolences.' Then, 'You know, if it's not . . .' He couldn't finish the sentence, like the people at the funeral.

Uncle Jesse helped him out. He said, 'It's not. And I will. Thanks.'

Harry's dad nodded gratefully. 'Funny, isn't it? After all these years – same grass, different kids. It's a long time ago.'

But Uncle Jesse didn't seem to think it was funny.

You didn't have to be a rocket scientist to figure out there was something weird going on. There was this freaky tension between them. They were sending each other messages without speaking, like they were paired on Bluetooth or something. Harry could see it too – he was giving me this look that said, *You know what this is all about?* And I did a little shake of my head.

Harry's dad dropped his chin. He said, 'Anyway, I just wanted to say . . .' And then he led Harry off to their car.

Uncle Jesse watched them go. But I was watching Uncle Jesse. He goes, 'You didn't recognise him?'

'Who?'

'That's Steve Vickers.'

'*Psycho Steve?*'

I couldn't believe it. I mean, as soon as Uncle Jesse said *Steve Vickers* I knew that's who it was, but I couldn't believe I hadn't recognised him, nor that the menacing thug I'd seen at the Odeon had got so fat. It's not like there's anything wrong with being fat. It was a surprise, that's all.

I said, 'You shook his hand.'

Uncle Jesse raised an eyebrow: 'What did you want me to do?'

'I don't know. It's just – after everything he did, after everything that happened . . .'

Uncle Jesse kept his eyebrow right up there. Then he said, 'You don't know what he did, Gabe. You don't know what happened.'

26

SOMETHING TO DO

Hannah got back from her outward bound camp in the Brecon Beacons. We picked her up from the school gym.

Even though we fight and that, I was totally buzzing to see her. I mean, she's my sister and I wanted to tell her all about Uncle Jesse – like, how he wrote (or is writing) Small Town Hero, about him and Mum and Psycho Steve, about his flash apartment and Daisy, and going to Nando's and stuff. I mean, obviously I couldn't tell her the mental things about black holes, the multiverse and Coral, and how I planned to save Dad. But, still . . .

Walking back from school though? That was mad awkward.

Uncle Jesse goes, 'Do you want me to carry your bag?'

And Hannah goes, 'Sure.'

And then he just did that thing, striding off at top speed with his long legs and me and Hannah running after him. She kept giving me these looks – like, *Who* is *this freak?* And it wasn't like I could say anything, so I had no choice but to do little shrugs that were meant to be reassuring but didn't really do the job.

As Uncle Jesse marched ahead, Hannah hissed at me: 'Why aren't I staying with Juliet? That was gonna be so cool. It's so unfair! Did you have another fight with P?'

And I was all, like, 'No!'

Uncle Jesse spoke over his shoulder: 'I spoke to your mother. The Adeyemis have a lot on their plate. I offered to step in.'

Hannah gave me this crazy glare, like it was my fault that Uncle Jesse has really good hearing and walks too fast.

When we got home, Uncle Jesse went straight to the kitchen and sat down at his laptop. Since the other night when he was drinking Guinness and we talked about Small Town Hero, he was working all the time. He said he'd had an idea.

Hannah got some apple juice from the fridge and some ice from the freezer. She was doing everything as loudly as she could, clunking the glass down on the counter, popping the ice into it and making these small tutting noises. But when Uncle Jesse didn't seem to notice, she rolled her eyes and huffed upstairs. I followed her.

Hannah lay on her bed staring at the ceiling. I stood in the doorway and she goes 'Yes?' in this sneering voice. She was being really annoying, but I reminded myself how strange I felt when I got back from London, that nervous feeling of moving between different worlds . . . And she didn't know Uncle Jesse at all, so it must have been crazy weird.

I said, 'How was the camp?'

She turned on to her side and propped herself up on one elbow, looking at me. 'Why?'

I was about to shrug and go, like, *Suit yourself* or something, but when she saw I was about to give up and leave the room, she started talking.

She said: 'It was all right. We did abseiling and orienteering and kayaking, but it was so cold, you know? Like, totally freezing. And there were these lads there. From Manchester. Proper scallies. And we got friendly with them – because, like, whatever – and then we found out they were actually all from Young Offenders and one of them, Marco, who seemed, like, really sweet at first was a total arsonist who burned down a shop or something.

'And then we went on a night hike in the pouring rain and I was on Marco's team and there was only one team leader with us, who was this Welsh guy called Daffyd, who was actually pretty cool, but all the same we're, like, marching through the middle of nowhere with this nutter who might have killed people? And I was all, *This is so not OK*. But I can't say anything because Marco's right there!

'And, when we get back, I discover that Sapphire's seeing Marco. And I, like, try to tell her she must be losing it, on account of he's an arsonist and stuff. And then she's all, *You're just jealous because you never had a boyfriend*. And obviously I'm all, *I don't think so!*

'So, I figure we can't be friends any more if she's going to be like that about it; only Marco dumped her the night before last. I'm thinking, *Serves you right*, yeah? But then she was so gutted that I actually felt sorry because we had final grading and she wasn't gonna get a certificate. So, we had to pair up for the last challenge and I went with Sapphire and we came third, which was actually totally amazing. And we beat all the boys except for Tony who's older. But, at least we beat Marco and we could be like, *whatever*.'

I didn't know what to say. So, I said, 'Sounds mad.'

And Hannah goes, '*Mad?* It was totally extra.'

And I nodded, because even though I didn't really know what she was on about, it did sound kind of freaky to go on a night hike with an arsonist even if it was pouring with rain – I mean, it wasn't like he could set fire to anything, right?

Then Hannah goes, 'So?'

And I said, 'So what?'

She didn't say anything. She just widened her eyes and did an exaggerated nod towards the stairs – *Uncle Jesse*.

So I told her all about his apartment that was so fancy it looked like nobody lived there, about Somers Town where him and Dad were born, and about Small Town Hero. I thought Hannah would at least be impressed about the game, but she wasn't that interested. She just goes 'It figures', like it wasn't even a surprise. I guess she's never played it and it's not such a big thing with her year anyway. In fact, her only comment was, 'He must be so loaded.'

Then she asked questions about Daisy, most of which I couldn't answer, which got her frustrated until she gave up and shook her head and said, 'Talk about punching above your weight.' And I nodded, even though I didn't get it. She goes, 'He's minted, all right. Trust me.' Then she said, 'So where's he been all our lives? Don't tell me you didn't ask him? I know you, Gabe. You totally asked him.'

I told her about how he went to boarding school for Sixth Form and then to college and how he worked in California for ages, so maybe he kind of drifted away. But she just pulled a face at me – *And you fell for that?*

So, I told her he was bullied by this guy called Steve –
like, really badly bullied – and how we saw Steve at Soccer
School, which was mental. But she was still pulling that
face. She goes, 'Yeah, right.' Then, 'And that's why he never
came back to see his brother?'

I shrugged. 'I don't know,' I said. 'I think it was kind of
a big deal.'

I explained about what happened at the Odeon (although
I didn't tell her I'd been there, obviously). I told her how
Uncle Jesse had a plan – how he took Mum to see *Men in
Black II*, how Psycho Steve gave him a load of grief and
Uncle Jesse sucker-punched him after the movie and Mum
was all vex. And Hannah stared at me and pulled a different
kind of face. This one was a disbelieving *Are you joking?*
expression, like the one she gave Grandy the time he was
looking for his glasses and they were actually on top of his
head. I didn't understand. I said, 'What?'

And Hannah goes, 'How old was Mum?'

'I don't know. Uncle Jesse was away for Sixth Form. It
was the first time he came back. They must have been, like,
seventeen?'

'So she was already seeing Dad?'

I shook my head. I didn't know. And I didn't know
what she was getting at. But she was still giving me that
same look. She goes, 'You're so cute, Gabriel.' Then, before
I could even get vex. 'Uncle Jesse was totally in love with
Mum.'

I stared at her. I was all, like, 'What?'

*

When Hannah said that Uncle Jesse was in love with Mum, it didn't even occur to me that she could be wrong – she sounded so sure and like I must be an idiot not to have realised. I was mad confused. I mean, I know that being *in love* means changing your profile status and sex and all that stuff, but that didn't explain why Uncle Jesse never visited and couldn't even get to know me until Dad died – what's that about? Mostly, I just felt vex with Uncle Jesse, like he'd lied to me or something. I can't quite explain that either, but I sort of understood. Like I said before, there are lots of things that don't make sense but are kind of obvious too.

Anyway, one thing was for sure: I didn't want to talk about it. I didn't want to talk to Hannah any more because she'd just make me feel stupid (and I already felt stupid). I didn't want to talk to Uncle Jesse because I didn't know if I could believe what he said. And there was no one else to talk to.

I thought about trying to step into that other reality again, the night before Dad went to Glasgow, to save him. But somehow I knew I wouldn't be able to get there because my mind was such a muddle. I knew that my 'stories' – whatever, I can't think of a better word – needed concentration and I couldn't get my head straight. So instead I played Small Town Hero for the first time in a few days. It was something to do.

In case you've forgotten, Prince Prince and the Fool had just gone through a black hole in Infinite Space before landing in Place Necessary, which turned out to be the very same spot they left from – on the edge of Just Desert. Only now they had the Lodestone.

The Lodestone turned out to be really cool. Basically, when your avatar holds it, it bends the game before your eyes, so that you can see everything you've already done and go back to the beginning of any chapter you've finished.

Like, I went back to Chapter One and it was just Prince Prince and the Fool at the citadel, except of course it felt different now, because I knew what was ahead of them . . . And they had the Kit Bag. I didn't want to start again from the beginning, but using the Lodestone, I could jump back to Just Desert; only now it said I was on Chapter Twenty-one. I went back to Chapter Five and the first time we met Juju the Witch. I went back to the Monstrosity, only it didn't seem so scary any more. I went back to Psycho Steve at the Lido, only this time I had the Unbreakable Shield and the Dagger of Ultimate Leverage, so instead of giving him half my snacks, I agreed to fight and eventually I killed him, but it didn't really solve anything, because then I had to decide whether to stay where I was or flip back to Just Desert. And every time I flipped back, it said I was starting a new chapter – Chapter Twenty-two, Twenty-three, Twenty-four, and so on.

I guess this sounds pretty boring, because I was just going over old ground, stuff I'd already done. But, actually, it was kind of fun too, a bit like seeing one of your favourite movies a second time. If you watch a wicked film, you get all caught up in the excitement of it, right? And all you can think about is what will happen next. But when you watch it again and you know what's going to happen, you can enjoy different things – details, jokes and clever bits you hadn't noticed before. It was like that, only a whole lot freakier . . .

Like, when Prince Prince went back to Chapter Five and saw Juju the Witch, do you know what she said to him? She goes, 'What are you doing, Prince Prince?'

And he goes, 'How do you know my name?'

And she goes, 'Why? Is it a secret?'

I don't know if you remember, but that's exactly what Coral said to me that night in Euston Station (only she called me Gabriel, of course). Mental, right? I mean, I know Uncle Jesse wrote Small Town Hero, but he wasn't there when I met Coral and I never told him about the conversation and, besides, I'd finished Chapter Five way before I went to London and it must've been written ages before that. I thought about asking Uncle Jesse about it then and there, only I didn't want to talk to him.

I suppose you might be wondering why I kept making Prince Prince use the Lodestone to go back to the beginning of chapters I'd already finished. Five reasons.

One, the only other option seemed to be for Prince Prince and the Fool to head out into Just Desert again (which would be like going backwards anyway).

Two, I couldn't think why there was a Lodestone unless you were supposed to use it.

Three, I remembered what Uncle Jesse said about a sandbox – 'You build your own world, find your own pattern.'

Four, like I said, it was actually kind of cool.

Five, it was something to do.

27

DO YOU WANT TO PLAY OR NOT?

When I came downstairs in the morning, Uncle Jesse was already at his laptop. In fact, he looked like he'd been there all night. I told him I was going to Soccer School. He didn't look up. He just said, 'I'll get my jacket.'

'It's fine. I can go on my own.'

Now he looked up. 'I'd like to take you. I'll get my jacket.'

'It's fine,' I said again. 'Really.'

He frowned, making his eyes all narrow. Then he looked back at his computer: 'Fair enough.'

So I went on my own.

Soccer School was pretty cool. We did the same drills as the day before and new ones. Some of the lads were grumbling that it was boring and kept going, *When are we gonna have a game?* But I could tell that annoyed the coaches, so I just kept my head down and remembered another thing Dad always said – *Practice makes permanent.*

When they split us up into squads for a match though, I was really disappointed. Today, there were three strikers in our squad – me, Harry Vickers and Darren – and I figured that at least one of us was going to have to be sub. Instead, the coach picked Harry and Darren up front and I was put at right back, which was where I used to play at school, but that was only because I was the youngest in the team. I must've looked kind of gutted, because the coach goes, 'What's up, Gabe? You played there before, right?'

And I said, 'Yeah, but I'm a striker now.'

The coach caught a right strop. He goes, 'Do you want to play or not?'

The game was rubbish. It started to rain and the grass was skiddy. I hardly got a kick. The kid I was up against wide left was fast, but he hadn't got a trick. Basically, he just pushed the ball past me, chased after it and then I made a slide tackle into touch, every time – push, chase, slide tackle. I only got decent possession once and I zipped it into Darren's feet, back to goal. But, like I told you, Darren's got no control, so it just bounced off him like a tennis ball and the defenders cleared it easy. That was annoying, but not as annoying as the coach bawling me out for playing the pass too hard – 'Come on, Gabe! Give him a chance, son!' It was so unfair. I mean, it's not my fault Darren's got a lousy first touch.

Uncle Jesse turned up to watch before half time. I don't know why he bothered; he doesn't even like football. It was raining pretty hard and he didn't have an umbrella or anything. He just stood there on the touchline, hands in his pockets, long hair plastered down around his face.

One time, the ball went off and landed right at his feet. Any of the dads would've seen this as a chance to show off their tekkers. They'd have flicked the ball up and volleyed it to the thrower or something. But Uncle Jesse bent down and picked up the ball and tossed it back, which was the kind of thing a mum would do. I mean, I'm not saying there's anything wrong with that, but it just seemed a bit weird. All the men looked at Uncle Jesse and I knew what they were thinking – *Geezer can't play football*. Not that I care or anything.

At half time I got my chance. The coach subbed Darren and put me further forward to play behind Harry Vickers, between the lines. But the game was still rubbish – I think because the pitch was so slick it was hard to play proper football. With a couple of minutes left though, I caught the other team's right back in possession. I drove him towards touch, he tried to knock it down the line and I slid in to make a block. Somehow, the ball got stuck in my legs and I was quickest to my feet while the right back was still on the floor. I accelerated away and drove across the line of the defence. Harry Vickers could see what I was thinking and made a good run off the centre half, so I could reverse a pass right into his path and he was in on goal. It was the chance to win the game. He should've taken it early, but as their keeper rushed out Harry tried to fool him with one of his fancy stepovers. He tricked the keeper all right, but it was too slow and the centre back got back to make a cover tackle and the chance was gone. It was really frustrating, but I didn't say anything, because I could tell by Harry's face that he knew he'd messed up. The game finished nil-nil.

Afterwards, the coaches called us all together. They told us that we should keep trying to do the things we learned, even if it was raining. They reminded us that Moses was coming tomorrow to watch the last day of the Soccer School and give out prizes. They clapped their hands and said things like, *Good effort, lads!* And, *Good game!*

I went over to Uncle Jesse. I was actually pleased he'd come because he brought my tracksuit in a plastic bag, so I could put on something dry.

By the time I got out of the changing room, most of the other lads had gone and the sun was poking out from behind a cloud. Uncle Jesse was waiting for me. He goes, 'You all right, Gabe?'

I just shrugged. I still didn't want to talk to him, because of what Hannah had said.

I think he was going to say something else, but we were distracted by Steve and Harry Vickers walking back to their car. They were having an argument, or rather Steve was. He was doing his nut, going, 'One chance, boy! That's what I'm saying! Just stick it in the back of the net!' That's exactly what he said, only I left out all the swear words.

And Harry goes, 'I was trying, Dad!' His voice was really upset and whiney, like he was scared or something.

Then Steve cuffed him round the back of the head. It was pretty shocking. I mean, it wasn't like hitting him exactly, but it was hard enough to make Harry's neck snap forward and he goes: 'Ow!'

I think Steve must have felt our eyes on him, because he looked round. When he saw Uncle Jesse, he cracked a smile and goes, 'All right, Jesse?' And then, of Harry, with a shrug, 'Kids, eh?' Only he didn't just say, 'Kids, eh?' but put another swear word in front. Then he nodded at me. He said, 'Great pass that, Gabriel.' Then, 'Good game, boy.'

As Steve marched away, Harry glanced back over his shoulder and gave me a really nasty look like I'd done something wrong. But it wasn't my fault he'd missed an open goal and his dad's a psycho.

I looked up at Uncle Jesse. I could tell he was angry because he had his hands at his sides and he kept opening and closing his fists. For a minute, I thought he was going to do something about Steve, maybe even deck him again. But he didn't. He just strode away across the kids' playground. I hadn't even done up my shoelaces yet and, by the time I had, he was at the gate. I was all, like, 'Wait up!' But he was already out into the street and I broke into a trot to catch him.

He was waiting for me on the pavement. It was like an ambush. He goes, 'What's the matter with you?'

I didn't know what he was on about. I was, like, 'What?'

He made an impatient tutting noise. He goes, 'For Pete's sake! You've been sulking since Hannah got home. What's going on?'

I didn't say anything. I didn't think he'd noticed.

He made the same tutting noise again, only louder, and turned on his heels to walk away. I said, 'Were you in love with Mum?' I blurted it out just like that and Uncle Jesse stopped with a jerk, like a dog on a lead.

He turned round and his face was a blank page. He goes, 'Excuse me?'

'Were you in love with Mum?' I said again. 'It's a simple question.'

I heard my voice like it wasn't my voice. It sounded angry and defiant, but I didn't feel angry and defiant; just embarrassed and kind of stupid.

'I love your mum,' Uncle Jesse said quietly. 'Always have, always will. But I'm not *in love* with her.'

'What's the difference?'

Uncle Jesse smiled. He goes, 'All the difference in the world, Gabriel.'

This was the fourth time I'd seen him smile (not counting the photo where he looked like he didn't want to be smiling at all and the two times he laughed about Nando's). The first was in the lift when I said that thing about apartments and flats, the second was when he admitted he was a fool, and the third was when he told me about stepping into other worlds. But this time his smile was different. It wasn't a proper smile. It was more like the one in the photo. It was that smile adults do when they know something you don't and, really, they're just showing how much smarter than you they are. I felt my face go all hot and my stomach go all cold.

I said, 'I told Hannah about the time you and Mum went to the movies, about Steve Vickers. Hannah said Mum was in love with Dad and you were in love with Mum. That's why you never visited. It makes sense.' Uncle Jesse wiped off his fake smile. He turned and stalked away. I said, 'Where you going?'

Uncle Jesse said, 'Penn Reservoir.'

28

BEFORE THE BEGINNING

Sometimes, when something really big happens, people say, 'It's like my whole world was turned upside down.'

In fact, I don't know if you remember, but that's what I overheard Uncle Olu say about me that night I found myself standing in the Adeyemis' hallway at the foot of the stairs – *'What he's been through, it's hardly surprising. His whole world's been turned upside down.'* It's a pretty good description, but it doesn't go far enough.

In fact, since Dad died, it's more like Grandy said: *'The world's an upside-down, inside-out, back-to-front kind of place, is it not?'* In fact, since Dad died, it's more like it's *me* that's been turned upside down, inside out and back to front. It's like the blood's rushing to my head and my feet are treading on air. It's like all my worst fears are on the outside for everyone to see, but the whole world's inside me, falling into the black hole. It's like, whatever I do, I keep coming back to the beginning – even before the beginning . . .

Uncle Jesse marched off up the street. He wouldn't look at me or talk to me. Or, rather, he did talk to me, but he didn't answer my questions properly.

I said, 'Where you going?'

'I told you, the reservoir.'

'Why?'

'Because.'

'Because what? It's not even on the way.'

'Because I want to. You don't have to come, Gabriel. You walked to football on your own, you can find your own way home.'

'OK,' I said. And I stopped. I kind of expected Uncle Jesse to stop too, but he didn't, and because he walks so fast it was, like, less than ten seconds before he turned a corner and out of sight. I thought about chasing after him, but then I said to myself, *Why should I?* So I decided to go home instead. I went back to the rec to cut across, because if you jump the wall on the far side it cuts the corner of Park Drive and that road with the garage.

The rec has the kids' playground, a bowling green (only it's not used any more), six football pitches and a cricket pitch nearest the wall. The cricket pitch is actually part of two football pitches and then the wicket is roped off. It was nearly summer so there was a groundsman dragging a big roller. He had no shirt on, even though it wasn't hot. The only other person I could see was this girl flying a kite – a big Chinese dragon. She was about my age, maybe a bit younger, but she was a real expert and the dragon swooped and soared, tail flapping in the breeze. I was so impressed that I stopped to watch. There was something really appealing about the noise it made on the wind – a kind of ripping, rushing, whooshing noise. It was exactly like the noise I hear when I step into another world.

'What are you doing, Gabriel?'

This is the girl talking. She's looking right at me as her hands jerk backwards and forwards on the kite rig. She has short hair and freckles. She looks really familiar even though I'm pretty sure I've never seen her before. I say, 'How do you know my name?'

She goes, 'Why? Is it a secret?'

I stare at my grandmother. I feel like I've been turned inside out, upside down and back to front (or maybe the opposite): 'Coral?'

'Yeah.'

'You're a kid!' I say. 'You can't be here! Not now!'

'Where is here? When is now?'

I must look really confused, because she goes, 'Everything's happening all at once, remember?'

'But you *chose* to be here,' I say. 'Like you *chose* to be at the station. So you must be in control!'

'Control? Are you joking? For Pete's sake, Gabriel!'

For Pete's sake – it's such a weird, old-fashioned expression. I guess Uncle Jesse got it from Dad, and Dad got it from their mum.

She asks, 'How is he?'

'Who?'

'Jesse.'

I shrug. What am I supposed to say – *Yeah, fine, considering*?

Coral pulls a right strop. In fact, she drops the rig and we both watch as her dragon loops the loop and plummets to the ground. She goes, 'Now see what you made me do.' Then, 'Is he happy?'

I shake my head. 'I don't think so.'

'Why?'

'I dunno. Ask him!'

'I can't,' she says. 'I can't get close.' Then, when I look confused, she gets all impatient again: 'You think I know how this works? I don't. I've no idea. I only know how it doesn't. Jesse told you about the fence around reality . . .'

'How do you know that?'

'How do you think? Because I saw you!' She frowns like I'm being stupid. 'You called them stories, right? I told too many, Gabriel! I tore down the fence. I thought I could go anywhere and now I'm nowhere! I'm *lost*! Is that what you and Jesse want for yourselves? Are you stupid? You're as bad as each other!'

I stare at her. What she's describing sounds terrifying, but I'm only going to think about that later, because, right now I'm kind of vexed to be called stupid by my dead (whatever) grandmother who's currently a kid flying a kite on the rec. I mean, how mind-bending is that? So instead I just tut at her. I go: 'What are you doing here anyway?'

She gives me this sharp little look. Then she starts digging in the pockets of her jeans, but whatever she's looking for she can't find it. She goes, 'Oh, shoot!' and bends down and picks something out of the grass – 'This'll do.'

She walks towards me and holds out her hand. She gives me a small, dull pebble.

I stare at her, bewildered. 'What's that for?'

She raises an eyebrow. She's the spit of Uncle Jesse. 'To weigh you down,' she says. 'Let's call it the Lodestone.'

The Lodestone? Like from Small Town Hero? I stare some more. I'm thinking two things at once: *What if what I thought was a game is actually real life?* And, *What if what I thought was real life is actually a game?*

A noise makes me jump. I turn round and the groundsman's started up a big lawnmower on the cricket pitch. He's staring right at me with this weird expression, like he thinks I'm a nutter – *What's that about?*

By the time I turn back to Coral, she's already picked up her kite and is walking away towards the playground. I shout after her, 'What about Dad? Have you seen my dad?'

But she just keeps walking. I guess she can't hear me over the sound of the mower. I could run after her but now I feel the groundsman's eyes boring into me and I wonder whether Coral's really there at all, or if I'm just shouting to myself. That makes me think something else – *What if I've completely lost the plot?*

I went to find Uncle Jesse. I caught up with him on one of the dykes at Penn Reservoir. He was near the pump house, standing by the low railing, looking out over the water. I was really on edge, but he didn't notice. He didn't even seem surprised to see me. He said, 'You know where we are, right?'

'No.'

He frowned: 'Billy – he never showed you?'

'Showed me what?'

'Your mum. This is where she fell. Right here.' I didn't know what to say to that. He said, 'I spoke to her. She thinks she can get away from her course early. She'll catch a train tomorrow.' Then, 'Must be a relief, right?'

It didn't sound like a real question, so I didn't answer it. Instead, I said, 'I spoke to *your* mum and all – Coral, I mean.' *Now*, he was surprised. I didn't know that by his expression, which didn't flicker; only by the way his eyes zipped towards me. 'She gave me this,' I said. I showed him the pebble. He looked confused. 'She said it's the Lodestone.'

He said, '*What?*'

He was looking at me like I was mad. I wasn't going to argue, but we didn't have time to get into it because a sound – a vague, distant buzz like a TV on standby – was suddenly swelling until it became a roar so loud it had me covering my ears: a ripping, rushing whoosh. I looked at Uncle Jesse. He'd covered his ears too.

The air was suddenly cold. The light was suddenly failing. I looked down at the pebble in my hand. It was just a pebble. Then I looked up at the sky. I could still see the sun, but it was disappearing. I don't mean it was setting; rather it was dimming like it was on the switch in the front room. It didn't change colour. It just got weaker. And then finally it blinked shut like an eye. In the inky blackness that was left, stars appeared – slowly, one by one – twinkling like the sequins in the dress Dad bought for Mum's birthday. The rip and rush and whoosh began to fade, only to be replaced by a great sucking noise: not as loud, but really weird and creepy.

I lowered my hands from my ears. I said to Uncle Jesse, 'What's going on?'

His eyes were wide. I realised he didn't have a clue. Then I saw that the level of the reservoir was dropping, the water draining away. And no sooner had I noticed that than it was all gone and you couldn't see the bottom in the darkness. I shivered. The air smelled of spring and cigarette smoke. We'd stepped into another world; or, at least, this world before the beginning.

29

THE FALL

It's years ago. There are other voices. Mum and Dad are right next to us on the dyke. They're so young. Dad's leaning against the wall of the pump house, lighting two cigarettes. He hands one to Mum. She has her hair pulled back in a pony and she's wearing that short top, cargo trousers and trainers. I know it's later the same night she went to the movie with Jesse. I remember what she said to him in the alley by the cinema: *I told you. I'm meeting someone.* Now I know who.

Dad looks at his cigarette. He goes, 'Stupid habit. I'm gonna pack it in. We should give up together.'

Mum goes, 'I hardly smoke anyway. It's not like I'm addicted or nothing.'

She doesn't know that one day I'll catch her smoking out of her bedroom window. If she did, I bet she'd stub out that cigarette right now.

Dad has a leather jacket on and he's blowing smoke rings. He looks like a rock star from the old days. I don't mean then, I mean, like, *before* then – the really old days: like the 1980s or something.

Mum says, 'Aren't you worried?' Then, when Dad shrugs, 'He's your little brother, Billy! You should've seen him! He totally lost it!'

'Good!' Then, 'He's gotta learn to look after himself. Steve Vickers had it coming. I'm not worried. I'm the opposite of worried. It's about time.'

Dad does this funny little chuckle and flicks his cigarette butt into the empty reservoir. Its burning tip disappears into the blackness. He goes to the very edge and peers down. I notice that the low railing has vanished. Then I realise that it hasn't been put in yet. That thought spooks me.

'I wonder why they emptied the water,' Dad says. 'How deep you think it is?'

Mum goes, 'Don't get too close to the edge!'

Dad makes this *Woooah!* noise like he's about to lose his balance and he does that funny chuckle again. He's showing off. Then he turns to Mum, grabs her by the wrist and pulls her towards him. He puts his arms round her waist and she has her hands on his chest; not pushing him away, just holding him there. He goes, 'Beth.' And it looks like he's about to kiss her, but then he suddenly pulls back a bit, like he's just thought of something. 'I'm gonna call you Elizabeth from now on,' he says quietly. 'Like the Queen.' Mum giggles and now Dad kisses her.

Before, whenever I saw Mum and Dad kissing, I'd always say, 'Gross!' But this time I don't. And it's not just because I know they can't hear me.

There is shouting somewhere in the distance. I don't look round, because I can't imagine this kiss being interrupted. It feels kind of unstoppable. I don't know. It's impossible to describe.

Then Uncle Jesse makes this peculiar, strangled noise

somewhere in the back of his throat and I glance at him. He looks like he's seen a ghost. I suppose he has in a way – we both have. But I figure it's because he's in love with Mum too, right? That's what Hannah said. Only Uncle Jesse's not looking at Mum and Dad, but across to a lamppost on the far bank where a dark figure streaks through the puddle of light. I say, 'What's going on?' But Uncle Jesse doesn't answer. Then I see two other figures run through the light. I recognise the one in front by his blond hair – Psycho Steve. Suddenly I know what's going on.

I turn back to Mum and Dad. They're not kissing any more. Dad's looking across the dyke. He says a swear word as his kid brother emerges from the darkness.

Jesse's out of breath. He looks scared, then surprised. He looks between Mum and Dad. He goes, 'What are you doing here?'

Dad doesn't answer, but steps past him as Psycho Steve and his mate Drew appear at full tilt. They hit the brakes when they see Billy Douglas.

There's a lot of insults and swearing. Steve is saying things like, 'Stay out of this, Billy!' And, 'You know what he done tonight? Blindsided me. At the Odeon. You think I'll let that go?' Drew's taunting Jesse – 'Got your minder, have you?' Mum's going, 'Just leave it! All of you!' Jesse – still out of breath – is muttering to himself – *Get me out of here! What's going on? Get me home!* He's clearly utterly terrified, but it's a moment before I realise that his fear has less to do with Psycho Steve than the fact he expected to open his eyes back in the armchair at the flat. He's just worked out that he's not in control. That this isn't a story.

Only Dad's not talking. He has his back to me. I can't see his face.

Psycho Steve and Drew are walking slowly forward. They only have eyes for Jesse, but they need to get by Dad on the narrow dyke. Dad is backing off. I can't get out of the way and he passes right through me, like it's me who's the ghost. Now I can see Dad's face. He looks very calm. He has a kind of half-smile. But I see the very moment when he decides he won't back away any further.

Then everything happens quickly:

Dad launches himself at Steve, knocking him to the ground.

Mum shouts, 'No!'

Drew flies at Jesse. He punches him in the guts and, as he bends double, brings a knee up into his face. Now he's got Jesse from behind, around the neck, choking him. Mum's trying to pull him away.

Back to Dad. He has his forearm in Steve's throat. But Steve manages to free an elbow and jags it into Dad's side. Dad groans and slips right to the empty reservoir's edge, but he doesn't fall over. Steve is up and tries to kick him in the head. Dad slips the worst of it but is still caught a glancing blow and now Steve's on top of him – punching and snorting and grunting and punching.

I look for Uncle Jesse. I realise he's hiding behind the pump house. He can't watch. I can't do anything else.

I turn back to Dad in time to see him wriggle his way

out from under Steve. His hands are still pinned down, but he thrusts his head forward right into Steve's already bloody nose. Steve squeals and tumbles off, properly dazed.

Dad's on his feet and over to Jesse just like that. Drew doesn't see him coming and now it's Dad who has *him* in a chokehold. He lets go of Jesse and Dad can tighten his grip. Dad falls backwards with Drew on top of him and I can hear him snarling, 'Enough! Say it's enough!'

Eventually Drew splutters, 'Enough!' And Dad lets him go, lying back on the dyke, gasping for breath.

'Jesse! Stop it!'

This is Mum's voice. I turn in time to see Jesse boot Steve right in the guts. Steve is trying to get to his feet, but he's winded and he can't see for blood. Jesse kicks him again.

Mum shouts again, 'Stop it!'

She tries to grab Jesse by the elbow. But he spits, 'Get off me!' He throws out an arm and it knocks her backwards . . .

It sounds crazy, but it's only now I realise that this is the very night Mum falls – because I didn't know Uncle Jesse was even there, because I had no idea what really happened. I can't look, but I can't look away. Mum stands for a moment on the very lip of the reservoir, trying to hold her balance, teetering. Then she screams and she's gone.

Silence.

Time jumps. I find myself standing on the reservoir's concrete bed. It's pitch black. I can't see a thing. I hear some grunting and can just about make out Dad's silhouette. He's found a place where he can scrabble down into the reservoir on his backside. He can't see me. He can't see anything. He strikes his cigarette lighter. He goes, 'Beth!' I follow him by the feeble light. He finds her body.

Obviously, he can't see Uncle Jesse standing over her. Uncle Jesse has his head in his hands and he's weeping. Honestly? I don't know why. Sure, it was crazy to see Mum fall but I've seen a lot of crazy stuff recently and, besides, I know what happens, right? And Mum doesn't look all that bad – there's a small slug of blood on her temple and she's deathly pale, but otherwise she looks kind of peaceful.

Dad starts shouting, 'Call an ambulance! Call an ambulance!'

At first, I don't know who he's shouting at, but then I can just about make out Jesse's figure above us on the dyke, a dark outline against a dark sky. But he doesn't move.

'What's he doing? Why doesn't he get an ambulance?'

This is me. I don't even realise I've spoken out loud, but I must have done, because Uncle Jesse says, 'There's no point. He knows she's dead.' I don't know what he's talking about. He says it again: 'She's dead, Gabriel. Look at her.'

I look at my mum. I don't know what I'm looking for. I've never seen a dead person before: I never saw Dad after the accident – Mum said it was for the best. I'm so confused. I'm starting to panic. I say, 'What did you do?' Then, pointing back at Jesse on the dyke, 'What's he doing? *What's he doing?*'

Uncle Jesse says: 'He's trying to find a new story.' Then, 'Part of me still hoped I was in control. I believed in stories. I made this happen. So I had to find another one. And another.

And another. And even when I found one where she lived, her injuries— But I was desperate and exhausted . . .'

Uncle Jesse's voice cracks and I understand why. He killed my mum by mistake and then stepped between worlds, again and again, until he landed in one where she survived. But right now, as I look at my dead mum, I realise I'm peering into a world in which I will never exist and I can't wait to get out.

30

FORTY-TWO TIMES OVER

Uncle Jesse and me walked home together. For once, it was no problem keeping up. In fact, it was more like *he* couldn't keep up with *me* – he was really dragging his feet, he had his hands in his pockets and this faraway look.

'It was an accident,' I said.

He made a strange, snorting, dismissive noise. He goes, 'Fair enough.'

I was puzzled. I said, 'Wasn't it?'

'I didn't intend it to happen if that's what you mean.' He sighed. Then, 'Look, Gabe. When life goes well, people think it's because they're so great. But when it goes wrong? Unless they can blame someone else, they usually say it's bad luck. I just don't buy that – either everything's an accident or nothing is, you can't have it both ways. I don't believe in luck and I don't believe in accidents. I believe in *patterns*.'

I turned round and stood in his way. I made him look at me. I asked him, 'What did Dad say?'

'About what?'

'About Mum's fall! I mean, I know she doesn't remember anything. But Dad was there. He knew what happened – at least in this reality. So, what did he say to you? Afterwards, I mean.'

Uncle Jesse shrugged. He looked uncomfortable: 'I hardly saw him. He went to the hospital. He was at Beth's bedside while she was in a coma. Term was starting and I had to get back to boarding school. I wanted to stay, to make sure she was all right, but he told me to go. He rang me at school when she woke up. He told me he'd asked her to marry him.' He paused, frowned. 'I mean, I hadn't even known they were seeing each other and now he was talking about getting *married*? I thought . . .' He tailed off.

'You thought what?'

He shook his head: 'I shouldn't be talking to you about this.'

I stared at him. Something was bubbling inside me. I didn't know what it was. 'What did Dad say?' I asked again. My voice sounded weird; kind of wobbly, but insistent too: 'What did Dad say to you about the fall?'

Uncle Jesse sighed. 'He said it was an accident.'

Now I knew what the bubbling feeling was – it was anger. I don't know where it came from exactly: perhaps the black hole inside me. But here it was, and I was so angry I thought I might burst. I was helpless to stop it. I was shaking, and the words came out of me double-quick and spiteful: 'You're so selfish! Hannah said you left because you were in love with Mum. I thought that was bad, but at least it kinda made sense! But it was guilt, wasn't it? You felt so guilty that you just ran away! What about us? What about Mum and Dad and Hannah and me? That's so selfish!'

Uncle Jesse did that face: the one where he looks like he can do all sorts of expressions but he's not doing them – only, this time he did. His face crumpled like a scrunched-up ball of paper and he buried his head in his hands like he was trying to hold it in place. 'Of course it was selfish! But you don't get it!'

'Get what?'

I was really shouting. I didn't mean to, but I was. It was like Uncle Jesse was shrinking before my eyes. I mean, I know he can't actually have been shrinking, but I swear it was like he was now no bigger than me, head in his hands, all scared and upset. And you know what? That didn't make me less angry; if anything, it made me angrier than ever.

'The reasons you do something,' he muttered. 'You think they all have to happen before you do it. But if time's an illusion – a story – and everything's happening all at once, how can that be true? Maybe the real reason can come later.'

'That's an excuse! It doesn't mean anything!'

I was still shouting, still shaking. Across the road there was a woman with a toddler. She'd stopped at the sound of my voice. She was looking at us curiously. I had this weird moment when I wondered what she'd think if she knew the truth.

I turned back to Uncle Jesse to find he'd dropped his hands from his face and was back to his real height – just like that. He glanced at the mother and child. He goes, 'Come on, Gabriel, let's walk.' And the way he said it was so forceful that it kind of squashed my anger, like a thumb squashing an ant.

He was on the move again, back to his usual pace, me

trotting after him. He said, 'I shouldn't be telling you these things.'

I tried a sarcastic laugh. 'Who else you gonna tell?'

He looked back at me and did a sniff and a shrug as if to say, *Well, you asked for it.*

So Uncle Jesse told me everything. He told me that I didn't know how it felt to kill Mum, not just once but forty-two times over – it haunted him.

Actually, I kind of did know how it felt because when I'd tried to stop Dad going to Glasgow it totally freaked me out. But Uncle Jesse didn't know anything about that.

He told me he visited from boarding school one weekend during Mum's rehab. It was supposed to be a surprise, but when he saw her learning to walk again, struggling with a frame, he was spooked. He didn't even say hello. He just got straight back on the train. 'I was scared, Gabriel,' he said. 'That's the truth.'

Dad came to the school soon after. He asked Uncle Jesse to be best man at the wedding.

Uncle Jesse fell silent. I said, 'What?'

'I told Billy he was crazy. I told him he didn't have to marry Beth just because he felt sorry for her.'

That stopped me in my tracks. I said it again, '*What?*' – only this time it wasn't really a question, just shock. But Uncle Jesse kept walking. In fact, he was going even faster and it was like I was chasing him. I said, 'Dad *loves* Mum!' It was as if I'd forgotten for a moment that Dad was dead.

'He does,' Uncle Jesse said, as if he'd forgotten too.

Uncle Jesse told me that he and Dad had a huge row. Dad said that Uncle Jesse was jealous – not jealous of Dad, like Hannah thought, but jealous of Mum for taking Dad away. Dad said that Uncle Jesse was seventeen, not a kid any more: he had to learn to stand on his own two feet. He said that Uncle Jesse thought the world revolved around him, but it didn't.

'But after what I'd done? I figured it kind of did. And that was the problem.' Uncle Jesse looked at me and raised an eyebrow. 'I told you we see gaps in the fence. Well, after what happened with Beth, trying over and over again to make it right, it was like I tore down the fence and I didn't know what reality I was in.'

Tore down the fence – that was exactly the phrase Coral used, and I remembered what she'd said about being 'lost'. But I didn't say anything because I didn't want to interrupt.

Uncle Jesse didn't go to the wedding. He meant to. But he hadn't been sleeping, because every time he closed his eyes, he found himself sliding into another world. It got so bad that he was scared to get into bed, sitting up every night at his desk until he just passed out from exhaustion. On the day of the wedding, he set an alarm. He put on a suit and caught the early train. But on the train, he was so tired that he couldn't help shutting his eyes and, before he knew it, he heard the great rushing, whooshing sound. 'I crossed into another world and I didn't come back,' he said. 'I crossed into a world where I slept through my alarm and missed the train and the wedding was over.'

That's some excuse. Imagine trying that if you didn't have

your homework – *Yeah, of course I did it, only in a different reality.*

Obviously, Dad was vex. He didn't have a best man, so he had to ask a guy he knew from the football and they'd been tight friends ever since – Olu Adeyemi. But according to Uncle Jesse, it was Mum who totally lost it. He didn't think Dad ever told her what he'd said about feeling sorry for her; she was just furious that he didn't show up for his brother's wedding – the brother who'd done everything for him, made so many sacrifices – and it wasn't like he could explain. Later, she wrote Uncle Jesse a letter saying she'd never forgive him.

I was shocked by this too. I couldn't imagine Mum writing a letter like that. I asked Uncle Jesse how it felt.

He shrugged. He said, 'I had other things to worry about.'

Uncle Jesse told me that all the time he was at university and then working at his first job in London, he never wanted to visit; he *couldn't* – partly because of unhappy memories, but mostly because he was scared those memories would cause more problems. 'I was on the edge, Gabriel,' he said. 'That fence around reality? I had to put it back up myself, now I knew I wasn't in control. So if I ever heard those noises, if I ever felt myself getting sucked in, I'd open my eyes straightaway: hold them open with my fingers if I had to. It was difficult at first, but I learned. And then one day they were gone. I don't know how I knew, but I knew. One day, I knew I couldn't do it any more, even if I wanted to.'

Uncle Jesse moved to America. He was in New York when Hannah was born. By the time I came along, he'd relocated to California – Silicon Valley. He only came back to England once in the next decade. It was when I was about four years old. By then, he and Dad were talking on the phone sometimes. Uncle Jesse told me he thought they could make it right. He goes, 'I was so young when I left England. But now I was my own man, standing on my own two feet, like Billy wanted.'

I remembered the picture Mum showed me – that one of Dad and Uncle Jesse at the rec, me on Dad's shoulders, the pair of them smiling weird, faraway smiles, like they didn't really want to be smiling at all. I knew they hadn't made it right, but I had to ask: 'What happened?'

Uncle Jesse told me he had a plan. Mum was still angry with him – about the wedding, about his absence. He said that he knew the only way to repair it was to tell her the truth – about the fall, about everything. 'But first I had to tell Billy,' he said.

I didn't get it. I said, 'But Dad was there!'

We'd reached our front gate. Uncle Jesse stopped. He gave me a look. He goes, 'No, Gabriel. I had to tell him the *whole story*.'

I got it. He wanted to tell Dad about the other worlds.

31

THE GOLDEN RATIO

It was seven or eight years ago when Uncle Jesse was living in California. He came to London on business for a couple of weeks. He rang Dad to plan a visit. He was worried that Mum might not be pleased to see him. Dad said it would be fine, but it wasn't. Mum wasn't actually rude, but she made it pretty clear she wasn't happy.

Uncle Jesse told me he understood. And that's why he needed to tell her the truth. But first he had to talk to Dad.

It was a Saturday. Mum was taking Hannah to a birthday party in the afternoon, so Dad and Uncle Jesse took me to the rec. Uncle Jesse talked while I pottered around after my football. Apparently, I was mad about football even then. I don't remember.

Uncle Jesse told Dad, 'I need to tell Beth. I need to tell her what I did.'

'What did Dad say?' I asked.

Uncle Jesse shook his head.

Dad didn't say anything. Not at first. He just lit a cigarette, kicked the ball for me to chase, puffed smoke, and looked off into the distance.

Uncle Jesse said to Dad, 'I don't want to live with it any more.'

That was when Dad started speaking. He said: '*You* don't want to live with it? You *don't* live with it!' He said that Uncle Jesse didn't know what it was like for Mum: how bad her hip was, the painkillers she had to take on a daily basis, the surgeon telling her she'd need a replacement before she was fifty . . .

Uncle Jesse said, 'I just want to tell the truth!'

But that just made Dad vex. Why did Jesse want to tell the truth now? Who would it help? According to Dad, Uncle Jesse still thought the world revolved around him – always had, always would. 'You left, Jesse,' he said. '*You left.* You go wherever you want. Do whatever you want. You think you're so special. I stayed. I picked her up. We have a family. We built a life.'

I looked at Uncle Jesse. I understood where Dad was coming from, but I could imagine how hurt Uncle Jesse must have been. 'What did you say?' I asked.

Uncle Jesse raised an eyebrow: 'I said, *Yeah, Billy, you're a real small town hero.* Just like that. Sarcastic.'

I asked what happened next. Apparently Dad was really calm; like, too calm. He just got out his phone and stopped a woman passing by. He hoisted me onto his shoulders and asked her to take a photo. He said, 'Me and my kid brother. We don't get together much.'

The woman said, 'Oh, that's a shame.'

And that's the photo Mum showed me. I was right. They really didn't want to be smiling at all.

I kind of assumed that was it. I imagined Dad telling Uncle Jesse to go away, back to America, to leave us alone.

I asked, but Uncle Jesse shook his head. 'No,' he said quietly. 'Billy would never tell me to go away.' Then, 'And I still hadn't told him, had I?'

So Uncle Jesse said he just came out with it. He told Dad how he'd stepped between worlds. He said, 'I didn't tell him about the multiverse, because I hadn't figured out the theories yet.' But he did tell Dad about getting his revenge on Psycho Steve for the years of bullying; how he'd sat in the flat and closed his eyes and was transported to the cinema where he sucker-punched Steve in the foyer. He told Dad he'd never have been brave enough if he hadn't thought he was in control, telling a story. He'd expected to find himself back in the flat, but he didn't. After Mum left him outside the Odeon, he didn't know what to do, so he began to wander slowly home, only Psycho Steve and Drew were patrolling the streets, looking for him. When they spotted him, he ran for it. He thought he might lose them on the reservoir and that was when he chanced across Mum and Dad. He told Dad he was spooked because he didn't know what was real. He told Dad it almost felt like a nightmare. And he told Dad about the fall – how Mum died at the reservoir and how he had to relive it over and over again until he found a reality where she survived.

I stared. I said, 'Dad must've freaked out!'

But Uncle Jesse shook his head quickly from side to side. 'No,' he said. 'No.'

Dad didn't freak out at all. Instead, he just lit another cigarette right from the last and he asked Uncle Jesse what he remembered about their mum, Coral.

'Why did he ask that?'

Uncle Jesse gave me a look – *Hold on*.

He told Dad he didn't remember anything.

Dad nodded. He said he didn't remember much either, but a bit: like the stories Coral told – crazy, terrifying stories of places she said she'd been. He remembered one about a pirate captain in the olden days, another about walking through Somers Town, only every building had been reduced to rubble. Dad said, 'All her stories were so scary – I must have been, like, five years old for Pete's sake! But I couldn't not listen! It was years before I realised how wrong it was!' Then, 'One time I asked Mum when she'd seen all these things and she just laughed – *Any time I want. I close my eyes and I just go.*'

Dad looked at Uncle Jesse and sighed. Then he told him something he'd never told him before. He said, 'You don't remember, but I do. Coral took us to the playground, back of Medburn Estate. We went there most afternoons. She brought her knitting and we could just play. I was with my mates on the monkey bars. I saw you by the roundabout, standing on your own, screaming and crying. You were always crying, so I ignored you for ages. But in the end, I looked for Mum and I couldn't see her. I started to panic. This older kid came over, a teenager. For some reason, I told her everything was fine, and I walked you back to the flat. I remember you wet yourself. I rang the bell again and again. I didn't know what to do. We just sat down on the doorstep. In the end two cops came. Someone must have called them. And that was it. Mum was gone.

'The first night we were taken to this house. I couldn't sleep at all. There was a woman called Mrs Gabriel. I guess she was a social worker. I wasn't worried about me. I was worried about you. I'll never forget what Mrs Gabriel said – *He won't remember this*. I thought, *You're so lucky; you can't remember and I can't forget*.

'For ages, I was sure Mum would come back. I mean, how come she just upped and left? But, years later, we had a visitor at Beedon Road – a police Family Liaison Officer. She told me they were very sorry but they were closing the file – Coral Douglas was missing presumed dead. It was almost a relief.

'But what you just said about Beth's fall, what you did, it kind of makes sense to me now. I always knew you were like Mum, Jesse. I always knew that. I just didn't know what it meant.' Dad lit *another* cigarette. He was chain-smoking. He said, 'I gotta pack this in.' Then, 'Maybe Coral didn't die. I think she left and couldn't find her way back.'

We were sitting either side of the kitchen table. I was staring at Uncle Jesse. It was really strange, but he'd started crying without crying. What I mean is that he wasn't sobbing or sniffing, but tears were pouring down his cheeks and he made no effort to wipe them away. You might think it would freak me out to see my uncle weeping like that, telling me about my poor, lost grandmother, stuck between worlds where no reality and no time would hold. But it didn't. I still had too many questions. And, besides, I'd seen my poor, lost grandmother as a kid, flying a kite, a couple of hours ago. Then Uncle Jesse stopped crying anyway.

He said, 'Now it was my turn to get angry.'

'Why?'

'Because he hadn't *told* me!' Uncle Jesse exclaimed. 'Because he hadn't told me any of this – about Coral's stories and the day she disappeared. Because he'd always known I was like her. Because when the cops told him she was missing presumed dead, he said *It was almost a relief*. But all I could think was that she was like me and for all those years he kept me in the dark! I could have found her!'

'What did you do?' I asked.

'What do you think I did? I left you and Billy at the rec. I had to start looking.'

Uncle Jesse went to the police and got the file detailing their investigation. It didn't add up to much, but it contained Coral's medical records. He discovered that – before she had kids, before she disappeared – she'd been in and out of psychiatric hospitals. At different times she was diagnosed with schizophrenia, delusional disorders and psychotic episodes.

I didn't know what any of these things meant, but they terrified me. I think that's why I said, 'So she was mental?'

'No,' Uncle Jesse said. 'No. But she took down the fence and she couldn't put it back up.'

Work took him back to the States. He began reading: quantum mechanics, Schrödinger's cat, the multiverse. He needed to step between worlds again – his great unusual talent – so he began to practise. He'd close his eyes, concentrate and wait to hear that rushing, whooshing, ripping noise but it was six months before he did, and even then, it was only briefly and a long way away and then it was gone. He figured he was making progress, but it was another five years before he actually managed it . . .

'Where did you go?' I asked. 'Did you see her?'

He shook his head: 'Actually, it was around here. The rec. By the pavilion.' Then, 'I know, right? What's that about?' Then, 'It was just for a second. It was night. I thought I was alone, but then I saw a pair of white trainers poking out from the shadows.'

'And?'

'And that was it. I was back in my bed.'

Uncle Jesse resigned from his job in California, found work that would let him live in London and rent the flat in Somers Town, and he moved home.

I said, 'Why? Why couldn't you do it from there?'

'Dunno,' he shrugged. 'A closer reality to the ones I was trying to find? It just made sense. It's not like I know how this works.'

'Then what?'

'You know *then what*. I've seen her. But I can't get close. I told you.' Uncle Jesse stared at me and there was something in his face that suggested I was being stupid. He said, 'This isn't a game, Gabriel; it's dangerous! I've almost been lost so many times. Look what happened to Coral!'

He was missing the point. I said, 'But what about us? Why didn't you visit?'

Uncle Jesse sighed and sat back in his chair. He said, 'Have you heard of the Golden Ratio?'

Now it was my turn to stare. This was typical: asking a question like this as if it were the most natural thing in the world – *obviously I'd never heard of the Golden Ratio.*

He nodded. He said, 'One to 1.618 more or less – it's called the Golden Ratio or Phi. You know Pi, right?' I nodded. I knew Pi from maths with Mrs Naidoo. 'So, Pi helps you describe the area of a circle, stuff like that. It's a cool number. But, Phi? I think Phi's way cooler. Because the things it helps you describe are much more important.'

'Like what?'

'Beauty, the universe, pretty much anything and everything.'

I kept staring. I didn't know where this was going.

He went on: 'You see a pretty girl? You can bet the dimensions of her face can be described using Phi, the *Golden Ratio*. Same with the Great Pyramid of Giza, the Parthenon, paintings by Da Vinci, Dali, Mondrian . . . And they were just the artists who knew they were doing it. But it's not just man-made things, it's everywhere in nature too – branches on a tree, leaves on a branch, veins on a leaf; sea shells, hurricanes, DNA, spiral galaxies, black holes—'

I interrupted: 'Black holes?'

'Sure,' he nodded. 'You know black holes spin, right? And, as they spin, they're either heating up or cooling down. But they can also go from one to the other, hot to cold. And when does that happen? At the exact moment the square of the black hole's mass is equal to Phi times the square of the angular momentum of its spin!'

Uncle Jesse was getting excited – typical; he got more

excited by ideas than people. But I didn't have a clue what he was on about. I said, 'I don't understand.'

'So what? I told you – you don't need to understand electricity to switch on a light! And you don't need to understand Phi to recognise a pretty girl when you see one!'

I shrugged – *I guess*.

'It doesn't need to make sense up here,' he said, tapping his temple. 'So long as it makes sense in here!' Now, he was patting his chest. 'You understand beauty because you're a human being!'

'OK,' I said. 'So what?'

'*So what?*' He sounded frustrated. 'Think, Gabriel!'

I thought. I still didn't have a clue. He sighed. He said, 'You asked me why I left. But if time is a story and everything that has happened, can happen and will happen is just happening all at once, what's the point in looking for reasons? I told you I don't believe in accidents, but I do believe in *patterns*. We know the Golden Ratio helps us describe natural phenomena, even beauty. But what if it helps us describe other things too?'

'Like what?'

'Like how we feel and think, what we do, the stories we tell . . . Maybe even our lives.'

'But you never visited!'

'Because I'm selfish! Because I'm a fool! Because I was in the States! Because I was looking for Coral! What do you wanna hear, Gabriel?' He was raising his voice, frustrated. 'Remember Schrödinger's cat? When you look in the box, the very act of looking affects what you find! The reason comes after the fact! When I saw you at the funeral, Gabe,

I glimpsed something – *a pattern*. I'm not talking about fate, I'm talking about acceptance: accepting your life is trying to lead you somewhere, not fighting it, but letting the pattern resolve.'

'Lead you where?'

He gave me a look like the answer was obvious. He said, 'Here!'

I stared. I kind of hoped he was joking. But the way his eyes were blazing? He was *so* not joking. I said, 'So you left and never visited your only family because of the Golden Ratio?'

His face changed completely. It kind of softened and he smiled at me for the fifth time ever (not counting the photo and Nando's). This one was a real smile, but it was sad and kind of embarrassed. He said, 'Well, it sounds lame if you put it like that.'

32

VICIOUS RUMOURS

I sat on Mum and Dad's bed. I knew I was ready. I knew that if I closed my eyes and concentrated, I could take myself to the night before Dad went to Glasgow. In fact, I was so sure that I felt like I didn't even have to close my eyes – all I had to do was decide. But I didn't; partly because I was scared and partly because something was bothering me.

I was scared by what Uncle Jesse had said: not that I might get stuck in a different dimension – in fact, if you think about it, that was the whole point – but that I'd get stuck in the wrong one; like the one where I smashed up the car or even worse. Or, what if I got lost all together, like Coral? As for what was bothering me, I couldn't put my finger on it, but it had something to do with Small Town Hero.

I was still psyching myself up when Hannah burst into the bedroom. The look on her face was kind of wide-eyed and jumpy, like she wasn't sure whether she was excited or scared. She goes, 'You heard about P?' Then, 'When did you last speak to him? You're supposed to be his best mate, Gabriel!'

I shook my head blankly, because my mind was elsewhere and she already knew I hadn't heard anything. 'He got arrested!' she announced.

It took me a minute even to get my head around the words. I said, 'What?'

And she told me; only I had to keep asking her to slow down so I could follow, because this story was *long*, and the way Hannah talks is, like, totally round the houses.

So, Hannah went down the Intu Centre to meet up with Sapphire and check out the summer stock at TK Maxx; only when she got there, Sapphire was bursting with gossip, so they went in Starbucks for a frappuccino.

Hannah goes, 'What's the sketch?'

Sapphire told her that Juliet and Shay Rockwell had split up while she and Hannah were away at the outward bound camp. Hannah said she was all, like, *And?* But, according to Sapphire, this was mega, because it had turned into a whole he-said-she-said kind of thing and it was totally going viral, although everyone agreed Shay started it, because he went round saying Juliet was actually, like, a real tease.

I didn't know what that meant, so I asked. Hannah pulled a stupid face, all circles – eyes and mouth. She goes, 'Oh! You did *not* just say that! I always forget you're still a kid!' Then, with a stupid giggle, 'Let's just say she won't do *special cuddles*.'

I didn't mean to, but I blushed; partly because I understood and partly because I didn't.

At first Juliet didn't retaliate. She just stayed off Snapchat and that. But when she ran into Chloe at the bus stop (she's seeing Dion, one of Shay's crew), and Chloe was all, like, *Shay's well out of order* (which was totally fake because she just wanted a reaction), Juliet said that Shay could say whatever, but why should she hang out with a total weedhead who isn't in college and doesn't have a job?

Sapphire said that personally she was kind of Team Shay, because Juliet was Nigerian, so she was probably, like, really stuck-up and totally born again or something and, besides, everyone knew that Shay had put college on hold for his music career.

I asked Hannah, 'What did you say?' Because Juliet and her are really tight these days.

But she was all, like, 'Shut up, Gabriel! I was just listening, wasn't I?'

Apparently Sapphire said, 'Let's face it, Han, Shay's fit. He could have any girl he wanted!' And, when Hannah goes, *I don't think so!* Sapphire was all, like, *You lie!*

I still didn't understand what any of this had to do with P getting arrested, but Hannah goes, 'All right! I'm getting there!'

So, when Shay Rockwell heard from Dion who heard from Chloe that Juliet was calling him a weedhead, he was seriously vex. Apparently, he told his mates, 'That's only because she don't want people to know the truth!'

So he changed his story about Juliet being a tease. Actually, he said, she was a right slag and she just got freaked out that he might tell his boys when she had this reputation for being so righteous or whatever. He said, 'I wasn't gonna breathe a word, but if she chatting like I'm a wasteman? That's jokes, fam!'

I knew what a *right slag* was, more or less. But I still didn't understand. I asked Hannah, 'Is it worse to be a tease or a slag?'

Hannah frowned. 'A slag,' she said. 'But they're both pretty bad.' Then she shook her head and goes, 'Men!', like that was the answer to anything.

Anyway, the point was that Jacob Rockwell was there when his big brother was telling his boys about Juliet. And Jacob and P are mates, right? So, no one knows quite what happened next, but they met up in the car park back of Asda and Jacob must have told P that his sister was a slag, because P, like, totally lost it. They had a fight and P does kung fu and stuff, so he gave Jacob Rockwell a proper kicking. Hannah goes, 'The people from Asda couldn't even pull him off! They had to call the cops!' And Jacob had to go to hospital to have stitches and P was arrested. Hannah goes, 'It's so brainless!'

And I go, 'What?'

And Hannah goes, 'Men!' again; although she was talking about P, who's only nine months older than me even if he's a lot bigger.

'Is he in jail?' I asked. And when Hannah did that stupid giggle again, I said, 'Or Young Offenders or whatever?'

'No!' Hannah said. 'But obviously, when the cops brought him home, he had to tell Olu and Femi why it happened, right? So, now they got Juliet and Pete on total lockdown for the rest of the holidays. They can't leave the house or have friends round or anything.'

I noticed that Hannah said *Olu* and *Femi* instead of *Uncle Olu* and *Aunty Femi*. I felt like that meant something, like they'd accidentally got pulled in to the next generation. I also noticed that she was calling P *Pete*, even though that's not his name at all.

Hannah said, 'Apparently Olu and Femi are thinking of taking the whole family back to Nigeria.'

'Who said that?'

'Who'd you think? Sapphire.'

I knew this was rubbish. In the first place, Sapphire doesn't even know the Adeyemis. In the second place, Uncle Olu was born in England and Aunty Femi came when she was a baby. I didn't say anything though.

Hannah goes, 'You think that's bad? That's not even the worst!' Then, 'You think Shay Rockwell's gonna let Pete get away with what he did to Jacob? I don't think so! I mean, Shay's all right and that, but he's a rudeboy! Everyone says he's well vex and he's all, like, *I'm gonna cut him up* and stuff!'

'Who says?'

'I told you,' Hannah goes. '*Everyone!* It's all over social media! Vicious rumours, Gabe!'

I took all this in. At least, I tried to. It was kind of hard because it all sounded so serious and so stupid all at once. I mean, it sounded serious because P (or *Pete*, or whatever) had beaten up Jacob and been arrested and now Shay was talking about cutting him up. Only it sounded stupid too because Juliet said Shay was a weedhead, but everybody knew that already – he boasted about it himself. And Shay said Juliet was a tease and then a slag, which basically made no sense, because one of them had to be a lie in which case they probably both were. Also, I didn't know what to think about P. There was definitely a bit of me that was all, like, *Serves him right*. But he's still been my best mate since for ever.

Hannah was still talking but I was thinking and kind of stopped listening by mistake. Hannah said, 'So?'

And I said, 'What?'

She tutted frustration. She goes, '*Tomorrow!* I told you, Olu will be at work and Femi's got a meeting so we can go round there.'

'I got my last day at Soccer School.'

'Afterwards, then.'

I shrugged – *OK*.

Honestly? I wasn't sure I wanted to go round the Adeyemis. I mean, what for? I didn't say anything because, if I had, Hannah would've gone, *They're our friends!* But since Dad died, P hadn't been my friend at all, and actually I only reckon Hannah wanted to go to involve herself. People do that. Like, if they haven't got a story of their own, they poke their noses in because it makes them feel important. That sounds really mean about Hannah, but it's not supposed to be. It's not just her, is it? It's people.

I wanted to change the subject. I said, 'Mum's back tomorrow. Uncle Jesse spoke to her. He told me.'

Hannah gave me a meaningful look. She goes, 'That'll be interesting.'

I knew what she was getting at because of what she said before. I said, 'He's not in love with her!'

But she just goes 'Gabriel, Gabriel!' in this sing-song voice like I must be the thickest and youngest kid brother in history.

I didn't say anything to that either, because what was the point? It's not like I could tell her the truth. But it did make me think that people don't just poke their noses into other people's stories, they actually tell them all over again to suit themselves. I was still thinking about going back to save Dad, you see, and when Hannah started talking about vicious rumours I realised what was bothering me.

I knew what I wanted to do, but first I had to talk to Uncle Jesse.

33

THE TORTOISE AND THE TORTOISE

Uncle Jesse was at the kitchen table, working of course. He didn't look up, but he goes, 'It's late, Gabriel. Haven't you got football in the morning?'

I said, 'I need to talk to you.'

He must have heard something in my voice, because he immediately sat back. 'Fair enough. Fire away.'

'Small Town Hero – there's one thing I don't understand.'

He raised an eyebrow. He goes, 'Just the one?' Then, 'Sorry. Tell me. What don't you understand?'

I wasn't sure how to explain. I mean, I knew what I wanted to say, I just didn't know how to say it. And then Hannah came in, so I couldn't say anything. She went to the corner cupboard and found a packet of biscuits. Then she turned and looked between Uncle Jesse and me like we were both mental and goes *What?* before doing this big tut and stropping out of the room.

Uncle Jesse goes, 'Gabe?'

I sat down opposite him. I shook my head. I was trying to shake my thoughts into some kind of order. But when I realised that wasn't going to happen, I just started talking. I said, 'Small Town Hero – some of it's true, right? I mean, Psycho Steve is basically Steve Vickers. And I guess the Lido is kind of like Penn Reservoir. And you told me that the Guy That Won't Die is someone you work with and the Backseat Driver is Dino, your boss. But what about the rest? Like the Monstrosity, the Small Giant with Big Feet, the Vicious Rumours?'

Uncle Jesse frowned. Then he shrugged.

I go, 'Juju the Witch? That's got to be Coral. And you're the Fool. And I'm Prince Prince.'

'If you say so.'

'No! Not if *I* say so! It's *your story*!' I was snapping at him and he looked at me in surprise. But what did he expect? He was being really annoying. 'I mean, I use the Lodestone and go back to Chapter Five, and when Prince Prince won't tell Juju the Witch his name, she goes, *Why? Is it a secret?* That's exactly what Coral said to me. And, come to think of it, what about the Lodestone?' I took the pebble out of my pocket and the total crazy madness of it all struck me. 'I mean, I met Coral down the rec and she gave me this. Forget the fact that I'm meeting my grandmother, only she's a kid – how's she giving me something from your game? What's that about?'

Uncle Jesse shook his head. He said, 'I don't know.'

'I do,' I said. '*I know.* I mean, it's got to be one of three things. Either I'm, like, totally crazy . . .'

'You're not crazy, Gabriel.'

I looked at him. Maybe it sounds stupid, but it was actually kind of a relief to hear that. 'OK. One of two things then. Either you're writing about stuff you know is true, or you're making it true by writing about it. It can't be anything else, right?'

'Maybe it's both,' Uncle Jesse said. 'Maybe it's something else too. Psycho Steve? The Backseat Driver? Sure, those were deliberate. But I never thought of Juju the Witch as my mum until you said so. I mean, *now* I see it but . . .' I rolled my eyes, but he leaned forward. 'No, I'm serious. Like, what Coral said to you – I don't remember writing that. But maybe it was a past me who'd come back from the future. And maybe I – I mean the one sitting in front of you – stepped into this reality from a position of relative ignorance compared to the me I replaced. Accepting that almost anything is possible? That's the easy part. Understanding the consequences – that's where it gets harder.'

I stared. I was way too slow for this. But Uncle Jesse wasn't even done.

'That's why I don't worry about it,' he said. '*That* would make me crazy. Stories are weird, mysterious, uncanny. Perhaps Small Town Hero is writing itself and I'm just . . . I dunno, like the pencil. I mean, we built an algorithm – machine learning. That's why you have to download every new chapter. It's why it feels unique to you. It's why I can't impose an ending that's *happily ever after* – it's against the whole point, what makes it interesting. Small Town Hero's an experiment, Gabe. A writer's not God. They can only manage so many variables – if you do a, then x, y or z. Using the algorithm, the outcomes are almost infinite, but maybe they'll still revert to a pattern – like the Golden Ratio . . .'

I wanted to say something, but I didn't know what because my mind felt like melted cheese – and I don't like melted cheese. Besides, when Uncle Jesse gets on a roll like this, you just have to let him talk himself out.

He goes: 'Human beings are storytellers, Gabe. We're hard-wired that way. Stories impose order on chaos; they're how we learn. But they're not obvious, even the ones that look it. Think of any fairy tale – 'The Boy Who Cried Wolf', 'Hansel and Gretel', 'Brer Rabbit'. When you read it, you gotta work out what it means for yourself. Like 'The Tortoise and the Hare'. You know it?'

I nodded. This was easier. You know it too, right? The tortoise and the hare have a race. Obviously, the hare gets miles ahead, so he thinks he can take a nap. But while he's sleeping, the tortoise overtakes him to win.

'But what does it *mean*?' Uncle Jesse said. 'You could just say, *Slow and steady wins the day*. But then you ignore the vanity and cockiness of the hare. And what about the dogged tortoise who won't be put off by the hare's insults? What I'm saying is it means different things depending on how it's told and how it's read. If it only meant *Slow and steady wins the day*, you'd just say that and you wouldn't bother telling the story.'

Suddenly I knew what I wanted to say: 'So what about Small Town Hero? What does it mean?'

He shrugged again: 'Like I said, look for the pattern. You gotta see it for yourself.'

I made this weird little groaning noise. It just slipped out. I was getting so frustrated. I said, 'But I can tell all sorts of different stories.'

'Sure. At least that's how it feels.'

'And Abdul? He just stayed in Small Town, so he never met Juju the Witch. If I'd done that, how could Coral give me the Lodestone?'

Uncle Jesse narrowed his eyes, thinking. He goes: 'There's a Swedish philosopher who's calculated the probability that we're all actually living in a simulation—'

'No!' I interrupted. I was raising my voice again, exasperated. 'No more hiding behind theories! I just want to know – *can I take control*?'

Uncle Jesse pursed his lips just for a second. I'd never seen him do that before. He said, 'That's a big question, Gabe . . .' I gave him a spiteful look. I just wanted an answer. He had no idea what I was planning, what I was capable of; he thought I was only talking about the game. He said, 'Well, I haven't finished the patch yet . . .' He sighed. Then, 'I mean, you control your own actions. At least that's how it feels. But that doesn't mean you can choose every outcome . . .'

34

OK

Again–

It's the night before Dad goes to Glasgow. I've managed to climb the stairs and I'm in bed. We have a routine – Mum will come to say goodnight first, then Dad.

I have my sticker album, but I'm not looking at it. I'm too nervous. I got too much on my mind. I'm going to try one more time. I've thought it through and decided it's worth the risk. This is only my sixth attempt to stop Dad leaving: not like the forty-two Uncle Jesse made before he found a world in which Mum survived the fall. I'm not going to get lost. I figure that if I really want something, if I control the controllables, I can make it happen.

Trouble is, I'm already having doubts. It's crazy, but if you really want something it's like you can't see all the consequences when you're planning, however hard you try. And then suddenly you can. Like, now I'm suddenly thinking, *If I stop Dad going to Glasgow, then what?* I mean, of course stopping him is the most important thing, but the idea is I'll stay in a reality where I know everything I know and I'm going to have to explain it all to Mum and Dad. It's like I'll make the world the way I want only I'll be totally different. I mean, it's fine but it's going to be hard too.

I put these thoughts out of my mind because I need to be clear and focused but, as soon as I do, I just realise something else that doesn't make sense. It's like this . . .

So Uncle Jesse told me about his conversation with Dad at the rec, the last time he visited, years ago, when he explained about stepping between worlds. But if it happened like he said, then how come Dad looked so totally spooked when I tried to stop him going to Glasgow before: those five times that took half the night and left me exhausted and confused? I mean, if Dad knew about Coral's stories, if he knew about Uncle Jesse's, then why did mine come as such a shock? Why didn't he call Uncle Jesse like I asked him to? Why didn't he listen to me? It doesn't add up, unless—

Mum comes into the bedroom. She does this little laugh and says, 'You look so worried, Gabe! What are you thinking about?'

I go, 'Nothing!' as she kisses me on the forehead. She smells different and I say so.

'Really?'

'Have you got new perfume?'

She laughs again: 'No. No new perfume.' Then, 'Five more minutes.'

'Is Dad gonna say goodnight?'

'He'll be up in a minute,' she says as she leaves the room.

So I still have to wait. Like I said, I'm nervous, but now I just want to get on with it. Like I said, I got too much on my mind, but I need to be clear and focused. So I open my sticker album to the Watford page. I notice something's changed straightaway, but it's a second before I realise what it is. Do you remember I told you about Kiko Femenia, the journeyman Spanish full back, whose sticker is the only one I'm missing? Well, now I've got it. In this world, the page is complete. For some reason, this totally throws me, but I don't have time to dwell on it, because Dad comes in.

Dad says, 'Time to put that away,' and he reaches for the bedside light. But I sit up, because I've got my plan. He goes, 'For Pete's sake, don't mess about, Gabriel. It's time to go to sleep.'

I take a deep breath. I say, 'Dad. I got something to tell you. You're not going to believe me, so I need you to promise not to interrupt and to listen, OK?'

He looks at me in surprise. I can tell he's worried. He goes, 'OK.'

'You can't go to Glasgow tomorrow. You're going to be killed in a car crash.' He furrows his brow. He tries to say something, but promised not to interrupt. I say, 'Dad, please! Listen!'

'OK,' he says. 'I'm listening.'

'I can't explain how I know. I just know. But there's something I can tell you that might convince you. You never see Uncle Jesse. You haven't seen him for years. But I know why. I know about what happened at Penn Reservoir with Steve Vickers, how Mum had her fall. You see, after you die, I'll go stay with Uncle Jesse in Somers Town. He comes to your funeral and Mum sends me there because she has to go away for a new job. He explains it all to me – Many Worlds Theory: it's not magic, it's science.'

Dad is staring at me, with a puzzled expression: not like I've told him he's going to die, more like I've asked for help with my homework. He says quietly, 'So you've come back from the future,' like I knew he would.

I say, 'From *a* future. It's more like everything that *can* happen, *has* happened and *will* happen is actually happening all at once.'

Dad gives a funny little laugh, like I knew he would. But then he says, 'I'll call Uncle Jesse.' I wasn't expecting that. That was my line.

He goes out of the room. Now I'm feeling really weird. In this reality, Mum doesn't smell like Mum, I've got the Kiko Femenia sticker and Dad rings Uncle Jesse without me even having to ask. I mean, I knew I was stepping into a different world – that was the whole point. But I didn't know it would be this different or what that means.

I can hear Dad on the phone, but I can't hear what he's saying. It's a short conversation, but he doesn't come back into my bedroom when he's done. I wait. I'm confused. I go to the top of the stairs. I can hear Mum and Dad talking in the front room. I pad quietly down. I arrive in time to hear Dad going, 'We have to talk to him.' It's a relief because I've heard this before – he's gone back to what I remember.

Mum says, 'So, let's talk to him.'

I hear Mum's chair squeak as she stands up. But I know Dad will say, *Wait! Just a minute! Let's think it through – what we're going to say.* Only he doesn't say that . . .

Before I know it, Mum and Dad have appeared in the doorway to find me listening from the hall and their eyes widen and they look sort of scared but angry too. I want to say something, but I don't know what. It's Mum who speaks first. She goes, 'We need to talk to you.' And they kind of usher me into the front room.

We don't sit down. Dad stands by the door, almost like he thinks I might try to escape. Mum's staring at me with this really strange expression – I can't explain it, a bit like a wild animal. I don't know what's going on, but I'm getting totally creeped out.

Mum goes, 'Billy told me what you said.'

Why's she calling Dad *Billy*? I mean, she'd never usually do that. She'd say, *Dad told me what you said*.

Mum goes, 'Where's Gabriel?'

'What?'

Now I'm really confused and Mum's suddenly so angry – like, so angry that *angry* doesn't begin to cover it – and she's talking really fast and I struggle to keep up. She goes, 'If it's true. If what you say is true. If you've come back from the future, another world, where's my son? You're not my son! You're not my boy! Where's Gabe?'

I stare at her. I'm terrified. I go, 'Mum! It's me!'

But she won't even look at me. She has her hands to her temples and she's shaking her head, going, 'No! No! No! If you're here in his place, then he must be somewhere else!'

And Dad says, 'Where did you take him? Where did he go?' And he sounds so menacing and I can see his hands are trembling and he looks like he wants to kill me.

I suddenly see they're right. The other Gabriel, the one they know, he's already branched off into a different reality with a different Mum and Dad. It was me that made this happen and *this* Mum and Dad, getting angrier and angrier – they don't want me, they want him . . .

The understanding washes over me like a wave and it's followed by a wave of nausea. It's like my head's spinning and so's the black hole inside me, only it's gone from cold to hot. I feel like I might puke. My eyes dart around the room and for the first time I notice all kinds of tiny differences – the TV's in the wrong place (not by much, but still), there's no coffee stain on the carpet beneath the dimmer switch, *there's no dimmer switch*. I glance at Mum and Dad's wedding photo on the mantelpiece. It looks exactly the same only there's an extra figure in the picture – Uncle Jesse. In this reality he attended the wedding. So, in this reality, Mum never wrote him that letter saying she'd never forgive him. In fact, maybe he's a regular visitor and the conversation with Dad where he told him about stepping between worlds never even happened. And the black hole inside me is spinning faster and faster, sucking me in.

Apparently, I was screaming. I sat bolt upright to find myself back in Mum's bed with Uncle Jesse standing over me. Hannah was at the door. She looked freaked, maybe even a bit worried. But when Uncle Jesse goes, 'It's just a nightmare,' she made this sighing-tut noise: 'You're so lame, Gabriel!' And she turned on her heels like she was in a black and white movie and went back to bed.

Uncle Jesse waited until he heard her bedroom door close, then he said, 'What's going on?'

So I told him – what I'd tried to do tonight, what I'd tried to do before.

He sat down on the bed and watched me as I spoke, but I couldn't tell you what he was thinking. Occasionally, he prompted gently. It was like he wanted to know every last detail. Eventually, when he was satisfied he'd heard everything, he sat back and looked away. 'I told you, Gabriel,' he said quietly. 'I told you this isn't a game. You'll get lost.'

'But I didn't!'

'Not yet,' he said. 'But I'm not just talking about getting lost between worlds.' He tapped a finger to his temple. 'I'm talking about in here. You think your brain can deal with this kind of uncertainty?'

'I'm fine!' I insisted. Honestly, I think I was protesting a lot because secretly I knew he had a point.

He said: 'You're making a terrible mistake. If you—'

'What about you?' I interrupted. 'What about you at the reservoir? You told me it took you forty-two times to find Mum alive! Was that a mistake?'

Then Uncle Jesse said something bewildering: 'I don't know. How could I? I'm not God. *You're not God.*' At last he turned to look at me and he said something even more bewildering: 'What about the world you just left? What about the Mum and Dad who think you're an imposter? What about you, the imposter?'

I stared at him. I wasn't following. 'But I didn't cross the point of no return.' He gave me a look. Clearly, I hadn't answered the question. I go, 'Hold on. The fence around reality – you told me that sometimes we peer over, sometimes we find a gap and climb right through and sometimes we can't find our way back. But I came back. So that world's gone. That's the point.'

'Maybe,' he said. 'But how do you know?' I started to form the word *because*, but he cut across me firmly. *'How could you possibly know?* Reality splits and branches every single second of every single day, Gabriel! Come on! Do you think the whole world revolves around you?'

I blinked. Suddenly I knew what he was saying. I thought about the me, the imposter: a me who was exactly the same as I am, who'd had exactly the same life to this very point but was now stuck on a timeline with a mum and dad who were scared of him, hated him even, because he'd replaced their son. How would he feel, that me? What would he do? Surely he'd try to flee – because *I* would. I'd step into another world, any world, as soon as possible, even if it risked being lost for ever. But would the imposter me work out what I'd just learned? That he may be leaving an identical version of himself to suffer the same fate and, no doubt, attempt the same escape, spiralling out of control, again and again and again . . .

I said, 'It's not my fault.'

'No?' Uncle Jesse said. 'Whose fault is it?'

I was feeling dizzy. My stomach was churning and I was feeling nauseous in this world too. I slipped out of bed and stumbled past Uncle Jesse to the bathroom and now I chucked my guts up until my stomach was empty. But I kept retching so violently that briefly I thought my body was trying to turn itself inside out.

When it eventually subsided, I was dripping sweat and light-headed, my vision blurry. I splashed my face from the cold tap and rinsed my mouth. I went back to the bedroom. Uncle Jesse hadn't moved. He was still sitting in the exact same spot on the bed, looking at the pillow, almost like he thought I was still there.

I said, 'I was trying to save Dad.'

'You can't.'

'What about Coral?'

'Coral's not dead, she's lost,' he said. He looked at me. 'Billy's not lost, he's dead.'

It took a moment to sink in. You might think it sounds kind of brutal, the way Uncle Jesse said that. But you know what? I was OK with it: not that Dad was dead, of course not, but that I was powerless to change it. I'd told myself I was trying to save Dad's life because it made me sound like a hero. But that wasn't true, was it? It was what Uncle Jesse called *a cheap trick* – no wonder it wouldn't hold. In fact, what I was trying to do wasn't for Dad at all; nor for Mum or Hannah – it was all for me. And there's not much heroic about that. It was like I'd been on a quest. I'd started out all cocky, like I'd get it done in time for tea, but it got so hard that discovering it was actually impossible was like a great weight being lifted. I felt calmer than I had for months: *it was almost a relief* – I don't know how else to put it.

I lay down in bed. Although I was on Dad's side, the

pillow smelled like Mum: *my mum*. It used to smell like Dad but it doesn't any more. That's probably for the best.

Uncle Jesse said: 'Do you want to talk, Gabriel? What are you thinking?'

'I'm tired,' I said.

35

MOSES HAYES

It was the last day of Soccer School and Mo Hayes himself was going to be there, which was major for me: partly because he's my favourite player and partly because he's a pro who knows what it takes to make it in the Premier League.

When I came downstairs to grab breakfast, Uncle Jesse was already working. In fact, I reckon he'd pulled another all-nighter. He looked well knackered. He pushed aside his laptop while I poured my cereal. He goes, 'How did you sleep?'

I said, 'Fine.' But he kept looking at me (on account of what I'd done, I guess), so I added, 'Really well actually.'

He nodded. He goes, 'I've finished.'

'Finished what?'

He pulled the laptop back towards him and touched a button to wake it up. 'With Small Town Hero, I mean. The *ending* ending. My patch. Thanks for your help.'

'Cool.' To be honest, I didn't know how I'd helped. Also, I was thinking about Soccer School.

Uncle Jesse raised both eyebrows, like he was surprised. Then he looked back at the screen. 'You mind if I don't come and watch today?' he asked. 'Just that I gotta tidy this up so I can send it to the coders.'

Now it was my turn to be surprised. At first, I was kind of vex – like, *didn't he know this was a big deal for me?* But the obvious answer was, *no, he didn't*. Besides, maybe it would be better if he wasn't there because I didn't want any distractions. I said, 'OK.' Then, 'Me and Hannah are going round the Adeyemis after.'

'Your mum'll be home about seven,' he said. 'Just make sure you're back.'

'Are you leaving tonight?' I asked.

'Probably,' he said. He nodded at his laptop. 'They'll want me in London. For any last tweaks.'

I was pulling on my boots in the changing room at the rec when Mo came in. He was wearing his Watford training gear. I'd met him in another world but never this one, and he looked different somehow. I mean, he's absolutely massive: not tall exactly, but even his muscles have muscles. He rubbed his hands together and goes, 'All set, lads?'

All the other guys crowded around him, asking for selfies and autographs. But I didn't have a phone and I'd already got his autograph off a friend of Uncle Olu's who's a club steward. Anyway, I didn't want to look like a try-hard – I was here to play football.

Mo took most of the drills. It was more fun than the other days because we practised volley finishes, one on ones and dead balls. But it was mostly fun because Mo's a cool guy. I mean, I already knew he's really down to earth and stuff from interviews I'd seen. What I didn't expect was that he'd be so funny. Like, when we were training, he was crazy serious, but he always had this twinkle in his eye and a joke ready. And he didn't talk to us like we were kids at all; he talked to us as footballers. Actually, he reminded me of Dad. He even looks similar, although Mo's a bit darker and, like, way more ripped.

When we divided into teams for a game, it went like a dream. I was playing in behind Harry Vickers again, between the lines. I mean, Harry wasn't happy about that at first. He'd been frosty with me all morning, probably because I saw what happened with his old man yesterday – like he was embarrassed or something. But he soon cheered up when I played the perfect lay-off for him to score the first goal.

I swear I was on fire. It was one of those days when I couldn't do anything wrong. My team ran out four–nil winners and Harry scored a hat-trick. I didn't score, but I played a part in all four.

After the match, Moses and the coaches gathered all the players and parents together on the bowling green outside the pavilion where there was a table set up with trophies and a certificate for every participant. He called out names and we went up in turn to collect our certificates and everybody clapped. Then he made a speech.

Moses said he was really impressed by the standard and Watford football club was lucky to have so much talent on its doorstep. But he said that it isn't always the most talented or even deserving players that make it. He told this story about him and his kid brother, Zeke. Mo was rejected by Bradford as a teenager, expelled from school and got in trouble with the cops, while Zeke was captain of the Leeds

United academy team. He said that if you asked anyone which of the two brothers would succeed in the professional game, they'd all have said Zeke. But Zeke snapped his cruciate at seventeen and, despite three operations, he never played again, while Mo was now captaining Watford. He goes, 'You can dream of being a pro, you can aim to be a pro, but you can't *plan* to be a pro – to make it takes a combination of talent, hard work and luck.'

I thought about something Uncle Jesse said – how people think that good stuff happens because they're so great and bad things because they're unlucky. Uncle Jesse doesn't believe in luck. Moses does, but at least he doesn't think he's so great.

Then, he said something I found so interesting: 'When I was a kid, I was a right tearaway. Mum and Dad split up and I was always in trouble at school and stuff. You know why? It's because I was always thinking how unfair it was – what had happened to me and what I thought was gonna happen in the future. Football saved me. I'm not talking about turning pro and earning money; I mean the game itself. Because football's a game of moments. You get the ball, you choose a pass and, whether you chose right or wrong and did it well or badly, the moment's gone and you gotta move on. The great players – like Messi or Scholes – they have vision, they see patterns. But even they only see two or three moments ahead. Pele, who's probably the greatest ever, called football *the beautiful game*, and I think he's right. It's beautiful because, whatever you plan before a match and whatever you regret later, the game makes you live in the here and now – you can't change what's gone and you can't see what's coming. That's how I try to live my life.'

Moses looked around the players and their parents and he did this embarrassed smile. I guess he figured people weren't really listening. He was probably right and all. But I was listening.

He moved on to presenting the trophies. There were two small tankards and a shield. The tankards were for Best Trainer and Most Improved, but the shield was the big one – MVP (Most Valuable Player). One of the coaches passed Mo each trophy in turn and then he announced the winner. I reckoned I had a chance for Best Trainer, but that went to this defender called Ben Tring. I was more annoyed that Harry Vickers won Most Improved: not because I thought I should've won, only because he'd been acting all vex with me. But when I thought about it, I had to admit it was fair enough, as he'd listened to the coaches and become more of a team player *and* he scored a hat-trick today.

I never thought I'd win MVP; really, I didn't. But that's what happened. I knew it as soon as Mo said, 'The youngest player at this year's Moses Hayes Soccer School . . .' I was shocked and I felt myself blushing. I had to go up and shake Mo's hand and there was a photographer from the local paper.

Afterwards, there were sandwiches and drinks in the pavilion. Loads of people patted me on the back and shook my hand and everyone was being really nice, but I didn't half miss Dad and I wished Mum was there; even Uncle

Jesse. I looked up at the clock on the wall. If I wasn't careful, I'd be late to meet Hannah. I didn't want to leave though. I mean, it's not every day you win MVP.

Steve Vickers came over. He was puffing a bit and pinker than ever: 'Good game, son.' I was still holding my trophy and he goes, 'Quite right too. You earned it.'

'Thanks.'

He was nodding at me. He wasn't finished. He goes, 'I just wanted to say . . .' And he leaned in like he was about to tell me a secret. His breath smelled like coffee.

I don't know why, but I had this idea that he was going to tell me something about what happened at the reservoir all those years ago. But he didn't. Instead, he goes, 'They invited Harry to the academy, to train with the youth team, a trial. I just wanted to tell you. I mean, I know he scored the goals, but you played the passes.'

I stared. It was a second before I understood. I managed to say, 'Great.' And Steve Vickers nodded and clapped me on the shoulder with a big pink hand before walking off.

I was glad he was gone. My face was hot and red. I felt so disappointed and let down. Harry had been invited for a trial at Watford and I hadn't; even though I'd won MVP.

Now I did want to leave. All the other lads were still messing about or chatting to their families, so the changing rooms were empty. I slipped on jeans and a sweatshirt. I was just zipping the shield into my kit bag when Moses came in.

He goes, 'Gabe, right?'

'Yeah.'

'You going already? You don't even say thanks or goodbye?'

'I was just grabbing my bag,' I said, in a way that suggested I was going to say thanks and goodbye after, which was such an obvious lie that I felt myself blush again.

Moses nodded. Then he said, 'You're the best player here, Gabe – head and shoulders. Me and the coaches, we talked about getting you down the academy. But you're too young, too small. You'll get knocked off the ball, out-run, out-jumped. Best thing for you is to keep doing what you're doing. We'll keep an eye on you. OK?'

And I said, 'OK.'

We shook hands again. He looked me in the eye. He frowned a bit. He goes, 'Have we met before?'

'No,' I said. For a moment, I thought about telling him how one day he might cross the ball for me to score the winner in the Champions League Final. But Watford winning the Champions League? He'd have thought I was a nutter.

36

BOYS

I met Hannah at the twenty-four-hour. I was only ten minutes late, but she made such a big deal of it and wouldn't talk to me the whole way to the Adeyemis, so I didn't even tell her about my trophy. And, when we got there and Juliet answered the door, Hannah goes, 'I'm so sorry, Jules,' and rolled her eyes in my direction like I was the biggest pain ever. Then she said, 'What time's your mum back?'

'Not till this evening,' Juliet said. 'Dad'll be home first.'

Hannah goes, 'Right.'

We were both staring at Juliet. There was something different about her, which was, like, really obvious and completely invisible at the same time. She looked sad, but that's not it. She looked kind of tired, but that's not it either. It was more like she'd been turned down – like on a dimmer switch or the volume on a stereo. It's hard to explain, but Juliet's usually a sparkler, like the ones you get on Fireworks Night that leave streaks of light when you wave them around. Not any more.

Hannah gave her a hug on the doorstep. Juliet didn't stop her, but kind of slipped away, heading back into the house and turning into the lounge. 'Come on in,' she said.

She settled onto the couch, curled up beneath a blanket.

Chibs was dozing in his pushchair. The electric fire was on even though it wasn't cold and there was an empty crisp packet on the floor. I reckon she'd been there all afternoon. 'I was sleeping,' she said.

Hannah sat down on the edge of an armchair, leaning forward, looking worried. I just kind of stood there. I put my hands in my pockets. I found the small, dull pebble that Coral gave me – the Lodestone. I turned it in my fingers, shifting from foot to foot, unsure whether to stay or go.

Hannah goes, 'What happened?'

Juliet looked at her slowly. She sniffed and wiped an eye. 'Nothing,' she said. Then, '*Really*. Nothing happened. That's why it's all so crazy.'

She pretty much confirmed Sapphire's story, only in this flat voice that made it sound a whole lot less exciting. The way she told it, Shay and her got on fine, but the truth was she didn't have time for a boyfriend – not with mocks coming up and her UCAS to complete. When they split, they even agreed what they'd say: that it was a mutual thing, because she had all that study and he wanted to get in the studio. She said, 'I didn't think any more about it until Shay started going around throwing shade and telling lies, you get me? Then I had a whole bunch of people I hardly know blowing up my timeline.'

Even then she was prepared to let it go, only Chloe got involved and she's always been jealous of Juliet and is well stuck-up. Juliet said, 'I dunno. I just lost it, you know?'

Hannah goes, 'You should ignore her, Jules. She's a total gossip.'

Juliet shook her head. 'It's too late for that. After what P did to Jacob.'

According to Juliet, the cops took P down the station and Uncle Olu had to go and pick him up. 'The look on Dad's face,' Juliet murmured. 'He was so ashamed. And then it all came out. I had Mum going through WhatsApp, Facebook, Instagram, everything. It was savage.'

Hannah did this nervous little laugh. Then she goes, 'P, though – it's kind of sweet if you think about it, standing up for his big sister.'

Finally Juliet's eyes sparked and snapped towards her. '*Sweet?* It's not sweet! Have you heard what Shay's saying? Threatening all this rudeboy business – *I'm gonna kill Pete Adeyemi*, all of that! He tells one lie and he can't back down! That's the reality! And it's all about nothing!'

Hannah goes, 'Men!' which was what she said to me.

But Juliet shook her head and goes, 'They're not men. They're boys,' which was what I'd wanted to say all along.

And Hannah goes, 'For real,' even though if I'd said that she'd have tutted at me and gone on about how I don't get it.

I said, 'Where's P?'

They both turned to look at me like they'd forgotten I was there. Juliet shrugged: 'Upstairs, I guess.'

I went up to P's room. The door was closed. I knocked and said, 'P?' He wasn't there. I checked the bathroom and other bedrooms and headed down again. I checked the kitchen. He wasn't there either. I went back into the lounge. Hannah was now sitting next to Juliet on the couch with her arm around her. Hannah looked up at me and goes, *'What?'* All irritable.

I said, 'P's not here.'

Juliet and Hannah followed me back upstairs – like it was possible I'd somehow missed him. Standing in the doorway of P's empty bedroom, Juliet put a hand to her mouth: 'Oh my God! What's he *doing*? Dad's gonna freak!'

I said, 'Can't we try his mobile?'

But Juliet shook her head – Uncle Olu had taken both their phones.

I had this sudden terrible thought – obviously, P knew what Shay Rockwell had been saying, about how he was going to kill him ... I dropped to my knees and reached under the mattress. I took out the box where P keeps his wushu dagger.

It was empty.

37

FOR PETE'S SAKE

Juliet and Hannah stayed at the house. It was a bit late for Juliet to be taking Chibs out in the pushchair and, besides, someone had to be there in case P got back. At first, Hannah wanted to come with me, but I told her to stay put – if I didn't think P would listen to me, he'd definitely get vex with my sister trying to boss him around. I said, 'I'll find him on my own.' I don't know how I managed to sound so confident, but Juliet and Hannah looked like they believed me and that helped me believe myself.

Juliet goes, 'Shall I call my dad?'

And I was all, like, 'Not yet.'

Looking back, it sounds stupid, right? Stupid that I said it, stupid that she listened.

I threw my bag over my shoulder and left the house. By the time I reached the bus stop, I knew it was a wild-goose chase – P could be anywhere. Even if I found him, what was I going to say? I mean, he may have been my best mate my whole life, but now he hated me.

I went into town to check out the Intu Centre, but that was a waste of time. The shops and walkways were packed and it was like looking for a needle in a haystack. I knew that Shay and his crew liked to hang round Game and that, but as soon as I found they weren't there, there was no point waiting on the off-chance.

I had to wait ages for a bus back. I was about to walk when one finally showed up. It was already getting dark. From the top deck, I peered out of the window and, just for a second, I thought I saw myself walking along the pavement with my kit bag over my shoulder. But I might have imagined it because I didn't hear any rushing, whooshing noise and, as I stood up to try and look back, the bus had already accelerated away.

I checked my watch. Mum would be home in an hour or so and if me and Hannah weren't there she'd be gutted.

I tried the car park back of Asda, Rock 'n' Roe (where Shay's mate Dion works part-time, only he wasn't there) and I walked the dykes at Penn Reservoir – no joy. So I made for the rec.

As I approached the gate I heard laughter. Shay, Dion and Chloe were in the kids' playground. It's right near the road, so it was the only bit that wasn't pitch black: streetlights bleeding over swings, slide and roundabout. Chloe was sitting on a swing; Shay and Dion mucking about, kind of play-fighting. If I went in the gate they'd see me, so I headed round next to the bowling green where there's this tiny gap in the fence. I could just about fit, but my kit bag wouldn't, so I had to hide it behind a bin, even though it had my shield in it. I squeezed through the gap and padded quietly past the pavilion. Shay, Dion and Chloe were now sitting on the roundabout, passing around one of those big plastic bottles – beer or cider or something. I could see the light from Shay's spliff.

For a moment I stood totally still. I realised I hadn't thought this through. I mean, I'd been looking round places Shay Rockwell might be, but it never occurred to me that I might find him before P did. In fact, when you think about it, even if I found him *after* P, it wouldn't have been much use, because whatever was going to happen would've happened. Basically, I hadn't thought it through.

I looked at my watch. It was already quarter past seven. Uncle Jesse would be doing his nut. I was about to give up when I realised I wasn't alone. There was a figure in the darkness beneath the pavilion. All I could see was a pair of white trainers poking out of the shadows – P's big feet. He hissed, 'Gabriel?'

I went over to him. I go, 'What you *doing*? Juliet's, like, totally freaking out.'

'He bad-mouths my family, what am I supposed to do?' he said. Then, 'Dion's got work at half-seven. I just wanna get Shay on his own.'

'You took your knife.'

P shot me a look. He kissed his teeth. He goes, 'I don't need no blade, man! You think I can't take him? Wasteman all front. You don't like it? Run along. It's not for kids, you get me?'

I stared at P. He was supposed to be my best mate, but now it was like I didn't even know him. Why was he talking like that, trying to sound gangster? It was so stupid. He was all twitchy, couldn't keep still, hyped. It was like he thought he was in a movie, or a game.

Obviously, we were whispering. But it was really quiet at

the rec and the next thing we heard was Shay going, 'Who's there?'

We looked round and he'd come to the edge of the playground, tugging on his spliff, peering blindly into the darkness. Before I could stop him, P was on the move, marching over. As soon as Shay saw him, he did this big fake laugh. He goes, 'Pete Adeyemi! Oh my days! You got a death wish, bruv!'

Immediately, they were trading insults – *You know you out of line!* And, *You bring that beef when you lay a hand on Jacob?* And, *Let's do this!* And, *I'm right here, bruv!* Only obviously I've left out a lot of swear words.

I think it would've kicked off right then, but three things happened. First, Dion goes, 'Shay! I got work, man!'

Then I put myself between them, going to P, 'Leave it! Let's go!'

Shay started laughing. He was, like, 'Yo, Gabriel! What you *doing*? Last time I seen you, your mate gave you beatings!' Then, at P, 'You got anger issues, bruv!'

I'm not saying I helped, only that I slowed it down enough for the third thing to happen, which was Juliet appearing with Chibs in his pushchair, Hannah at her side.

Juliet took one look at the situation and goes, 'You're both so lame!' And both P and Shay were kind of frozen to the spot.

P goes, 'Stay out of this! It's got nothing to do with you!'

'*Nothing to do with me?*' Juliet shot back. 'It's all *about* me!'

There was no arguing with that, and P suddenly looked

kind of unsure. Shay sneered, 'Mummy come to save the day?'

But Juliet turned her fire on him: 'You're so tired, Shay! We both know what happened. Giving it all *she did this, she didn't do that*. We both know the truth! Tell it to my face, Shay Rockwell! Be a man about it!'

Juliet was well vex. There was nothing Shay could say. That was the end of it. I looked around the faces – just a bunch of teenagers having an argument, no big deal. Juliet turned the pushchair. She goes to P, 'Come on!' and started for the gate.

I was following her. P was too. But then Shay goes, 'Sket!' Under his breath, just loud enough for everyone to hear.

I can't tell you what happened next, because I can't quite remember. All I got in my head is a bunch of snapshots and these brief samples of sound, like from a drill tune or something . . .

P turns with a snarl of unlocked rage, reaching into the pocket of his hoodie, the glint of metal. Someone shouts, 'No!' Shay, eyes wide and crazy, striding towards him. Me, between them, hands up, trying to stop it, but I'm not strong enough and P pushes me backwards. Someone shouts, 'Come on then!' Me, stumbling into Shay, eyes still on my best mate, the knife in his hand. 'For Pete's sake!' This is me too – I don't know why I said that, I'd never said that before in my whole life. Hannah, bent over, hands on her knees, head up, mouth wide. Screaming. Me, kneeling, looking up at P, the terror on his face and I don't know why. Someone gasping, 'Oh God! Oh God!'

I don't remember pain. I remember I couldn't breathe, but I hadn't a clue what had happened. I remember this taste in my mouth – metal, like I was sucking a coin. I remember how my vision seemed to close in from the corners of my eyes, dark circles until it was like I was looking the wrong way through a pair of binoculars. I remember thinking that the black hole inside me must have torn itself open again and this was how the world looked as it was sucked inside. There was a ripping, rushing, whooshing sound.

I am high in the sky, a bird. Everything is slow, so I can take it all in. I relive the action. I see P push me backwards and I stumble into Shay; Juliet, half-turned, hands still on the pushchair; Dion barking encouragement; Chloe petrified; Hannah bent double, screaming. And now I spot the small knife in Shay's hand just as it sinks into my side, beneath my ribs. I fall to my knees as Shay reels back. He drops the bloody knife as if it's electrified – 'Oh God! Oh God!'

Another figure is approaching. I recognise the young girl at once. She walks purposefully, but without panic. It's like she knows what she's got to do, like she's done this before; maybe more than once, maybe several times. And now the whole world disappears: first the people – Hannah, Juliet, P, Shay, Dion and Chloe, clicked out of existence like somebody pushed a button; then the playground, pavilion, streetlights, trees; and the stars last of all. All that's left is Coral, standing over my dying body, and me, watching from above. She turns, looks up at me and smiles. For the first time, I see the rig in her hands and she reels in the thread and I'm looping the loop and plummeting downwards. I'm not a bird, I'm a kite.

And now everything is slow. I'm lying on my side. My hand's in front of my face. I can't feel my hand. I can't feel anything. But I watch my fingers open and the Lodestone is in my palm, weighing me down. I must have been holding it all along.

38

HEAVY SKY

It must have been about ten days later that Uncle Jesse was staring out of the window at a heavy sky. 'What do you mean by real?' he asked. 'Define your terms.'

I didn't know what to say so I didn't say anything.

He sighed. Then, he goes, 'You know how eyes work? People think they're like cameras – light hits them and makes a picture in your brain. But that's not true. In fact, your brain's already made a picture based on what you're expecting, the model in your head. Your eyes just fill in the gaps and they don't even do it that well. That's why, if you get a new coffee table or something, you're always banging your shins – because your brain doesn't expect it to be there.'

I peered at him. He appeared to be frowning. I couldn't quite tell. Maybe that's just what I expected. At least he'd started talking.

He said, 'You know about dark matter? What about dark energy?' I didn't need to shake my head. They weren't real questions anyway. 'Dark matter makes up about twenty per cent of the universe, dark energy about seventy-five. We can't see them, but we know they're there because we can mathematically prove it and, if they weren't, we'd always be banging our shins. But as we can't see them, they're not part of the model in our heads.' Then, 'Everyone's got two realities – related but not the same.' He pointed out of the window. 'There's out there.' He tapped his forehead. 'And there's in here.'

'Everything that's happened,' I began. 'You're saying it's real in my mind, but not out there? You might as well tell me it's all in my imagination.'

'And what's wrong with that?' he said. 'Where else would it be? We can't escape our imagination, Gabe! That's as real as it gets!'

I looked at him. I didn't know what he was on about. Typical. I was so exhausted. I get tired really quickly at the moment.

'Those clouds,' he said. I followed his gaze out of the window. 'Can you see a face in those clouds?'

'No.'

'Keep looking.'

I kept looking. I saw a face. 'There!' I said. 'It's a kid wearing a beanie!'

'Good. Find another one.'

I looked some more. I saw a castle, a map, a dragon, and finally another face. It was in profile, head thrown back, laughing. 'Dad,' I said. 'That looks like Dad.'

Uncle Jesse stared out too: 'I can't see him.'

I let my head fall back against the pillow. I felt my eyes closing. I couldn't help myself. 'So I see Dad's face in the clouds?' I said. 'That supposed to make me feel better?'

Uncle Jesse smiled sadly. It was the sixth time I'd

seen him smile. I think I know why he doesn't smile much – because so many of his smiles are sad. He said, 'No, Gabe, you're missing the point. The point is that what you're looking at didn't change, what changed was what you saw.' He thought for a moment, then, 'Nobody sees reality, Gabriel. We build it. From our senses? From our intellect? Sure. But also from what we believe in, the stories we tell, the people we love . . .'

39

A STITCH IN TIME SAVES NINE

Since I came round, Mum's hardly left my bedside. It's beginning to do my head in. She feels guilty for not listening to me about P, for going on that orientation course, for sending me to Uncle Jesse, even that I got stabbed. Obviously, it's stupid and I told her so, but it's like she can't hear me at the moment. Like, when we talk about what happened, she goes, 'Gabe, love, what were you thinking?' So I tell her what I was thinking – that I was trying to stop my best mate doing something terrible. I mean, I'm not saying it was a brilliant plan, but that was the idea. But Mum just looks at me and says it again – 'What were you thinking?'

I've been worrying about Mum even more than usual. At the hospital, she's been crying all the time. I said to her, 'Mum! Why are you crying?'

And she goes, 'I just miss your dad, that's all.'

I told Hannah about this. She said that Mum's been crying a lot at home too, but she reckoned it was a good thing. She goes, 'At least she's stopped saying she's stressed.' Then, 'You know how it's been, Gabriel. She starts crying and then switches it off just like that. It's like she can't let herself go because she thinks she's gotta be strong for us. Now? I think it's like she said – she's missing Dad. It's about time.'

I looked at Hannah. I spend so much time thinking she's lame that sometimes I forget she's actually pretty smart.

After my operation, the surgeon came to see me. He said I was really lucky. He said a stab wound like mine would have been fatal nine times out of ten.

Grandy was with me, and after the doctor left, he goes, 'Why the devil did he have to say that? He's watched too many films, has he not?'

There's something funny about the way Grandy can get shirty about, like, anything, so I started laughing. But laughing really hurts. It was only later when I thought about what the surgeon said that I started to wonder if Coral had to step through ten worlds to find me alive in this one.

Right after the surgeon, the cops arrived. Guess what? There were two of them, but the one who asked all the questions was Shilpa, the policewoman who came to the house after Dad died. I figured it was a coincidence, but when I told Hannah, she goes, 'Gabriel! They sent her because she knows you!'

That hadn't occurred to me, but I bet Hannah's right and all. Like I said, she's pretty smart.

Shilpa asked me what I remembered. I told her I didn't remember anything from the time I got to the rec. That wasn't true and I could tell she didn't believe me, but I'm not a grass. She didn't seem that bothered though. She said, 'We'll come back another time, when you're feeling stronger.'

I told Hannah about this too, that I hadn't grassed, and she rolled her eyes. She goes, 'You know how many of us were there, who saw what happened?' Then, 'Considering everybody knows you're the clever one, you're, like, totally thick.'

She told me they all told the cops the truth. I mean, apparently Shay gapped it – *fled the crime scene* – but when they caught up with him, even he confessed straightaway. Hannah told me he's been charged with aggravated assault and P with carrying a weapon.

I asked Hannah, 'What's gonna happen?'

'To Shay?' Hannah shrugged. 'Don't know, don't care. You make your choices, right? He stabbed you, Gabriel!'

'I thought you'd be glad to get rid of me.'

This was supposed to be a joke, but it wasn't funny. Hannah looked horrified. 'Don't say that!'

I tried another one. I did a sneaky smile and said, 'Everybody knows I'm the clever one?'

Now she smiled too. She goes, 'Yeah. You got brains and football. But don't get too cocky. I got everything else.'

The Adeyemis visited. To be honest, it was kind of weird, because they treated me like I was some sort of hero. Like, Aunty Femi started crying (which I couldn't even believe), Uncle Olu did this solemn speech about how Dad would be proud of me, and Juliet gave me a big kiss on the cheek. Only P didn't say anything. He just hovered in the background. But then the others melted away and I realised this had been their plan all along.

It was awkward at first. He goes, 'Juliet – I think she likes you.'

This was a joke too – I mean, she's, like, in Sixth Form – but it still made me a bit embarrassed and that didn't help.

He said, 'Mum wants to send me away. She wants me to go live with my grandparents.'

I was shocked. 'In Nigeria?'

'What?' He frowned. 'No. Southampton. I think Dad's talked her round.' He shrugged, then he goes, 'I got a solicitor; some friend of Mum's. She says that so long as I plead guilty and tell the truth, I'll get off with a caution and community service. But Shay's gonna get sent down – Young Offenders.' Then, 'I was gonna stab him, Gabriel. If you hadn't been there.'

'Why?'

He shook his head. He goes, 'I thought it was what he said about Jules, but that wasn't the real reason. I only saw the real reason later – I was just angry.'

'About what?'

'I dunno. Everything. Like, Juliet's the golden child and all they talk about is her going to university. And Mum's always working and busy with Chibs. Then you're in my bedroom and Dad takes you to Watford . . .'

I protested: 'Only when you got kung fu!'

'I know! But that's the truth. I was so angry I wanted to kill Shay. If you hadn't been there . . .'

I kept quiet. I was thinking about the time I'd stood over P while he slept and wished he was dead.

P sniffed and turned away. I realised he was nearly crying. He wasn't looking at me when he goes, 'You're fam, Gabriel. And you almost died and it's all my fault.'

'It's OK,' I said, which sounds lame, but I didn't know what else to say. At least P looked back at me and nodded.

Mum had arrived. I could see her through the glass door,

talking to Aunty Femi. P saw her too and he was about to leave. But then he goes, 'Dad says I got a second chance. He says I'm lucky. You don't always get a second chance.' Then, 'Dad's been really sound. I told him how angry I felt. He said it's OK. He said it's just being a man. He said that when men get angry like that it's usually because they're scared of something. I was all, like, *I'm not scared of nothing!* Stupid, right? Only, Dad didn't say it was stupid. He just goes, *Everyone's scared of something, P.* And he gave me this look and I knew he was right, even though I didn't want to admit it.'

Now it was P's turn to look embarrassed. He glanced at Mum, peering through the glass, getting antsy. He cracked a smile and raised an eyebrow. He goes, 'Laters, bruv, yeah?'

I thought about what P's dad said and how Uncle Jesse had said the exact same thing. I wondered if there's a moment when a boy understands what it means to be a man and how old you are when it happens. But then Mum came over and she was fussing about my pillows, checking my dressing and asking why I hadn't eaten the apple she left.

The only person who hasn't visited is Uncle Jesse. I mean, he was at the hospital the night it happened and he stayed all the next day, but I was in intensive care and unconscious. I haven't seen him since I came round. Mum said he had to get back to London because of the deadline at work. She said he hadn't wanted to go, but when it was clear I was going to pull through, she told him he must. She said he'll come see me in a couple of days.

I thought about how it would've been when Mum got

home that night and Uncle Jesse was there and we weren't. Apparently, it was Juliet who called them from Chloe's phone after ringing for the ambulance – Hannah was too cut up, in shock. I was worried that Mum might blame Uncle Jesse, but actually she was too busy blaming herself.

I remembered that letter Mum wrote to Uncle Jesse years ago where she said she'd never forgive him, so I told her what a brilliant time I'd had in London and how cool I thought he was. Maybe I overdid it, because she gave me this funny look and goes, 'Sounds like you made a friend.'

'I just want him to come visit sometimes,' I said. 'Not at the hospital. I mean, when I get home and stuff.'

She goes, 'He knows where we live, Gabriel.'

Mum's said that before, but last time she sounded all vex. This time, even if she didn't smile, her face stayed soft. I left it at that. I guess it's a start.

40

THE INEFFABLE, UNSTOPPABLE DRAGON

Hannah let me have the tablet at the hospital, which was pretty decent. She goes, 'Don't worry about it, me and Juliet have decided to take a break from social media anyway. We're, like, so over it.'

Then when Mum went to refill my water jug, Hannah leaned in: 'Guess what? You're gonna get a new mobile!' Then, off my surprise, 'I know! Mum's totally freaked out and she wants you to be able to call her any time – you're so lucky!' She raised both eyebrows at me and goes, 'Jokes, Gabriel! Just jokes!'

I opened Small Town Hero but it said I needed to update the app – Uncle Jesse's patch. It was a free download, but it took ages on the hospital Wi-Fi and one time it froze and I had to ask Mum to buy some more data on her card. She grumbled a bit, but she'd just got a new job and I'd just been stabbed so she was never going to say no.

I felt kind of uneasy going back to the game. After all our conversations and everything me and Uncle Jesse had been through and done, I'd started to agree with him – *happily ever after* was totally lame. But honestly? After I spent a whole day using the Lodestone again and again, working through chapter by chapter, finding nothing new and returning to Place Necessary every time, I was getting pretty frustrated and I just wanted to reach the end.

It was Chapter Forty-one before I made a breakthrough. If you're still playing yourself, you might want to skip this next bit; not that it'll necessarily be the same for you, but just in case.

So I took Prince Prince back to the Lido to face Psycho Steve. It was the fourth time. The first time, Steve killed Prince Prince – end of story. Then, we negotiated our way past by giving him half our snacks; then, when we had the Lodestone, the Unbreakable Shield and the Dagger of Ultimate Leverage, Prince Prince got revenge. What else was there to try?

Prince Prince opened the Kit Bag, strapped on the shield. We had another tough battle. Psycho Steve has mallets for hands. You can't avoid them altogether and the shield buckled but didn't break. Prince Prince had to wait until Steve tired and then he ran him through. It was kind of satisfying, but it didn't really solve much – if we walked out of the Lido, we'd be on to our first meeting with Juju the Witch; if we used the Lodestone, we'd be back on the edge of Just Desert.

But then I noticed something I hadn't seen before – a small gap in the fence around the Lido. Maybe this was a new feature of Uncle Jesse's patch. Prince Prince went over and I tried to steer him through, but he couldn't quite fit because of the shield. I tried to drop it, but it was twisted and bent and my avatar couldn't get it off his arm. I had an idea. I used the Lodestone.

Sure enough, returning to the edge of Just Desert, I found

the Unbreakable Shield back in the Kit Bag. Now, I knew what I had to do; though first Prince Prince had to kill the Guy That Won't Die for, like, the twentieth time.

I took us to the Lido again – Chapter Forty-two. This time Prince Prince left the shield in the Kit Bag when he went to challenge Psycho Steve. Immediately, I thought I'd made a mistake. The Dagger of Ultimate Leverage was too short to get close and Steve had Prince Prince staggering with one punch, which took a third of his vitality just like that. The Fool was cowering in the background as we tried to dodge past, only for another blow to send us reeling. One more and it would be game over. I dragged my avatar to his feet, fearing the worst, but at last the Fool was marching forward. He had no fighting skills – he just swung his sword randomly, and Steve battered him – but it gave Prince Prince the chance to run for the gap in the fence. The Fool was on his knees as Prince Prince slipped through the opening.

It was a few moments before the world materialised around us and my heart sank. It looked like Prince Prince was back at Place Necessary. It was almost pitch black but I could see the precipice over Infinite Space.

I didn't have time to think because suddenly Prince Prince was under attack and knocked to the ground again. As the sun began to rise on another false dawn, I could see we'd actually been pitched headlong into a full-scale battle and I could make out shadows fighting to the death. However, the light revealed no faces, only these mysterious silhouettes.

I did a special move to avoid a thrusting spear, knocked my attacker to the ground and he dissolved into smoke. It got lighter still and I began to recognise the silhouettes by their shape – Vicious Rumours, the Small Giant with Big Feet, the Backseat Driver, even a shadow Prince Prince. And there wasn't just one of each, but dozens – maybe a hundred dark, faceless figures doing battle on the precipice.

My avatar was attacked again – another shadow Prince Prince, but this one had a broad sword and the Unbreakable Shield. I thought we were finished, but then came the earthquake. The ground began to shudder and threw everyone to their knees. Then the earth itself started to slip away over the precipice and figure after figure slipped with it into Infinite Space. I heard a great whooshing noise and recognised it at once as the beating of the Ineffable, Unstoppable Dragon's wings. I looked at the false dawn still rising over Just Desert and the burning red semi-circle of the sun on the horizon seemed much closer. It looked like an eye and it blinked at me as we took flight.

You're not going to believe this, but we were on the back of the Ineffable, Unstoppable Dragon: an indescribably huge creature, flying through the darkness. One by one the silhouettes tumbled away until they were all gone. The noise was crazy and terrifying, wind was rushing, and my avatar was slipping too. I had an idea. Prince Prince drove the Dagger of Ultimate Leverage into the dragon and we hung onto that. The dragon shut its eye and screamed but it didn't stop.

And that was it. We were in a cool End of Story sequence. Prince Prince used the dagger to lever himself up and look down. We were soaring over Small Town at night and could see the rebuilding – new structures reaching high into the sky but still far below. Then we went even higher and I realised it wasn't night at all; rather the whole world had been in the dragon's shadow. But now, as we rose, Small Town began to be washed in sunlight and I could make out people emerging from the buildings, crowds filling the streets, all cheering as the dragon flew away. And I saw the dragon's shadow below, an outline that shrank as we climbed to the very edge of the atmosphere. And now the world disappeared, and I could see nothing but the sun looming ahead. And the dragon kept flying towards it as the credits rolled – 'Small Town Hero by Jesse and Gabriel Douglas'.

I told Uncle Jesse I'd finished the game on Chapter Forty-Two as soon as he arrived. He goes, 'What did you think?' He'd forgotten to ask how I was feeling but I didn't care. I was too excited and I sat up, even though it hurt. I was all, like, 'I can't believe you put my name on it! I'm gonna get such mad props!'

'But what about the ending?'

'It was cool,' I said. 'Not happily ever after, but believable and still an *ending* ending.'

'And Chapter Forty-two? What's it about?'

I shrugged. I said, 'Everything.'

He raised an eyebrow instead of smiling. 'Life, the universe and everything,' he said, like it was a joke. I didn't get it. He shook his head. He goes, 'But specifically, I mean – what's it about? What's the pattern?'

Honestly? I hadn't given it a moment's thought, but I could

still answer just like that. 'It's about death,' I said. 'It's the beginning and the end. That's the pattern. You can't describe it, because you only get to see it up close and it's way too big. But when you're right next to it like that, you can look down and see the whole world.'

Uncle Jesse nodded. 'And you can't stop it.'

'Coral did!' I exclaimed. I didn't mean to say it then and there, but it just slipped out. So then I had to plough on. I said: 'She was at the playground. She saved me. I don't know how exactly, I just know. I wanna go back. I want to ask her but I can't make it work. However hard I concentrate I'm just stuck in this bed.'

I was talking really fast. I mean, I thought this was big news. But Uncle Jesse didn't seem surprised. In fact, he didn't even seem interested. He just gave me a look and muttered, 'Best place for you,' before sitting down in one of the orange plastic chairs by my bed and peering off out of the window.

I stared. I was shocked. It was like he'd shut down the conversation and I didn't know why. This is a thing grown-ups do to kids, a known phenomenon – like, if they don't want to talk about something, they just stop, and, if you try and keep going, it's like you're being deliberately annoying. Mum does it a lot – when I want to discuss getting a new phone, or how Dad was when he was younger, or staying with the Adeyemis. But I thought Uncle Jesse was different.

I wondered if he felt bad about everything he'd told me and shown me. I even wondered if he was somehow jealous that I got to see Coral up close, spoke to her even, and he never did. But I couldn't ask him because he'd shut down the conversation. Instead he goes, 'Daisy's here. She wants to see you. We came in her car. She's still looking for parking. I told her we should just take the train, but she wouldn't listen.'

I was so vex. He was making me feel stupid – like what I wanted to say wasn't even worth hearing. I said, 'Uncle Jesse!' And I sat right forward, but I got this sharp, screaming pain in my side and I made a weird, strangled noise and I was suddenly, like, totally exhausted. I said, 'Coral saved me! It happened! It was real!'

Uncle Jesse still didn't look at me. He was staring out of the window at a heavy sky. This was when he asked, 'What do you mean by real? Define your terms.'

41

PUNCHING ABOVE YOUR WEIGHT

When I woke up, Daisy was sitting by my bed. She always looks like she's stepped straight out of an advert. *Glamorous*, Hannah would say.

'How are you feeling?' Daisy asked.

'OK.'

She stood up. 'Can I give you a hug?'

I remembered her bony hugs, so I said, 'I'm a bit sore actually.'

'Right,' she said. 'Sorry.'

She bent over to kiss me instead. She kind of smells like an advert too, if that makes any sense. She sat down again. She smiled at me.

I go, 'Where's Uncle Jesse?'

'He went for a walk?'

'Is he OK?'

'Why'd you ask that?' She was still smiling, but it was like she'd forgotten the smile was there; like she'd left it by mistake.

I shook my head: 'I don't know. It's just—'

She interrupted. 'He's worried about you.' Then, 'You know how busy he's been with Small Town Hero.' Then, 'You've exhausted him, Gabriel.'

Exhausted him? I stared at her: 'What do you mean?'

She finally took down her smile. She did this little shrug, almost like she was shy about something. She said, 'You know he told me what he could do the first time we met? I didn't believe him, of course. I said he must be joking. It was a while before I realised he wasn't.' She was talking in this easy, relaxed kind of way, as though Uncle Jesse had told her he could juggle or something, not step between dimensions. She looked at me like she expected me to say something, but when I didn't she pressed on: 'At first, I didn't see what was happening. How was I supposed to know that he was sliding into another world every night, looking for his mum? But I did see how he changed in *this* world – he was absent-minded, losing things, forgetting people he'd met and greeting strangers like old friends. Once, he turned up on my doorstep because he said we'd made a plan the day before, but I hadn't seen him for a week. In the end I asked him, and he admitted what he was doing. He said, *You think I'm losing it?* I told him – *Not yet, but you will*. He said he'd stop and he did. I'm sure he did.' She paused. 'But then your dad died and it began again. I know you saw what happened at the funeral. And when you came to stay, he spotted you talking to Coral in the street . . .'

It wasn't like she finished talking, more like she just petered out. I was trying to make sense of it. 'Are you saying it's my fault?' I asked. 'I didn't mean any of this to happen. It just started.'

'No!' Daisy was shaking her head quickly. 'No, that's not

what I'm saying. You brought Jesse back to his family, opened up a whole new world for him.'

I said, 'I don't want Uncle Jesse to lose it. *I* don't want to lose it.' I was thinking it through. I realised what she was saying. 'I don't want to end up in a psychiatric hospital!'

'Gabriel! That's not gonna happen!'

'These other worlds. I'll stop too.' The words came quickly, tumbling out of me. 'I've already stopped. Since the operation, since I've been in here – it's not working any more.'

'Oh!' Daisy looked surprised. 'Right.'

'What?'

'It doesn't matter.' She was frowning. Another short shake of the head. 'It's just I wanted to ask you to do something.' She was looking at me. It was like she was waiting for me to speak but, when I didn't, she sighed. She said, 'I don't think he'll let it go, Gabriel. And I thought you could find Coral.'

Uncle Jesse came in with Mum and Hannah. They'd met in the corridor.

Mum and Uncle Jesse were mid-conversation. Mum was going, 'No, the wing where I was? It's oncology now. That whole rehab centre's moved to Watford General. All change.' Hannah was giving me a look, like this chatting was significant. I guess it was in a way.

Daisy greeted Mum with a hug. It looked awkward. She said, 'Beth, I haven't seen you since . . .'

It wasn't just at the funeral that people couldn't finish their sentences, but even talking about it months later. Luckily, Hannah goes to Daisy, 'Can I visit you in London?'

Mum goes, 'Hannah!'

And Hannah goes, 'What? Gabriel went. I want to go to TK Maxx in Oxford Street. Apparently, it's off the hook.'

Daisy said, 'No problem.' Then, glancing at Mum, 'I mean, if it's OK with you.'

Uncle Jesse goes. 'You should all come. Stay a weekend.'

Mum said, 'That sounds nice.' And me and Hannah both looked at her, because the way she said *That sounds nice* made it sound like she didn't really mean it.

Uncle Jesse didn't seem to notice, but Daisy did. She turned to Uncle Jesse and goes, 'We should probably . . .' Then, to Mum, 'Thursday afternoon. Motorway will be hell.'

Mum said, 'Sure.'

Daisy gave me another kiss. Uncle Jesse didn't even come over to the bed. He just lifted a hand and said, 'I'll see you soon, Gabriel.' It was OK. I kind of know what he's like now.

Mum and Hannah watched Uncle Jesse and Daisy walk to the door – him with his long, lolloping stride and her clip-clopping like she's on TV. Hannah goes, 'Talk about punching above your weight.'

Mum goes, 'Hannah!' And then they both started laughing.

42

LIFE, THE UNIVERSE AND EVERYTHING

It was months later. I was at the rec. I was still wearing in my new boots. The night I was stabbed, someone nicked my kit bag from behind the bin with my boots, MVP shield and all my stuff. Can you believe that? I mean, why would you want a trophy that wasn't even yours? That's so lame.

I came down the rec with P, but he got well frustrated and stomped off in a strop. The taller he gets, the worse he is at football. He's the Small Giant with Big Feet. I mean, obviously he's not a giant, but he moves like one – all clumsy, like he doesn't quite know where his legs begin and end.

After P left, I decided to train on my own. I saw this interview with Kieran Trippier who took free kicks for Spurs and England and he said that he practises for forty minutes every single day. I figured I could do the same, but I'll tell you something – I bet Trippier has ball boys and more than one ball. I swear I spent about a minute practising free kicks and the other thirty-nine retrieving the ball. In the end I got frustrated too and decided to head home. Besides, none of it would make any difference if I didn't start growing – Watford aren't going to look at me. I said this to Mum and she goes, 'For goodness sake, Gabe! Kids grow! That's what they do!'

I passed the playground on my way to the gate. I paused where I almost died. There's no trace of blood or anything, but I know exactly where it is. I reached into my pocket for the pebble Coral gave me, the Lodestone, and turned it in my fingers – it's become a kind of superstition to stop there and do that.

I had the beginnings of an idea and I closed my eyes and really concentrated. I'd been trying for ages with no joy, but maybe I hadn't been looking in the right place – it's not like I know how this works. And this time I heard the rushing, whooshing, ripping noise.

Another playground. It's packed – all these kids who laugh and run and fall and cry and then their mums scoop them up and five seconds later they run away again, laughing. But I see this one little boy who's really screaming and I know it's different. No mother scoops him up. Nobody's taking any notice. I go over. He's, like, four years old. I go, 'What's up? Where's your mum?' But that just makes him scream all the more. I take his hand and look around.

Over on a bench by the seesaw, there's this woman whose head is turning left and right. I lead the kid across the playground. As we approach, I can hear her barking at an older boy who's messing about with his mates on the monkey bars. She's going, 'Billy? Where's your brother?' But Billy just shrugs.

I say, 'Excuse me.'

She turns round, but the boy's already slipped my hand and is running towards her. She goes, 'Jesse!' And she has to drop to her haunches to hug him because he's just a little kid. I get a good look at her face for the first time. Before, I've only seen her as a girl or an old lady, but I still recognise her no problem – she's got locks, freckles like mine and she's put her knitting down on the bench beside her. She looks at me over Uncle Jesse's shoulder as she squeezes him to her. She mouths, 'Thank you, Gabriel.' I nod and mouth 'Thank you' back – after all, Coral saved my life. I have a thought. I reach into my pocket for the Lodestone. I hand it to her and she takes it with a nod of understanding – perhaps it will weigh her down in this world.

I don't suppose this is what Daisy expected me to do and I don't know if the story will hold. I wonder if this little boy will get to grow up with his mum. I wonder if my Uncle Jesse will ever know either way. Almost anything is possible, I guess.

I remember what he told me, that sometimes the reason something happens can come later. I've thought about this a lot. Dad died, I began to see the multiverse, I got to know Uncle Jesse, I was nearly lost, nearly killed, I reunited Coral and her son. I reunited Coral and her son, I was nearly killed, nearly lost, I got to know Uncle Jesse, I began to see the multiverse, Dad died. Either way you look at it, there is happiness and sadness, failure and success, hope and regret. But, if time is an illusion, with practice you can give everything a different, better meaning.

I don't believe in happily ever afters but I do believe in patterns. And I believe that sometimes a black hole stops spinning and becomes a star again.

WHEN *you* REACH *me*

REBECCA STEAD

I am coming to save your friend's life, and my own. I ask two favours. First, you must write me a letter.

When Miranda starts receiving mysterious notes, she doesn't know what to do. The notes tell her that she must write a letter, a true story, and that she can't share her mission with anyone – not even her (former) best friend, Sal. It would be easy to ignore the strange messages, except that whoever is leaving them appears to have an uncanny ability to predict the future. And if that's the case, Miranda has an even bigger problem – because each note brings her close to believing that only she can prevent a tragic death. Until the final note makes her think she's too late.

'Smart and mesmerising'
The New York Times

9781783449637